Murder on the Mountain

By

T. D. Maughold

Published by Infopath (IOM) Ltd

www.infopath.co.im

First published in Great Britain in 2006 by Infopath (IOM) Ltd.
Web Site: www.infopath.co.im

ISBN 978-0-9552330-0-5 (From Jan 2007)
ISBN 0-9552330-0-3

Printed in the Isle of Man by
Mannin Printing.

Acknowledgements

I would like to thank Mike Smith and Amanda Paull for their painstaking hard work in proof reading the original manuscript and for their comments, suggestions and encouragement.

\- TDM

Front Cover: The Mountain Road, TT Course, Isle of Man
                       – Copyright of Peter Killey
                       http://www.manxscenes.com

Inside Front Cover: Map of the Isle of Man
                       – Courtesy of the Author
                       Photographs courtesy of Peter Killey,
                       Grant Matthews, Jan Thomas,
                       Derek Matthews and Jean McAleer.

Inside Back: Photographs courtesy of the Author
                       and Grant Matthews.

Back Cover: The publisher's co-sponsored bike ridden
                       by Mark Parrett, and owned by the
                       "Undertaker" coming 3rd in the 2004
                       400 cc TT –
                       Picture courtesy of the Picture Box, Onchan.

Contents

Chapter One

Monday Morning (Practice Week)

Five am. A pale light crept into the eastern sky as the darker night receded westward. Around them the grey slopes of Snaefell dozed sleepily as the thin strands of early morning mist slowly lifted to reveal the dark ribbon of tarmac that was the mountain road.

Jonathon Price stamped his feet and shivered. It was a cold morning for the end of May, but the road was now closed and the first practice of the annual meeting was about to start. He stood by the roadside at the Veranda in silence, but eight miles further down that road the sleepy town of Douglas awoke to a raucous cacophony of noise as motorcycle engines sparked and crackled into life.

It was the Isle of Man. The TT Races had begun.

The practice session began at five-fifteen. Two bikes at a time roared off the grid at ten second intervals. Engines screaming, front wheels pawing the air as the slick black rubber of the fat rear tyres squirmed to hold the grip of a hundred and eighty horses. A rising wail rose from the exhausts as the machines tore off down the Glencrutchery Road, Grandstand on one side of the road, cemetery on the other, then down the steep drop of Bray Hill, between the houses and the lampposts, Quarter Bridge Road, Quarter Bridge then off into the dew laden early morning Manx countryside.

It would be fifteen minutes before the leading machines reached Price who was at the Veranda, a series of four sweeping right hand bends, thirty miles out from the start and high up on the Mountain Road between Ramsey, the Island's second town and Douglas, its capital. He was on a busman's holiday of sorts. A surgeon by profession and an infrequent attendee at sporting events, he had been talked into coming once again to the TT by a colleague in the large District General Hospital in northern England where he worked. If coming to watch the races had not been mistake enough, he had found himself signing on as a race medic the day before and was now standing there stamping his feet and shivering on a bleak mountainside at a time when all sane and sensible folk would still be fast asleep in bed. He looked around; it was lighter now. Behind him the heather and gorse flecked bulk of Snaefell, the Island's highest peak rose smoothly to its still mist-shrouded summit. The road before him ran from left to right and in front of that the land fell steeply into a scree-scarred valley which itself dropped away until it reached the village of Laxey and the sea far below. In the distance he could just make out the great waterwheel, the Lady Isabella, built in the nineteenth century to pump water from the lead and zinc mines of the surrounding hills.

Price turned to Kinnish: he had worked with the man for five, maybe six years: Kinnish had gassed for him for more than half of that time and only now did he begin to realise that the man who had invited him to that little plot of earth by the side of a road in the middle of nowhere had little, if anything, really in common with him. Kinnish was a colleague, but certainly not a friend.

"So Steve, you got me out to this godforsaken place. What are we looking for, where, when and why?"

[Stephen Kinnish was a Manxmen. He was also a Consultant Anaesthetist who worked in the same hospital as Price and returned year after year to the Island of his birth to act as a race doctor and (as he had told Price some weeks earlier) "just stand by the roadside and watch the races," Price had asked dubiously "and if there's a crash?" Kinnish had muttered something about lending medical assistance, but that it didn't happen often and there was a helicopter ambulance and a casualty could be in the hospital in Douglas in next to no time. Come to think about it he hadn't said anything about this five am start business either. Price was different: he was not a Manxman: he was born and bred on the adjacent Island (as they say in the Isle of Man), but he had been to the TT Races once or twice many, many years before: he vaguely remembered the scenery, the racetrack and the bikes, but only now, in the early morning light, did those memories come alive once again.]

"This is a great spot Jonathon. Bikes come from way over there to your left – up the climb from Ramsey, Guthrie's Memorial, along the Mountain Mile, East Mountain Box then the Black Hut then this series of bends – four right-handers taken as one at speed then down to that left-hander over there," he pointed to their right "that's Bungalow Bridge or the Les Graham Memorial Shelter to give it its proper name. And then on past the Bungalow, over the tram rails, Hailwood's Rise, round the Brandywell then on down the mountain to Douglas"

"At speed?" Price asked raising his eyebrows just a little.

"Hundred and thirty, forty maybe, the top boys, but don't worry no-one crashes up here; just enjoy the racing today and tomorrow we'll have you out somewhere on your own."

"One on its way" someone shouted and Price, Kinnish and the small knot of marshals and spectators turned to their left and craned their heads, staring northwards for sight of that first machine. Suddenly there it was: only a black speck at first, but growing larger and clearer with the rising note of its engine and whine of its exhaust growing louder as it drew nearer and nearer. The bike and rider swooped into the left-hander before the Veranda, cranking over so hard that the rider's leather-clad knee scraped the tarmac, then in an ear-splitting crescendo of noise burst past them and was gone, the howl of the machine's exhaust Doppler-shifting into the distance.

"Number six, Dai Jones," someone commented.

Price shook his head. These guys were crazy. If they came off at that speed…..

A few seconds later, the rising whine of a racing engine cut through the still morning air; the shrill note rose and dipped and rose and dipped; a split second later, in a heady crescendo of sound, it flew past Price and his companions in an indescribable blur of noise, colour and motion.

"Number eleven, John Davis," the same person commentated. Another bike shot past: fast, furious, but safe. Price began to relax: another bike came past, then another, then another. They were all travelling at seriously high speed, but they seemed to know what they were doing.

Then, suddenly, he heard the screaming note of another machine, but this time everything was wrong. Men were running, waving flags and a frisson of fear clutched the pit of his stomach as he watched the rider fighting with the handlebars in what almost seemed slow motion, before the bike and rider left the road and disappeared over the mountainside. Kinnish grabbed the orange emergency box which stood by the roadside and dashed forward shouting:

"Help me Jonathon…. You others get the stretcher, someone get onto Air-med." There was no time for conversation. Price was aware of other machines approaching from his left, but the riders obeyed the waved yellow flags and slowed allowing him and the others to cross the road in relative safety and start off down the hillside to where the crashed machine and its rider were lying.

The bike had travelled two hundred yards or more gouging a scarred track down the mountainside. With some difficulty Price followed the others down the steep and rutted heather-clad bank until he reached the machine which was lying on its side, engine still running and rear wheel still turning. He was panting and sweating and his heart was still pounding with the adrenaline of the moment by the time he reached the rider, but Steve Kinnish was already in action; the local man had seen incidents like this before and knew exactly what to do. The rider's helmet was already off and lying beside him, but the signs did not look too good.

"I'm going to have to intubate him Jonathon; his resps are going off and he's starting to look cyanosed. Looks like a major chest injury"

"And the rest!" Price replied; he had now had an opportunity to look at the leather clad figure lying there on the bleak hillside and could see the other injuries: the leg bent over at a fantastic angle, the glistening shards of white bone poking through the black and gold leather, the unmoving chest, the greying skin.

It took a second or two for Price to get his breath back and take on board the locus of the crash site and the body of the victim. On that amount of reflection, the injuries looked bad, but he had seen worse in his career: the rider had a pneumo- or haemo- pneumothorax, no doubt, but the injury had been recognised, a helicopter had been summoned and within minutes the man would be dealt with by skilled personnel – he had a chance, at least. Far more than he would at virtually any other racetrack in the world.

"I've got an Ambu bag on him," Kinnish said, "can you just ventilate him while I get an IV line in, some colloid up and then I'll tube him. His pneumothorax doesn't look like a tension, so I don't think we need to put in a chest drain here and now. He'll probably need one once he gets to Nobles, but it'll be far too risky to do it up here. Not much else we can do here, but the chopper should be here in a few minutes".

Price did what he was told and as he held the breathing mask over the man's face and methodically squeezed the bag forcing air into the injured lungs, Kinnish went to work. Price looked again at the unconscious rider; not a particularly young man, probably early thirties; he recognised the face, maybe he had seen it before in a paper, or a magazine or something, but could not remember the name.

"Rob Taylor, won 6 TTs, used to be a works Honda rider, rides for Petromax now," someone spoke in answer to his unasked questions. "Never crashed on the Island in his life," the same voice continued, "been riding here for twelve years, a really safe rider, this is not like him at all."

"But didn't you see what happened?" another voice cut in, "he got it all completely wrong: it didn't look like he knew the course at all. He was on the wrong line when he went through the Black Hut; didn't you see him fighting with the bike right the way through the left hander? He'd lost it before he ever got to the Veranda; there was something wrong with him or that bike or there was something on the road."

The flat drone of an approaching helicopter brought the conversation to a premature close. The marshals knew that they had a job to do and instructions were barked against the loud chat of overhead rotors. The aluminium stretcher halves were slid beneath the rider and locked together and within minutes Kinnish and Price had transferred their charge to the airborne medical team. The helicopter had been on the ground for less time than it took to describe the medics' actions, its rotors barely slowing before the engine whined and it was off on its way to Douglas and Noble's Hospital.

Kinnish, Price and the other men collected their equipment and climbed back up the steep slope to the road where racing motorcycles were still flying past under the watchful eye of a marshal holding a stationary yellow flag. They were slower than before the crash, but not much and soon after Price and the others had come back across the road, the yellow flag was withdrawn. Someone had inspected the road and said it was safe; Price didn't know who, but normal service was resumed and the

Practice session continued without further incident until the Roads-Open car flashed past sometime shortly before seven. Price yawned and walked to his car. He opened the door, fell into the driver's seat and started the engine. He had been up since before four; time now to go back to the hotel, have breakfast and then a couple of hours sleep.

Price was rudely awakened by a shrill repetitive bleat; he lay there for a moment wondering what the sound was before his senses returned. He reached out for the telephone beside his bed, picked up the receiver and answered:

"Yes?"

There was a long pause before a hesitant reply:

" Dr Price?"

" Speaking."

Another long pause and then, "Are you one of the doctors who was up at the Veranda this morning when…when Rob Taylor…" The voice sounded tense, nervous and tailed off without finishing the sentence.

"Who are you?" Price demanded. Apart from Steve Kinnish and a handful of others, no-one knew where he was staying. The information certainly wasn't common knowledge. He suspected a reporter. He continued: "If you want any information, I suggest you contact the Press Office at the Grandstand." He was bullish, angry that the caller knew who he was and that his privacy had been invaded.

"I…I don't want information…I don't want anything…I want to tell you something…something I think you should know…I….I…" the voice hesitated again.

"What?" Price asked. His tone was less than sympathetic.

" I……I work at the hospital and I thought you should know something….I've heard that you're investigating Mr Taylor's death."

"Death!….he died? Are you sure?"

"Yes, I'm sorry Dr Price…you didn't know?"

"No I didn't, of *course* I didn't, and anyway what makes you think I'm investigating anything? I saw the man crash, but I'm a doctor, not a policeman…or any sort of investigator. What makes you say what you just said?"

"Well, Steve Kinnish has been asking around and he sort of, well, he mentioned your name. I can't say my name over the 'phone, but I…well I was the radiographer who dealt with Mr Taylor when he was admitted and I, er, x-rayed him in casualty and intensive care."

"And?" Price asked.

"I was really surprised when I heard that he'd died."

"Why?"

"He didn't really seem that badly injured……and they'd stabilised him by the time he got to hospital."

11

"So what went wrong?" Price asked.

"I don't know, I really don't….look I can't speak any more…someone's coming."

There was a pause of a few seconds, then a click and the line went dead. Price frowned, then shook his head; he wondered who the caller was, but knew he needed to speak to her. He tried 1471, but the caller had declined to leave her number. He was about to go back to sleep when the telephone rang again; he picked it up immediately.

"Price here," he said, this time far more pleasantly, "go on, do you want to tell me a little more?" There was a pause, but it was a different voice that spoke: a firm, confident voice with a tone of some authority:

"Constable Kneale, Sir, Isle of Man Constabulary. I believe that you witnessed an incident on the Veranda this morning, an incident involving a motorcycle ridden by a man called Taylor?"

Price frowned for the second time in the space of as many minutes before replying:

"I was there Constable. Why? Riders crash at the TT, don't they? I didn't realise that the police took an interest in motorcycle racing accidents?"

"No Sir, we don't as a matter of course, but, well you may not know, the rider, Mr Taylor died in Nobles Hospital earlier this morning and we do need to take statements when a fatality is involved, for the inquest. You'll appreciate, Sir, that we have to try and build up as accurate a picture…" the policeman carried on in this vein, but Price was no longer listening. So the rider really had died and the call he had received a few minutes earlier had pre-empted even the police. That Taylor had not made it was a shock and yet Price was also surprised – when he had helped lift that stretcher into the helicopter he really had thought that the man would survive. "…and so would it be convenient for you to come up to Police Headquarters later today to make a statement?" Price realised that the policeman had stopped speaking and wanted a reply.

"Er yes, yes certainly; what time?"

"Would two o'clock be convenient Sir?"

Price glanced at his watch – it was half-past eleven. He told the policeman that he would be there and put the 'phone down.

Price showered and dressed; he thought about phoning Kinnish, but then decided against it. Something was not quite right here; somewhere, in the back of his mind, he knew it. He closed his eyes and mentally smelt the faint and far off odour of a sour and long-dead rat. He would travel to Police Headquarters, but he would be on his guard. In theory, it would be a simple enough statement to make: he had been there, he had seen the accident (well he had seen the end of the accident), he had tried to help, but somehow Price knew that something was not quite right. To paraphrase Hamlet: was there something rotten in the state of Mann?

He had a coffee in the hotel lounge and then set out for Police Headquarters. It was a long, long time since he had been on the Island, but for some strange reason he remembered exactly where Police Headquarters lay. It was a fine and sunny day and he was in no hurry so he decided to walk. He made his way northwards along the Promenade for half a mile or so before turning his back to the sea and entering one of the little streets that ran at a right angle to the promenade, making the steep climb up to Nobles Park, location of the TT Grandstand, paddock area, campsite and start and finish of the races. Adjacent to the Park stood a large squat modern building: The Isle of Man Police Headquarters. It would win no prizes for architectural merit, but it served its purpose well enough, Price supposed.

He walked into the reception area and rang the bell. He waited for a minute, two minutes before someone appeared.

"Can I help you, Sir" It was a young uniformed female officer. She had a pretty smile and Price replied:

"Jonathon Price....I've come to make a statement about the accident on the Veranda this morning."

"Oh yes Sir," she stepped back out of sight and a moment later Price heard a click and a buzz and the door to the left hand side of the counter swung open. Price stepped forward through the now open doorway and descended into the bowels of the Police station. The door clicked shut behind him.

"Dr Price?" a voice to his right asked. Price turned and caught sight of a man of medium height and probable early middle age. He was wearing a shabby brown sports jacket, brown trousers, a nondescript shirt and tie. Price was a little surprised. He had assumed that a member of the uniformed branch would have been called to deal with what must have been a very mundane task.

"Detective Constable Kneale," he continued, "please come this way."

Price followed the man down some steps into a gloomy basement corridor. Steel doors, some closed, most opened revealing empty cells beyond, punctuated the walls and the reek of stale sweat, vomit, alcohol and cigarettes hung in the air. Price grimaced; it was an unintentional reflex action, but the policeman noticed and apologised.

"Sorry about the surroundings Sir; this is the custody area, but it's the only place available at the moment. We won't be long, just a quick statement and then you can be on your way."

The quick statement took longer than he expected; it was almost as though there was a hidden agenda and the policeman wanted to prolong the whole gloomy affair. In answer to a direct question from Price, the policeman told him that they had not spoken to Kinnish. For some unknown reason, he seemed to have no knowledge of the existence of Kinnish at all.

"We must have a word with him Sir; where did you say he was staying?" he asked politely, but seemed to take little interest in the reply. He asked Price a number of questions which Price was unable to answer in any detail, technical questions about the state of the road, about oil, about whether the machine had skidded or whether the engine had seized. Strangely though, it seemed to Price, reading between the lines and judging from the body language of his inquisitor that the man didn't really care about what Price said in his answers, just so long as Price was kept in that dank and miserable basement for what was left of the afternoon. Price got the distinct impression that the officer wanted to keep him there. Was it merely because he wanted to kill time so he could enter it on his time sheet for the afternoon? Maybe that was how they did things in the Isle of Man.

He ventured a question. "What do you think happened then, Officer?"

Constable Kneale stared at him blankly.

"Can't say at this stage, Doctor, no doubt we'll learn more by the inquest." The voice was devoid of emotion, but Price could see from the policeman's face that further questions would not be welcome. At long last the interview came to an end and Price was allowed to go.

Something was not quite right and, whatever it was, it added to the doctor's growing suspicions about the entire incident. The policeman hadn't asked him a single pertinent question about Taylor's injuries and the medical treatment he had received on the scene. Price had thought about bringing up the 'phone call from the anonymous radiographer, but decided against it. At this stage, he wasn't quite convinced that the Isle of Man Constabulary were singing from the same hymn sheet as he was. A disinterested observer may have thought him a little paranoid, but things were to get far, far worse in the very near future.

Nobles Park and the Grandstand basked in the golden late afternoon sunshine as he stepped out of the dark building. The evening Practice session would soon be underway, but Price was no longer in the mood for motorcycle racing. He had not volunteered for that evening's session and fancied a walk and possibly a drink. He turned to his left and walked down past the old prison, crossed a busy road then made his way along a quiet tree-lined lane until he came to a low wall. He found himself on a cliff top and gazed out over Douglas bay. It was a beautiful sight: the bay was an almost perfect semi-circle; the sky overhead was cloudless and the sea was blue and calm, too calm for the yachts dotted about it whose sails hung limply as the vessels drifted. The dark squall of depression which had drifted close to the edge of his mind passed on and his spirits lifted. A rough path twisted and turned down from the cliff top to the promenade a hundred and fifty feet below. Price looked down and thought he could see an encouraging sign.

The descent was quickly made and Price's intuition and eyesight proved to be good enough. It was an old pub, separated from the promenade by a flagged forecourt on which half a dozen rough trestle tables stood. A swinging signboard hanging from a pole announced: "The Queens Hotel" and another smaller sign standing by the edge of the pavement added: "Open all day for food and drink" Price walked in through the open door to be greeted by the sound of raised voices. A heated argument was raging between a group of men sitting at the bar.

"Oil on the road, I don't believe a word of it. I know some of the marshals up there and no-one saw anything. Anyway where's this oil supposed to have come from?" a red-faced balding man demanded.

"I dunno, diesel from a lorry the day before? oil from an earlier bike? All I know is what they said on the radio," another answered almost apologetically.

"If it wasn't oil what else could it have been?" a third added.

The red-faced man held out his hands in a gesture of apparent despair: "what do you think? The bloody usual of course, trying too hard, going too fast."

"He was a really experienced rider, six times a TT winner," the second man, taller and older than the first replied in a soft Irish accent, "wouldn't have been rider error with him, and they've taken away the bike for inspection, but they don't think it was machine failure."

"I've heard it was a seizure; engine failure," another man said.

Price realised that he had walked into a debate on the morning's tragedy. He had no desire to take part so he ordered a pint of Okells bitter from the barman and took a seat in a quiet corner of the room. The heated voices continued for a few more minutes then the topic of conversation drifted onto something else.

The beer tasted good and Price's mood improved with each passing mouthful. When he returned to the bar, the red-faced man acknowledged his presence.

"Over for the races?"

Price nodded, took a gulp from the freshly-poured pint and said: "Yes." It was a terse reply and the other men at the bar were having none of it.

"First time?"

"Where are you over from?"

"Enjoying it?"

"You not out for the evening practice?"

Price was a little daunted by the barrage of questions. He had come out for a quiet, relaxing pint, but he did not wish to offend so he smiled and told the men that he had been before, but only once and that had been many years ago. He told them his name and said that he liked the Island and that he was not watching the practice that evening because he had been up for the early morning one and anyway, he fancied a drink

15

instead. The red-faced man whose name, he discovered, was Richard, asked him where he had watched from. Price was wary about telling too much and simply said that he had been up on the mountain. He did not specify where. He made no mention of the accident and he did not tell them that he was a doctor, but this was the Isle of Man where, as Price was already learning, nothing was secret for long.

"You're a doctor aren't you?" Richard demanded, "and you were up on the Veranda this morning. You can tell us what happened."

Price was flabbergasted. "How, in the world?" he uttered.

Richard smiled. "Know most things" he replied intriguingly. His companions nodded. "And I do tend to keep a CB radio tuned into the appropriate frequencies when the TT is going on. Heard your name, *Doctor* Price, up at the Veranda this morning. Good work, by the way; by all accounts you did a sterling job. Shame the guy died."

After that short, but friendly, interrogation Price was accepted. At first he eyed Richard with a degree of suspicion, but when the man seemed harmless enough he relaxed. He listened to the local gossip and learned a great deal about the Island, about the TT races and in particular about the late Rob Taylor, not all of it complimentary or good. Richard had obviously very little regard for the man and made vague allusions to a susceptibility to bribery and corruption which Price was not prepared to entertain without far, far more evidence. The result was that he ended up staying far longer in the pub and drinking far more than he had intended. When he finally left it was gone ten. He walked back to his hotel, swaying a little, content, full of local beer and ready for bed.

With some difficulty he pushed the key into the door and turned the key and the knob; the door opened and Price stumbled into his room. It took him a moment or two before he realised that the light was on and someone was sitting on a chair in the corner. It was the anaesthetist, Steve Kinnish. Price knew straight away that something was wrong.

"Sit down Jonathon," Kinnish said, quietly, but firmly, "you and I need to talk." Price swayed a little, but did as he was told, finding a seat on the edge of the bed.

" I take it you've heard that the racer, Rob Taylor, died?"

Price nodded and replied: "I heard about it sometime late this morning," he said. His tones would have been a little angrier, but the beer had mellowed them, "telephone call from a young lady: a radiographer at Nobles Hospital who knew my name, telephone number and seemed to think that I was investigating the death of the late Rob Taylor. Now, I wonder how she got hold of that particular information?"

Kinnish raised his hand. "Sorry Jonathon," he said, "there were reasons; I can't tell you now, but it had to be said. Did you speak to the police?"

"The Police asked me for a statement this afternoon and I gave them one. They said that Taylor died in hospital, tragic, of course, but these things happen...I was rather more concerned about the call from the radiographer. I take it that you know her? what's the big mystery?" through conscious effort he managed to avoid slurring his speech, but only just. The shock of finding Kinnish in his hotel room at that time of night helped sober him up. The man's actions were positively furtive; how had he got into Price's room and more to the point why? Price voiced his concerns out loud.

"I got into your room," Kinnish replied, "because I know the hotel manager and I told him that I needed to speak to you....urgently. Apart from the police, and this radiographer, have you had any other calls today?"

"No, I haven't; should I?" Price replied.

"No calls from...er...anyone who sounded Russian?"

"Of course not; don't think I've ever had a call from a Russian in my life. Why?" Kinnish ignored the question and countered it with one of his own.

"This radiographer, what did she say?"

Price recalled the strange, anonymous call which woke him and repeated the brief words the caller had spoken.

"How did the voice sound?," Kinnish urged, "I mean what was its manner?" Price thought for a moment then replied:

"Nervous, anxious, guilty; like she and it was definitely a she, was afraid of somebody or something; she said that you had spoken to her and she said that neither she not anyone else in that hospital had thought that Taylor was going to die. I think that she would have said a lot, lot more, but she was obviously scared, really scared. Whatever else it was she wanted to say, she couldn't bring herself to say it and she put the 'phone down on me."

"Was it a local accent?"

"No, not Manx. I would have said southern England."

"She called me," Kinnish revealed, "but she spoke for a little longer. Didn't tell me her name, but I'm pretty sure I know who she is. She didn't put the 'phone down either, well, not straight away, not until she told me something...."

Price was listening closely now; the slight intoxication of a few moments ago appeared to have passed, his thoughts grew keener, more attentive.

"What?" he demanded

"Listen Jonathon," Kinnish continued, "let me take you back to this morning when Taylor came off his bike; can you remember what exactly happened?"

"No, I told the police as much, I didn't see the accident, only the result."

"Which was?"

"Well, he went straight off the road and down the mountainside."

"Did he try to get round the corner, but couldn't make it? was his bike over on its side?" Kinnish asked excitedly.

"No," Price shook his head, "come to think of it, he didn't seem to be trying to go round the corner at all. He seemed to be struggling just to stay on the bike. The marshals said that he was on the wrong line for the previous corner, but it didn't look as though he was trying to correct his line. He went straight on at the apex of that first bend...."

"What do you remember about the bike and about him, when we got to them?" Kinnish asked.

"Engine was still running, back wheel turning, so it wouldn't appear to have seized, You'd taken his helmet off by the time I got down there; he was unconscious so I assumed some sort of major head injury, chest injury, compound lower leg fractures," Price reeled off the injuries he could recall. "Nothing that you wouldn't expect in a high speed motorcycle crash."

"I looked at the crash helmet," Kinnish said slowly, "and there was hardly a scratch on it. That mountainside is all heather and peat bog; it's all soft ground. He didn't hit a wall or anything so why was he unconscious? I can accept the leg and the chest injury, but there was no head injury and besides....."

"Yes?" Price asked encouragingly; he sensed something important.

Kinnish's voice had shrunk to a conspiratorial whisper. "I checked his pupils before we put him in the chopper, Jonathon and they weren't dilated, they were constricted, in fact, Jonathon, they were *pinpoint*." He emphasised that last point; they both knew its significance.

Kinnish stood up.

"It's getting late. We're both up early in the morning, I'd better go." It was like a book snapping shut.

"But the radiographer, what did she say? Who was it?" Price needed to know more; half-confidences were not enough.

"No, Jonathon, not now; it might be nothing. I need to make some more enquiries. Please keep what I've said to yourself...for now."

Price pleaded half-heartedly for a few moments, but could see that Kinnish had made up his mind; he would learn no more that night. The door opened, closed and Kinnish was gone.

Chapter Two

Tuesday Morning (Practice Week)

Price had asked for an early morning call at half-past three. When it came, he swore and dragged himself from his bed. The few hours sleep he had snatched had not been peaceful. He pulled on yesterday's clothes and made for the hotel car park. He had agreed to be at Ballaugh Bridge for early morning practice and the roads closed to normal traffic at five.

The car started and he drove through the dark empty streets of Douglas until he reached Quarter Bridge. There he joined the TT Course and the headlights of his car, a powerful Alfa Romeo saloon, picked out the dark tarmac ahead as he accelerated into the Manx countryside. He drove through tiny villages with their street lights twinkling by the roadside, interspersed by long stretches of black emptiness: woods, fields and silent spaces. It was still too dark to be sure where he was for most of the journey: he hazarded a guess at Braddan, Union Mills, Glen Vine, Crosby, Ballacraine, Glen Helen, Cronk-y-Voddy. The sky was beginning to brighten as he drove through Kirkmichael, the village before Ballaugh and it was light enough to see by as he slowed into Ballaugh village, swung to the left over the famous hump-backed bridge then turned sharply left off the main road and parked. He was not the first on the scene. It was half-past four and a handful of figures were already there, roping off side roads ready for the Course closure in half an hour.

Price got out of his car and made himself known to the marshals. He was greeted enthusiastically and gratefully received a piping hot mug of coffee, his first refreshment of the day, as a reward for his appearance. Ballaugh was a little over seventeen miles out from the start of the Course and the fastest machines and riders took about nine minutes to get there. As the first machines weren't away until five fifteen, he had nearly fifty minutes to wait before he could expect any action.

He looked around. This was a different scene to the mountain: lowland country. Small rows of neatly whitewashed cottages lay on either side of the main road which appeared from his right over the narrow hump-backed bridge and then snaked off through the village. Across the road in front of him, stood an inviting country inn. Its sign said "The Raven". Behind the pub the land rose steeply into what, in the early morning light, still remained a shadowy grey hinterland: the dark craggy interior of the Island. Somewhere on the other side of those hills lay Douglas and on the Glencrutchery

Road, racing machinery would now be getting ready for the start of practice. Over there it would probably be a little noisy now, but in Ballaugh it was different. Scarcely a sound could be heard save for the faint rustle of a light wind in the trees and the gentle muted birdsong of the dawn chorus. Things would change in about fifty minutes time.

Time ticked on slowly. After what seemed an age, the course inspection car shot through the village at frightening speed, its tyres squealing as they fought for precious grip. The car was followed by a procession of travelling marshals on high-powered Honda motorcycles, each bearing the large and solitary capital letter M. The bikes flashed through the village and were gone. Silence returned. The road was now closed and the scene was set for the first machines of practice.

They were not long in coming. Somewhere, far in the distance, Price heard the rising whine of a racing engine. Its pitch undulated as the engine revs rose and fell, but the volume grew ever louder. Suddenly, in an explosion of noise it burst onto the scene and leapt over the bridge. The machine flew through the air for twenty yards or more, then landed. Its front and rear suspension compressed heavily, but its rider managed somehow to stay in the saddle. The engine note changed as the rider notched up a gear and raced on, but before that machine had disappeared from sight another had jumped the bridge, then another, then another. In a relentless stream of colour and noise, large and brightly painted racing motorcycles, their leather clad riders crouching behind fairings as they hung on to their bucking metal steeds, leapt the bridge and shot through the village. Shock waves of ear-splitting sound reverberated across the narrow street and the air was full of the heady smell of high octane fuel and Castrol R.

Then, as suddenly as it had appeared, the noise was gone and the smell drifted away on the early morning breeze. Price looked at his watch; the morning session had come to an end. Somewhere over to his left a radio crackled with static. It was race control telling the marshals that the "Roads Open" car had set off and would be with them in a few minutes.

"Dr Price should be with you; someone wants to speak to him." the radio added. Surprised to hear his name, Price moved across and took the microphone.

"Price here. How can I help you?"

"Jonathon?" It was Steve Kinnish, "Race Control have just patched me through; can you talk?"

Price looked around. The marshals had moved away and appeared uninterested in his conversation. "Go ahead Steve, I'm on my own."

"We need to get together. Can you meet me straight after practice?"

"Where?"

"Car park at the new hospital; know where it is?"

"Yes, I think so. Why? What's the urgency? I was planning on going back to bed."

"Can't say over the radio, Jonathon. See you there in half an hour"

Price reluctantly agreed and with a final crackle the radio went dead.

A short while later the "Roads Open" car shot past. The barriers and ropes which had blocked off the side roads had already been taken down so Price made his way to his car and set off back to Douglas. He had not been to the new hospital, but knew roughly where it was: on a hillside a mile or two outside and to the west of the Island's capital. It was on the inside of the Course and he supposed that if he drove back to the village of Union Mills and then turned left he would find it easily enough. He couldn't for the life of him understand why Kinnish wanted to meet him there, but he supposed that the man had his reasons and that he, Price, would learn those soon enough.

Price reached the traffic lights at Ballacraine and turned left joining the road to Douglas from Peel. He met a steady stream of early morning commuter traffic, some of it travelling a little too slowly for his liking. There were 30 and 40 mph zones in the villages and towns, but most of the roads in the Island had no upper speed limits and Price loved the opportunity to put his foot to the floor and listen to the growl of his car's powerful V6 engine as he accelerated along the awesome straights and swept through the fast bends of the famous Mountain Course. He was travelling in an anti-clockwise direction, however, and against the flow of the many two-wheeled visitors who streamed around the open course at high speed. Overtaking could involve an element of extreme risk, particularly at times like this. Reluctantly, he eased off the accelerator and took his time.

When he reached the hospital, the car park was already filling up as day staff arrived to begin their shifts. He found an empty space and parked, looking around for his colleague. Kinnish arrived a few minutes later. He was wearing full racing leathers and riding his thousand cc Yamaha. He had obviously spotted Price's Alfa and swung into an empty space beside the car. The burbling motorcycle engine coughed and was still; Kinnish put the machine on its stand and dismounted. Seconds later his crash helmet was off and he spoke:

"Good man, Jonathon; we needed to meet. You know what it's about?"

"Taylor, I assume," Price replied, "but why the drama Steve? If you think that something funny is going on, why don't you just tell the police?. They are investigating the death. "There will be a post-mortem and an inquest. If, as you seemed to be suggesting last night, there are suspicious circumstances, it'll all come out, surely?"

Kinnish shook his head. "There won't be a post-mortem Jonathon; never is. Taylor's body will be flown back to England, probably still in his race leathers. In the fullness of time there'll be an inquest, yes, but that'll be weeks after the TT and it'll just return the usual verdict - 'Accidental Death'."

"What about the police then? Why not just tell them your suspicions?"

"Because that's all they are at the moment: suspicions. We have no evidence; we don't know," he emphasised the word *know*, "anything. As you can probably imagine the TT races are a sensitive issue and not just here. There are some extremely vociferous critics of this meeting, both on this Island and off, who will use any possible reason or excuse to get the whole thing stopped. *That can't be allowed to happen.* I love the races, Jonathon and I'm not going to hand the detractors any ammunition whatsoever, not if I can help it, anyway. I propose that we investigate this ourselves and if we find out what really happened, if we get some real evidence, then we talk to the police, but not before."

Price listened to this little speech with some surprise. It had been delivered with unexpected passion. He felt that he owed Kinnish some support, if nothing else. He had been down this route before, of course, albeit a number of years earlier. Deep down he knew that he was going to regret this decision, but with deep reservations he reluctantly agreed.

"Well okay, I'm in. What do you suggest we do first?"

"We start here, at the hospital," Kinnish announced, suddenly and boldly. He looked Price in the eye and continued: "You and I both think that Taylor's death was no accident. I think he was drugged and that's what made him crash the bike….but we know that the crash didn't kill him, don't we?". If Kinnish was asking a question, it was surely a rhetorical one. "Taylor was injured when we saw him, his injuries were pretty bad, but I reckon they weren't life-threatening. When we got him off in that helicopter, he should have survived. I'm really pissed off about what happened next; it looks bad on the TT and the medical team; there must have been something else".

"Something else?" Price asked.

"Yes, Jonathon, you heard what that radiographer had to say. I think that something else happened to him after he left us. I don't think that the injuries he sustained were severe enough to cause death. That's why we need to start our investigation here at the place where he died."

Price shook his head; memories of a different set of events which had taken place some years before had been re-awakened. He knew the problems that lay before them.

"How can we do anything Steve? We don't work here; no-one knows us; we have no official status; we can't simply walk in and start asking questions."

Kinnish smiled grimly. "No-one knows you, Jonathon, but I'm a Manxman, don't forget, I grew up on this island. On top of that I was a Senior House Officer in the old

Nobles Hospital ten years or so ago and even when I left to go to England, I kept in touch with everyone. Most of the staff here moved over from the old hospital and a good proportion of them know me. We'll get a lot more out of them than the police could, I can assure you. This is what we'll do…"

Kinnish explained his plan to Price; it was embryonic at that stage and still evolving, but in essence it involved Kinnish exploiting his contacts and concentrating on the hospital whilst Price made enquiries amongst the riders and race teams in the Paddock. They agreed to meet up that evening at Price's hotel; by then they might have information to exchange.

Price got back into his car and turned the key; the engine burst into life. As he glanced over his shoulder to reverse out of the parking space he saw the leather-clad anaesthetist striding confidently towards the large new hospital. Someone at least, Price said to himself, seemed to know what he was doing. He drove out of the hospital grounds and onto the road back to Douglas, giving no further thought to Kinnish or Taylor or hospitals or plots. A shower, or better still a bath, then breakfast was what he wanted now; only then would he begin to consider the task which he had in front of him.

Dr Steven Kinnish, Consultant Anaesthetist was talking to the senior nurse in charge of the hospital's Accident and Emergency Department. The two of them had been friends (but never, to Kinnish's lasting regret, any more than that) for years.

"You see Julie," he continued, "it's a type of clinical audit. As you know we're always trying to improve our performance and in cases like this where we're, well, less than one hundred percent successful, it can be invaluable to actually trace the exact path of interventions that the patient experienced, before the, er, terminal event. I was present at the accident and performed first aid and emergency procedures at the scene, but I need to speak to the guys in the helicopter and whoever was involved in the care of Taylor when he arrived at the hospital."

Sister Julie Quayle nodded; she could see what Kinnish wanted to do and fully approved, being (as Kinnish well knew) an enthusiastic supporter of the modern doctrine of evidence-based, research driven nursing practice.

"You can count on our full co-operation, Steve," she said firmly. "The medical records will probably have been taken by the Coroner's Officer by now, but we always keep copies; I'll get someone to dig them out for you. You'll want to speak to the nursing staff and doctor who were on duty, but I'm afraid it would have been the night shift and they all went off duty a few minutes ago. I'll check, but I don't think anyone's still here."

She got up and left the room leaving Kinnish to quietly congratulate himself; the plan was proving easier than even he had dared hope. Minutes later she was back. Again; his luck was in. The doctor, who had been on duty during the night and early morning before had finished his shift, was still in the department finishing paperwork, and was more than happy to speak to Kinnish, provided, of course, the interview didn't take too long; the doctor was tired and wanted to go home to his bed. Sister Quayle would introduce him.

Price had finished his breakfast and was sitting in his hotel room reading the TT Race Guide and Official Programme. It didn't contain much information, but he had to make a start somewhere and he quickly discovered that the slim, but glossy brochure contained brief biographies of each of the competitors taking part in that year's meeting. He slowly read and re-read the relevant entry:

Taylor. Robert Andrew

Born 31 August 1965. Single. Professional Motorcycle Racer from Guildford, Surrey, England. Currently No 2 rider with Petromax Racing. Rob makes a welcome return to the TT after a gap of three years when he competed successfully in the British Superbike Championship, finishing in second place two years ago before being taken on by Petromax and moving up to the World Superbike Championship. He finished in a disappointing fifteenth position at the end of his first season in the world event, but hopes for great improvement this year and indeed is currently in third place in the series.

Rob first rode in the Manx Grand Prix in 1987 and moved up to the TT in 1990. He was formerly a works rider for Honda at the event and has won 6 TT races.

It was short and told him little more than he already knew. He was thinking about what to do next when the telephone rang. It was Kinnish. He was making progress and wanted Price to come back to the hospital.

"What, now?" Price exclaimed wearily.

He listened for a minute, then replied "Do I really have to?"

Kinnish insisted. He wouldn't say more over the phone. "Be at the main entrance in twenty minutes", he told Price curtly, then put the 'phone down.

Price met more traffic than he expected on the short drive out to the hospital and it was some forty-five minutes later when he met the anaesthetist.

"Come this way," Kinnish said, leading Price to one side of the brightly lit entrance hall. "They have quite a good coffee bar, what would you like?"

"Eh, Oh, anything Steve, just make it black so I can try and stay awake. What have you found?"

"All in good time," the anaesthetist replied, but a gleam in his eyes told Price that the man was onto something.

A minute or two later, Kinnish returned with two large mugs of steaming black liquid. The powerful aroma of ground coffee beans filled the air and Price found the need for sleep receding.

"I have spoken," Kinnish said slowly, "to the doctor who first saw Taylor in the Casualty Department. He did not think...," he paused to take a breath before continuing, "that the man's injuries were life threatening. He ordered X-rays, and scans and Taylor was transferred to the Radiology Department."

"And?" Price demanded.

"Sometime later, whilst he was in Radiology, he had a cardiac arrest and died. Its now all a little bit controversial, but, as far as he's aware, Taylor was alone with a radiographer when it happened; she called the crash team who were there within minutes, but when they put the monitor on him he was in asystole. They tried adrenaline, atropine, magnesium, all the usual stuff, but to no avail and he died. Cause of death is being put down as massive blunt force trauma to the chest with cardiac arrest secondary to that." He stopped for a moment.

"But?" Price asked.

Kinnish looked him in the eyes and said, slowly: "There is, however, another version of events."

"Which is?"

"A rumour, nothing more, is circulating in the hospital that someone visited Taylor in Radiology while he was having his X-rays and scans. The rumour suggests that this visitor was alone with the man for a minute, maybe more."

" What does the radiographer say?" Price asked.

"That's just it, Jonathon," Kinnish replied slowly, "I haven't been able to talk to her."

"Why?" Price asked, continuing without waiting for a reply, "on night shift, I suppose, gone home."

"No Jonathon," Kinnish responded, "the day shift had started by this time and this particular radiographer was on day shift, but you're right in one respect, she has gone home. She's been sent home."

"Why?" Price asked, yet again. The reply, when it came, could not have been more unexpected.

"Would you believe it, on a routine radiation exposure check, which they just *happened* to have yesterday, her radiation exposure badge, you know the thing they have pinned to the front of their uniform, was found to show excess exposure."

It was several minutes before either of them spoke again. Price broke the silence: "There are plenty of possible explanations for that."

Kinnish raised his eyebrows. "Such as?"

"The usual reasons," Price replied, "excessive cumulative exposure, spent too long by the CT scanner, that sort of thing."

Kinnish shook his head and snorted in a derisory fashion. "You know as well as I do that no-one gets overexposed these days; there are far too many safety procedures in place. The radiographers either sit behind leaded glass screens or wear lead aprons whenever they do anything. There is no way that sort of thing can happen."

"Well, it must be a mistake then, faulty badge or something." Price replied.

"That is the most likely explanation," Kinnish agreed cautiously, "but there are other possibilities…" his voice tailed off in mid sentence

"Such as?" Price demanded.

"Someone wanted her out of the way, just in case there were any awkward questions, questions like the ones we're now starting to ask, questions like how seriously injured Taylor really was. Questions like who this mysterious visitor actually was."

Price shook his head. "Hard to believe, Steve, all this conspiracy theory stuff; what concrete evidence have we got?"

Kinnish stood up, pushing his chair sharply backwards. "I think we should go and see the body," he announced firmly.

The mortuary was sited towards the rear of the hospital. Price followed Kinnish along a wide and brightly lit corridor. They walked past the entrance to a number of wards before coming to a halt before a plain green windowless door. It bore neither sign nor handle, but Kinnish seemed to know where he was going and pressed a small button on the wall. Somewhere on the other side of the door, Price heard the muted ringing of a distant bell, followed a short while later by footsteps. The door swung open.

"Yes? Can I help you?" It was a high-pitched, creaking, faltering voice, but a familiar one to Kinnish.

"Norman!" he exclaimed.

"Well, I never… if it isn't young Dr Kinnish!" the voice within answered. Its owner stepped out into the corridor. He was an old man - in his prime he would have been tall and strong, Price thought to himself, but now the frame had withered and the back had bowed. Wisps of white hair still clung to the sides of a nut brown but otherwise bald scalp. The man smiled, adding fresh lines to the heavily creased and weather-beaten face.

"Can I introduce you to my friend and colleague, Jonathon Price, Norman?… Jonathon this is Norman Kermeen… Norman's been the mortuary attendant at Nobles, here and the old Nobles that is, since, well, since er just about time began."

There was a curious rasping chuckle; the old man was laughing.

"Eh, it maybe seems like that to you young fellahs, but the customers in there do seems to be getting younger." It was the old man's attempt at humour and the two doctors laughed. After a few more pleasantries, Kinnish got down to business and explained what they were doing. He stuck to the same story as that he had fed the staff in Casualty, expecting, if anything, an easier time with the old mortuary attendant, but when Rob Taylor's name was mentioned, the old man's countenance furrowed into a frown.

"Yes, we've still got him, but he won't be here for long," he told them, adding, "his team manager has made all the arrangements."

"Can we see him?" Kinnish asked.

The old man's frown deepened. "Why would you want to do that, Dr Kinnish?" he asked.

Kinnish patiently went through the story about research and audit again, but the old man seemed less than convinced.

"I don't know about that, young man," he answered, shaking his head gloomily, "you won't learn much by just looking at him...and there's to be no post-mortem," he added, almost as an afterthought.

Kinnish tried again. "We just want to confirm the external signs of injury, Norman, it'll only take a few minutes." The old man shook his head again; his resolve hardened and with it the tone of his voice.

"No Dr Kinnish, its against the rules. I'm sorry, but if you want to see that young man's body, I want to see some sort of written authority." The conversation had come to a rather sour end and the door snapped shut leaving Price and Kinnish standing in an otherwise empty corridor.

"Damn!" Kinnish exclaimed bitterly, "I thought old Norman would be an easy touch; someone's been tightening up the rules in this place. We'll need to think of another way to get in there now."

The two men turned and walked back along the corridor. Meanwhile, in an untidy office somewhere on the other side of the green door, gnarled old fingers grasped a telephone.

"Hello, yes, it's Mr Kermeen from the mortuary," the voice creaked, "You said that you wanted to be kept informed. Well, I've got something to tell you..."

Price pulled off the Glencrutchery Road and parked his car at the end of the Pit Lane. It was Tuesday, the second day of practice and the midday sun was beating down on the brightly coloured flags which fluttered above the TT Grandstand. He climbed over the low brick wall and made his way towards the Paddock. The area to the rear of the Grandstand was still quiet; the marquees and caravans whose boldly painted banners and signs proclaimed the sale of cut-price clothing and helmets here and hot dogs and burgers there stood empty and idle; such would not be the case when the crowds arrived at the end of the week.

Price passed through a gate and in doing so moved out of the public area into a restricted zone. A large notice warned that only pass-holders were allowed entry, but the place seemed to be deserted and no-one challenged him. Moving on past the Mike Hailwood Riders' Centre, he noticed some activity by one of the large articulated trailers parked on the tarmac. The trailer was emblazoned with the logo of one of the world's most famous tyre manufacturers and before it stood a short and orderly queue of men in overalls pushing motorcycles. Price stopped and watched with interest as a bike was pushed onto a metal podium. A paddock stand slid beneath its rear wheel and with a sudden effortless movement on the part of the man holding the stand the bike jerked backwards, its rear wheel lifting off the ground. The high-pitched scream of a power tool momentarily ripped through the air and a second or two later the wheel was off and another, its rim greedily clad in fresh black rubber, slid onto the axle to take its place.

Price broke out of the hypnotic trance that watching others working often seemed to induce and walked on. He had now reached the area he was seeking: a large and, for most of the year empty field between the Grandstand and Police Headquarters. It was no longer empty. Vans, trucks and transporters with their tents and awnings filled every inch of available space. Price knew what he was looking for, however and it was not long before he found it.

The largest and grandest race transporters stood at the head of the field, closest to the start and finish line. This was the exclusive domain of the elite of the motorcycle world, the official works teams with their "factory" bikes. Honda, Suzuki, Yamaha, Kawasaki, Ducati, Triumph and now, making its first appearance at the TT, a new addition to the fold. Price gazed at the largest and grandest transporter of them all: in bold gold lettering against a matt black background, it logo proudly announced "Petromax World Racing".

"Impressive piece of kit, isn't it?" a voice behind him said. Price turned to face a short stocky man in bright red overalls. He had a friendly face so Price ventured a question.

"Do you?…are you…with them?" The man smiled and shook his head pointing to the "Honda" logo on his overalls.

"Sometimes wish I was," the man continued, "seem to have all the money in the world nowadays, them Russians. Don't know where they get it from; wasn't that long ago they were all broke, but look at 'em now: luxury yachts, football teams, they own everything, those bloody Russians."

"Russians?" Price enquired, raising his eyebrows just a little.

"Russians," the man confirmed. He spat out the word with a measure of disgust. "Owned by some Russian billionaire who fancied the idea of going bike racing. They spend money like water. Who else," he asked, "could afford to do Moto Grand Prix, World Superbike and the TT in the same season?"

"Well, your lot, for a start," Price replied, "and Yamaha, Suzuki, Kawasaki, Ducati…"

"That's different," the man added hastily, "we're all manufacturers. We need to do those races to sell bikes. Petromax don't manufacture anything, not for sale anyway. They only make bikes for themselves. Expensive hobby if you ask me."

Price smiled inwardly; this man could prove a useful source of information, provided that information was extracted carefully. He did his best to look unimpressed. "Can't say I've heard that much about them. They've never won anything, have they?"

"Not yet," the man replied, warming to what was evidently a favourite topic of the paddock, "but this is only their second full season. Their machinery is fast enough; all they need now is reliability and then the results will come."

"If they've got all that money, I suppose there's a danger that they'll poach the best mechanics and riders off the other established teams?" Price asked.

The man laughed. "Not them. Keep themselves to themselves do the Russians. They never speak to the rest of us, not that any of 'em seem to speak English, anyway. Only one who did mix with us lot was Robbie Taylor, God rest his soul, and it was pretty obvious then that their team manager didn't like it."

"Wasn't he the rider who got killed yesterday?" Price asked.

The man nodded. "Good rider. Not everyone's cup of tea, but I got on alright with him. God knows why he joined up with Petromax, but I suppose it was the usual story, money. It changed him, though, riding for that lot. His hair started to fall out; must have been the stress of having bloody Russians shouting at him day and night. In the end he got sick of it and shaved the whole lot off."

The conversation carried on for a few more minutes before the Honda mechanic looked at his watch, announced that it was time to take the number two bike to the "dyno" (whatever that was) and left. Price looked again at the black and gold Petromax transporter. As the Honda man had said, it really was an impressive piece of kit.

There was a crackle of noise as somewhere in the background a racing motorcycle engine burst into life. The noise grew louder and louder filling the paddock with a high-pitched screaming. Price wondered if the noise had something to do with the "Dyno" that the Honda mechanic had referred to and turned to walk towards it, failing to notice a tall burly stranger with dark glasses who had been standing watching him and listening to his conversation for the last ten minutes. When Price had disappeared from view the stranger pulled a mobile phone from his pocket, punched in a number and, after a momentary pause, began to speak in a low monotone. His words were in Russian.

Chapter Three

Tuesday Evening (Practice Week)

Tuesday evening had arrived and with it the fourth Practice session of that year's TT races. Price had made the eighteen mile drive out from Douglas to Quarry Bends, had parked his Alfa in the large car park that served the neighbouring Wildlife Park and was now sitting on the bank by the roadside waiting for the first machines to arrive. The roads had closed on schedule and the weather was reported fine all around the course. Quarry was the next named corner after Ballaugh Bridge. Approached by a longish straight, it consisted of a sweeping combination of right, left then right hand bends. The road surface looked good and to Price (who had never watched from here before) it looked fast.

Behind him the grassy bank dropped away steeply to the car park and beyond that an area of pasture and deciduous woodland in which he could see a number of animals roaming. Australian marsupials were not a field in which he claimed any degree of expertise, but at this range he tentatively identified them as wallabies. A gaggle of marshals stood over to his left by a small tower-like shelter, which rose from the car park such that the road passed in front of the second storey of the structure. To his right sat a handful of leather clad spectators; their conversation quite clearly marked them out as German as did the bold letter D on the number plates of the half-dozen or so motorbikes in the car park.

The travelling marshals flashed past and the small crowd fell silent waiting for the first racing machines to come into view. Necks craned out from the safety of the bank as each and everyone, spectator, marshal and doctor alike stared over to their right, down the road towards Ballaugh. Suddenly, in the distance, they heard a sound. At first a distant hum, like a far off swarm of bees, it grew louder as the seconds passed; rising then falling in pitch as the bees grew closer. One of the marshals seemed to be providing a running commentary, although to whom was unclear.

"On the approach to Ballaugh...braking...braking...jump the bridge...back down...hard on the throttle through the village...up through the gears...second...third....fourth.....fifth......hard on the gas.....top.....roll it off for Ballacry....the jump..hard on..."

Price had stopped listening. When the first rider made the jump at Ballacry, he had burst into view, rounding an oblique corner some three hundred yards or so down the road. In a gathering crescendo of noise those yards were eaten up and the motorcycle screamed past, inches from the roadside. Price flinched backwards. Then, suddenly, another shape arrived, pirouetting as if in slow motion across the road, a huge and menacing hunk of hot metal. Price dived backwards and slithered down the steep and unforgiving slope. A fraction of a second later a chunk of the machine flew over his head. Around him were screams and shouts and then a heavy silence.

When he came to his senses he realised that he was still alive and, as his brain slowly began to think again, unhurt, but lying on his back in the car park at the bottom of the bank. The Chief Sector Marshal and a handful of his staff were clustered around him; they looked worried, but they seemed to cheer up when he opened his eyes.

"Are you OK, doc?" they asked.

Price tried to move his arms and legs; found he could; nodded and waved them on their way. When they had gone, he tried again. It seemed harder, but slowly, and with a little bit of difficulty, he got to his feet. A motorcycle was lying half a dozen yards from his feet. It was on its side and appeared badly damaged. Remembering, albeit at that stage only vaguely, the reason why he was there, he looked further afield; the small group of spectators and marshals at the top of the bank appeared to have vanished. He got to his feet and shouted: "Medic here. Anyone need any help?"

When there was no response he continued: "What happened…..anybody?" A voice close by him responded.

"You Ok Doc yes?"

The accent was hesitant, but unmistakably Russian. Price turned around and faced the speaker. He was tall and powerfully built, wearing black racing leathers with the logo "Petromax" picked out in striking bold capitals of a vivid gold design. Helmetless, his facial expression appeared, if anything, sheepish and he continued:

"Doc…sorry…bike lose front..er….end…after jump…da!" He turned and pointed back down the road towards Ballacry.

"Are you OK?" Price demanded. The Russian rider nodded and, without waiting for further comment, the doctor struggled up the bank to the roadside. The marshals had yellow flags held aloft, but they were not being waved; in Price's limited understanding of the rules that was a good sign. He broached a question to the Chief Sector Marshal:

"Er…Is everyone OK" The Chief Sector Marshal nodded.

"You had a lucky escape there, Doc!"

"What happened?" came Price's tame reply.

"That rider there Rorletski, came over the jump at Ballacry and lost the front end when he landed. He was just behind the works Honda guy as well….started ten seconds behind him so must have been going like absolute stink to catch him on the road. Anyway, looks like a front end seizure to me…Rorletski's bloody lucky…or unlucky…I suppose you could say….way those Petromax bikes are going…"

"But no-one's hurt?"

"Yeah, luckily the bike didn't hit anyone. Think a couple of the German spectators got twisted ankles diving out of the way, but there you go!" He wore a bemused expression as he shrugged his shoulders. The couple of Germans were clearly not his problem.

The bikes were flying past now, thick and fast; after twenty minutes or so Price began to realise that most of them seemed to know what they were doing and did not appear to be particularly suicidal. He noticed that the strongly built Russian rider was still standing beside him. The phrase "Never look a gift horse in the mouth" clearly sprung to mind so he ventured a question:

"So you ride for Petromax…..Yes?" The Russian smiled.

"Da…..Yes"

There was a certain innocence about the manner of his response. Price felt that a few further questions could be tried.

"Good bike…the Petromax…very fast…doing well in World Superbike…could do very well here…..You like the TT?" They were easy questions, teasers, but Price wanted to engage the man.

The Russian beamed. "I know of TT races since I was boy.Greatest motorcycle race in World…..I have videos…." His tone dropped to a conspiratorial whisper,"Pirate videos, not legal in Russia…Duke…Hailwood…Agostini….Dunlop…. Hislop….Fogarty….I always want to ride here."

Price could see that the sentiments were genuine. There was no doubt about the man's commitment: the light shining from below those bushy eyebrows spoke of that. He nudged matters on a little further.

"Is the bike…er…..reliable enough for the Island?"

The response was as surprising as it was unexpected.

"World Superbike Da….TT Niet….the….." he seemed to struggle for words before announcing, proudly, it seemed and emphatically, " *Bloody* thing, it break whenever we seem to get it going right…it seize engine with Rob Taylor, it seize front wheel bearing with me."

"That's what caused Rob Taylor's crash then, did it?" Price asked curiously (his mind recalling the still-running engine and rotating rear wheel as he knelt by the prostrate body on the mountainside).

"Engine seize." The man confirmed emphatically. "that is what my team tell me happen. And today front wheel bearing seize. Very, very bad luck or…."

"Or what?" Price prompted. The Russian dropped his voice again.

"Sabotage," he whispered lowly.

☆　☆　☆　☆　☆　☆

It was ten o'clock and Price was back in his hotel room. An appointment had been made sometime earlier and dead on time Kinnish arrived. Price told him about the incident at Quarry Bends.

The local man had some feelings about the way the investigation was going and spoke about them with a degree of passion.

"It's pretty obvious Jonathon," he stated boldly, "the Petromax guys are getting knobbled. Don't know quite how yet, but that is the only possible explanation."

Price was sceptical. "How…and why?"

"Like I said, I don't know yet, but that can be the only explanation."

"So, Taylor?….do you believe it was a seized engine?"

"Well, I can't say I'm convinced, but that's the story they believe in the Paddock."

"But you know as well as I do that the engine was still running when we got to him."

Kinnish shook his head; he had evidently considered this question and dismissed it. "Engine might have nipped up and thrown the rider off, but still kept on running when it hit the deck."

"How could anyone possibly have rigged that then?… surely, if a saboteur, to give them their proper title, had done something to the bike then it would have been picked up by the scrutineers before Taylor set off on the lap?" Price demanded.

Kinnish shook his head again."I don't know Jonathon, but word in the paddock is that the crash was down to engine seizure."

Price remained unconvinced. He recalled a conversation with Kinnish which had taken place a few hours earlier.

"So what about the pin-point pupils, the lack of obvious head injury and the radiographer being sent home? A guy I met in the Paddock told me that Taylor was ill: he'd been sick for a couple of days before practice started; what do you say about that?"

"Can't really see any possible link; I'm afraid it must all be down to sheer coincidence." It was a lame explanation and Kinnish knew it, but he could offer no other.

Price decided on a change of tack. If they couldn't say with any real degree of certainty *how*, what about the remaining questions *who* and *why*? "So who in the hell knobbled them?"

"Dunno. Big money on these races nowadays."

"Come off it, Steve. What do the guys get if they win a TT? Twenty Grand? Thirty? You can win more than that in a second division darts match these days, never mind snooker, football, tennis, golf…and those guys ain't risking their necks."

Kinnish stared at his friend blankly. Price obviously had no idea of what was involved.

"Not the *Prize Money* Jonathon. That's obviously crap. The money is in *betting*. You must have heard about the syndicates in the Far East. They bet on anything…everything nowadays…just so long as someone will set the odds. I've been talking to a few people today and I've learnt a few things. The TT has been….well it's been *noticed*. Serious, serious money is being laid on some of these riders and, well, from what I have heard, the sort of people involved are not, shall we say, to scrupulous about the methods they will use to get the right result."

"Are you *serious… betting*?" Price exclaimed loudly and incredulously. "Are you sure, I mean where are you getting this information from? Are these people you've been talking to….er….reliable?…who are they anyway?" Price was becoming irritated and he knew that it was beginning to show. He was tired. It had been a long day and the theories which were now being thrown into the hat by Kinnish seemed to raise more questions than they answered.

"Get real Jonathon," Kinnish responded angrily, "you saw what happened to Taylor, you saw what happened to the Russian guy. That wasn't coincidence and those weren't accidents." His voice was raised now and the look of disbelief on Price's face made matters worse.

"I can see that you don't agree with me," Kinnish continued defiantly. "I can't prove anything…yet, but give me time, I think I can find out." Without further word, he turned and stormed out of the room. The door slammed shut behind him.

Price sighed. Kinnish had clearly become obsessed with Taylor's death and more worryingly seemed now to be developing definite signs of paranoia. Still there was nothing Price could do about it… or maybe there was. He, Price, was, after all, on holiday and there was no reason why Kinnish should spoil that. He looked at his watch – ten thirty – just enough time. Picking up his jacket he left the room and made his way out of the hotel.

Dusk had fallen by the time Kinnish and his Thousand cc Yamaha R1 joined the TT course at Quarter Bridge. He had been fuming with anger at Price's apparent disbelief and, worse, apparent lack of interest, when he left the hotel, but after a couple of miles on his motorcycle those negative thoughts had already started to ebb away. He was staying with his family in their farm out near Kirkmichael, so a thirteen or fourteen mile ride lay before him. It was a pleasant thought. The bikers who circulated the Course at insane speeds for most of the day had returned to their hotels or campsites and the road was quiet. He accelerated off towards Braddan Bridge, rode smoothly through the S-bend then on towards Union Mills. Slowing for the 30mph zone, he glanced in his rear view mirror whilst passing the *Railway* public house. The only traffic in sight seemed to be a large car some thirty or forty yards behind him. The car's headlights were on full beam and Kinnish swore under his breath – why did some car drivers have to be so discourteous, didn't they realise that bikers could be dazzled too? He accelerated out of the village and up the hill, the digital speedometer climbing rapidly to one hundred miles per hour. Passing Glen Lough campsite he slowed again and glanced in his mirror. To his surprise the car was now closer. He rode through the villages of Glen Vine and Crosby with his speed dead on the regulation 30mph. The car followed 20 yards behind him, its headlights still on full beam. Kinnish wondered if the driver was one of those individuals who felt uncomfortable driving in the dark and sought the false security of playing follow-my- leader. If so, he would soon have to cope on his own, for Kinnish would not be hanging around when the 30 mph zone came to an end.

Kinnish rode up the hill past the Crosby public house and glanced to his right. It was a warm evening and a smattering of people could be seen clustered around the small, but varied collection of motorcycles in the car park. The lights of the pub twinkled invitingly and Kinnish wished for a moment that he had pulled in for a pint. Too late, the opportunity had passed. The familiar white circle with oblique black line appeared; he notched down a couple of gears and opened the throttle. With a deep, but muted roar the Yamaha leapt forward. The digital speedo climbed again, on through 100mph, 120mph, 140mph. Kinnish tucked in behind the fairing as The Highlander Restaurant flashed by on his right, before sitting up at the last moment to brake for Greeba Castle. He glanced in his mirror: the car was still there, but had fallen back and now lay several hundred yards behind him. Kinnish was puzzled: he had expected it to be out of sight; no car on earth could live with the acceleration of a modern superbike, but whoever was driving that car was trying. He glanced in the mirror again and saw that the gap was closing. Gritting his teeth, he tucked in and wound on the throttle.

The two vehicles sped on through Appledene and Greeba Bridge. Drinkers sitting outside the Hawthorn pub looked on in amazement as motorcycle closely followed by car flashed past at over a hundred miles per hour. They were used to high speed action in the races, when the roads were closed, but not at this time of the night. Meanwhile, on the motorcycle, Kinnish was getting worried and was starting to make mistakes. He knew now that he was being followed, worse still that he was being chased. He would soon be on the twisty, wooded Glen Helen section of the Course. In the daytime, he would have been able to leave the car for dead, but it was night and the Glen Helen section would be dark and lonely. A modern superbike could kill a car in daylight, but in darkness?…were the headlights really up to the power of the machine? He toyed with the idea of turning off and making his way to Kirkmichael via Peel, but when the green traffic lights of Ballacraine crossroads appeared in front of him, he instinctively threw the bike into a right turn and thundered up the hill. He knew almost as soon as he had turned the corner that it was a mistake. He was on the Glen Helen section: the only possible escape would have been the back road to Peel at Ballig Bridge, but that road had been closed because of a rock fall a few days before and there would be no opportunity to turn off now for several miles.

The thousand cc motor was singing as he rounded the left hander at Ballaspur and accelerated on through Ballig Bridge. His twin headlights picked out the road ahead of him, but they were the only sources of light apart from the occasional fleeting glimpse of a far off and solitary farmhouse. It was the most dangerous section of the Course and Kinnish knew it well enough, bad enough in the daytime, but a thousand times worse at night. The trees were oppressive; they seemed to crowd in and overhang the narrow road, soaking up the luminance of his headlights and sapping the strength of his machine. His speed fell and those other headlights in his mirror grew ever closer.

He raced through Laurel Bank, throwing his body and machine through the left hander then the right and accelerated on to Glen Moar and the infamous Black Dub. Many good men had died there and feelings of impending doom swept into his mind like so many gathering dark grey clouds. He glanced in his mirror yet again, hoping against hope, but the blinding white lights were almost upon him. Suddenly he felt an agony of pain, a searing blinding knife wound to his right thigh as the car struck once…and then again. To his left, the black jagged shape of a cliff appeared out of the night, then darkness, everlasting darkness came……..

The silver car drove on for a short while, then pulled over to its right into the large car park that lay before the Glen Helen Lodge. It stopped for a few moments then turned around and set off back down the dark road towards Douglas. Twenty minutes later it pulled into the car park, behind a large hotel; after a few moments its ignition cut and its engine was silent. The driver door opened momentarily then slammed shut.

Price opened his hotel room door, fell onto his bed and was asleep before he had even thought of undressing.

Chapter Four

Wednesday (Practice Week)

The door opened with a deafening crash and the room exploded with light. Price opened his eyes and looked up.

"Jonathon Price?" a voice shouted from somewhere outside his peripheral field of vision. Price pulled his body into a sitting position. He had been lost in a deep and dreamless sleep, but the loud noise, sudden bright light and barked urgency of the strident tones addressing him dragged his unconscious mind into waking reality.

"Who…what the ….who in the hell are you?" he demanded angrily.

"Police," came the response, "Police Constable Quilliam. I ask again, are you Jonathon Price?"

Price was fully awake now and glared angrily at the uniformed policeman standing beside his bed. The policeman was accompanied by another uniformed, but as yet nameless representative of the local branches of law and order. He replied:

"Yes I'm called Jonathon Price. Why? What do you want? What gives you the right to burst into my hotel room at (he hesitated for a second to look at his watch)… at four o' clock in the bloody morning?

Police Constable Quilliam stood back for a moment as though formulating his speech and then proceeded: "Jonathon Price, I'm arresting you on suspicion of the murder of Dr Stephen Kinnish. You do not have to say anything, but it may harm your defence if you do not mention now something which you later rely on in court. Anything which you do say may be given in evidence….and, by the way, my colleague's name is Constable Carter."

"Murder of Steve Kinnish?" Price said, "what the hell are you talking about? Steve is fine; he was in this room only…(he looked at his watch)…six hours ago. There was bugger all wrong with him then and I doubt very much whether things have changed so much whilst I've been asleep."

"Things have changed, Dr Price," Quilliam replied, "as I believe you know full well. The main change is that Dr Kinnish is dead and we believe that you were involved in his death. Now are you going to come with us, or do we have to use force?"

Price did not reply. He shook his head, believing that the episode was no more than some extremely bad dream. Unfortunately the dream seemed to be an interactive one which led to Constable Carter seizing his shoulder and pulling him from his bed.

Offering no resistance, Price felt himself dragged to his feet, his arms swivelled behind him and with a dull click, cold metal bracelets were applied to his wrists.

"Okay Dr Price, I think its time for you to come down with us to the station," Quilliam announced with a degree of finality. Price saw no point in struggling, but asked if he could at least be allowed to change his clothes. The request was denied. There was no further conversation and he was bundled unceremoniously out of the room, down the stairs and into the white police van which was waiting in the car park at the rear of the hotel. It was, he thought, at least discreet: they had not dragged him out through the front entrance.

Handcuffed, Price sat alone in the back of the van whilst it made the short journey to Police Headquarters. He racked his brain to try and guess what had happened, but it was no good, he could not even begin to speculate without certain minimum information. Quilliam had said *murder* and *Kinnish*; surely there must be some mistake, Kinnish had been alive and well six hours earlier when he left Price's hotel room. Kinnish couldn't be dead...he just wasn't the sort of person who, well *died*, he was far too boring for that. And why had they come for him? What had happened to the anaesthetist? Price knew that the man was a bit of a lunatic on that motorcycle of his; it certainly was quite possible that he had crashed and wiped himself out. If that was the case then Price would maybe shed a tear or two (but no more than that...Kinnish had never been a close friend and the grief Price had experienced over the last couple of days seemed to outweigh any residual feelings he still had for the man). If Kinnish really was dead, though and it was not an accident, what possible evidence could they have which would implicate him? These questions and a dozen more swirled around his mind. The van lurched to a halt and minutes later the rear doors were flung open to reveal a dimly lit yard at the rear of the police station. Price was told to get out and, seeing no reason to object, did so without speaking.

The next hour passed slowly. Price was taken into the station and escorted down that same gloomy corridor he had walked in such different circumstances less than forty hours earlier. The stale, repugnant smell which hung about the place seemed even more overpowering. He reached the desk and was booked in by the custody sergeant, cautioned again, searched, breathalysed (and found to be well over the limit), stripped of his possessions and led to a cell. He was advised of his right to see an advocate, but nothing more was said about the alleged offence and he was not told when he would be interviewed. He understood that the Isle of Man had its own legal system. Maybe they did things differently over here? An advocate (which he took to be the same as a solicitor) would surely be able to help; he took up the offer and was told by the custody sergeant that the duty advocate would be called and would come and see him in due course.

The hours dragged on. Price lay on the uncomfortable bed (if that was what they called the thing) in the corner of the cell and waited…and waited. He was desperately tired, but sleep was impossible. They had taken his watch and the cell was windowless so he had no real idea of time, but hours must have passed before eventually he heard voices in the corridor outside. There was a click as the lock was turned and the heavy steel door opened. It was the custody sergeant again. The duty advocate had arrived.

Price was led down the corridor into another, larger room. A table lay against the left hand wall. On it stood a twin deck tape recorder and around it five plastic chairs, of a utilitarian as opposed to a comfortable or elegant design. He was told to take a seat and the door closed behind him. He heard voices in the corridor again; the conversation was muffled and he could not make out clearly anything that was said, but after some minutes it came to an end, the door opened again and a youngish woman walked into the room. She was tall, of slender build, had short dark hair and wore a reassuring smile.

"Dr Price?" she asked. He nodded. "I'm Louise Templeton, duty advocate," she continued, "how are you bearing up?" She spoke quickly, but in a confident, reassuring manner.

"I'm okay," he replied, "well, as okay as I could be under the circumstances. What's going on? Why have I been arrested? what's this rubbish about Steve Kinnish?"

"I've just been given some disclosure," she said, "and I understand that the police want to conduct a preliminary interview based on that. I'll discuss it with you in a minute and take your instructions, but please understand that you're in a police station and anything that you tell me in this room may not be totally confidential."

"You mean we could be overheard?" Price asked.

"It's possible," she replied, but added nothing more.

The meeting between advocate and client lasted twenty minutes or so. Miss Templeton outlined the case against Price. Kinnish had been found by the roadside in Glen Helen just before midnight. He was dead and the motorcycle which was lying nearby had been badly damaged. An autopsy would have to be performed and the bike examined forensically, but on the face of it, the signs pointed to impact with another vehicle. A car had been seen turning into the car park at the Glen Helen Lodge and then driving away at speed some time earlier. Witnesses outside the Hawthorn Inn had seen a car following a motorbike at high speed. The descriptions of the vehicles seemed to tally. The car was a silver Alfa Romeo saloon. A silver Alfa Romeo saloon had been seen entering the car park of the hotel where Price was staying some twenty minutes or so later. It had been recorded on CCTV. The night manager of the hotel had walked past the parked car, had noticed the extensive damage to its front nearside, damage which he knew had not been there the day before and had noticed something else, something which had caused him to pick up

41

the phone and dial 999, something dark and red and smeared over the crumpled silver bodywork of the car.

"What?" Price had asked incredulously.

"Blood," came the monosyllabic reply.

And, of course, the car had been Price's. The hotel register had confirmed that fact, as had a quick check on the Police National Computer. In addition, the hotel's evening receptionist had stated that Dr Kinnish (she knew his name well enough) had visited Price late the previous evening. A statement from a guest in a neighbouring room had ·described raised voices and a slamming door. Kinnish had been seen leaving the hotel just before ten-thirty. Price had been seen leaving not long after. That was all the evidence which had so far been revealed, but it was enough, Miss Templeton advised Price, for the Police to have acted as they did. It was time now to take his instructions and then the interview could begin.

A couple of hours had passed. The interview under caution was coming towards an end. Price had answered the questions put to him in as full and frank a manner as he thought possible, but the investigating officers did not seen remotely satisfied.

"So," the older, taller, grey haired officer inquired sarcastically, "you're telling us this, Dr Price. You were with Kinnish and had a row....er, sorry, a discussion, with him about some matter that you're not prepared to go into because *you* don't think its relevant to this investigation. Kinnish then stormed out of the room closely followed by you. He jumped on his motorbike and rode off, but you just calmly walked off down the promenade, having a late night constitutional as it were and *precisely at that moment* someone broke into your car without setting off the alarm, hotwired the motor, followed, no, chased, Kinnish, knocked him off his bike and killed him. They then calmly brought the car, your car, back here, parked it up for you so it was all nice and ready for the morning and then they walked off, all without anybody seeing them. Do you really think I, we, let alone the man in the street, could be expected to believe that?"

Miss Templeton interrupted firmly. "Officer, this *is* an interview. You are here to put questions to my client about his involvement or suspected involvement in an alleged criminal offence, *not* to ask him to indulge in idle speculation about what you, your colleague, or indeed the hypothetical man in the street could or should be expected to believe. Now, may I assume, by the degree of repetition which appears to be creeping into your questions, that you have substantially completed this interview?"

"Miss Templeton," the officer protested, but the female advocate stood her ground.

"I think my client has answered all your questions, officer."

The older man reluctantly agreed and the interview came to an end. The tapes were removed from the machine, sealed in the usual way and the policemen left the room.

Louise Templeton turned to speak to Price. "So far, so good, Dr Price. I don't think that the evidence they have against you would be anywhere enough to convince a jury, not at this stage in any event. Especially as so far they don't have any positive identification of you driving the car, but that might change."

"Miss Templeton," this time it was Price's turn to protest, "how many times do I have to tell you and them, I *wasn't* driving the car. I never went near it again after I came back from evening practice. I went out for a walk along the promenade and I stopped in a couple of bars and had a couple, well more than a couple of drinks. I'm a bit shocked at the moment; maybe you believe me, maybe you don't! I've been told this morning that a guy I've known for quite a few years has been killed; I don't really think that's sunk in yet, but I've also been told that I'm suspected of murdering him. You may not quite understand, but I'm pretty upset at the moment. On top of that, I'll tell you now that I had a shed load to drink last night, got back to my hotel room late and got pulled out of my bed by the police in the early hours of the morning. I've had virtually no sleep for over twenty-four hours and, at the moment I feel pretty stressed and pretty depressed. Okay I can't give you the names of the bars I went to or the names of the people who saw me, because I can't remember, but someone, somewhere is bound to know."

"Okay Dr Price," the advocate replied supportively, "where were the bars again? If you can't remember their names, just try and describe where they were. The police have said that they'll look into your alibi, but I think we'd better not take any chances, so I'll look into it as well."

"Look, I went to a load of places, but I think I remember ending up at an old-fashioned pub with woodened panelled walls. I visited it a couple of nights ago, I think. Somewhere on the Prom. Spoke to a guy called Richard. He'll remember me."

Price was taken back to his cell and the door clanged shut. He had learned that it was just after twelve noon and the custody sergeant informed him that they had sent out for lunch. "Fish and chips," he had added cheerfully. Price had just shrugged his shoulders; food was the last thing on his mind at that particular moment.

Miss Templeton had already begun her investigation. She had asked to look at the vehicles and as Price sat in his cell feeling sorry for himself, toying gloomily with battered cod and chips, she was outside in the yard being shown the damaged Alfa and wrecked Yamaha. The Senior Vehicle Examiner pointed out the details and the advocate took notes. Obviously, as the expert had stated, a full forensic examination would have to be made with microscopic and chemical analysis, but it did look likely that the traces of silver paint found on parts of the motorcycle came from the car and the traces of blue paint found on the car came from the motorcycle and then, of course, there was the blood. Miss Templeton felt a little sick; she had seen enough and asked to leave.

It was several hours later when Price awoke. How he could possibly have fallen asleep on such an uncomfortable resting place, he found difficult to believe, but total exhaustion had done its job and the rest had served him well. Those feelings of shock, frustration, anger and fear seemed to have gone, replaced by a deeper, stronger feeling, of resolve to see things through. He had been this way before. On that occasion, albeit in the dim and distant past, things had looked just as bleak, if not bleaker than they did now. Price smiled grimly to himself as he recalled those far off events and his manner steeled. If Kinnish really had been murdered (and he was not yet convinced) then the murders of Taylor and Kinnish had to be related; his task now was to solve the puzzle and in some way avenge the death of the guy who had brought him to the Island. Paper, pen, telephone and computer he had not, but an active mind and photographic memory he had. Slowly and methodically he recalled every single thing that had happened to him since his arrival on the Island three long days before. Every detail was considered, evaluated and logged. When he had finished he sat back. He had formulated a theory, well a hypothesis at least. It was implausible perhaps, but nevertheless it was a possibility and in considering it, a distinct train of thought had been set in motion. He needed further information, evidence and he needed help, but first and foremost he needed to get out. His thoughts turned again to Miss Templeton.

At that very moment Louise Templeton was on the case. Her afternoon had been spent in the office working through the mountain of paperwork that every day seemed to bring. She had made a few telephone calls on Price's account, but they had proved unsuccessful. The local private investigator was busy; he had told her that he would have no spare capacity for at least a couple of days, *not even* to help with a murder. She had pleaded with him, pointing out that it was a privately paying client and not one on legal aid, but his resolve had stood firm; he was unavailable. This time she and she alone would have to try and find the alibi witness.

There would be little point, she reasoned, in scouring the bars and pubs at too early an hour. The evening practice session would keep most of them empty until half-past eight at least. Most people were set in their ways and kept the same sort of hours when they went for a drink. Price had gone out at half-past ten the previous night and had returned some time after twelve. It would seem logical to look for witnesses at about that time. He had tried to describe his route, initially at least, so she parked her car outside his hotel and began to retrace his steps. It was a balmy summer evening. May had moved into June and the promenade was busy. Groups of leather clad bikers meandered along the pavement admiring the gleaming rows of two-wheeled machinery, parked in orderly phalanxes at right angles to the kerb on either side of the road. Louise Templeton knew that it would be busier still in a couple of days time when the real crowds arrived for race week.

Every bar was busy, the legions of drinkers spilled out from open doors, but these were happy revellers. The beards may have been long and the attire unusual, but the conversation, which flowed freely in all manner of accents and tongues, was friendly and the faces wore universal smiles.

The advocate moved on, pausing only to enter each establishment and question the bar staff and any customers who would listen. She showed them a photograph of her client; had they seen this man last night? At about this time? Time after time her questions met with the same response: a shake of the head; an emphatic no. Sometimes her questions provoked other questions, irrelevant, but not altogether unexpected:

"Lost your boyfriend, Pet?"

"Stay and have a drink with us, darlin'"

"Wanna come for a ride on my bike?"

She smiled, shook her head and moved on.

It was nearly midnight when Louise Templeton reached the last place on her list. She walked through the open doors of The Queens Hotel and approached the bar. Her enthusiasm for the task had now faded and with it her earlier confident belief in her client's story. Deep down, she had become quietly resigned to failure. She voiced her standard questions and thrust the photograph forward just as the landlord uttered the traditional words: "Come on gentlemen and ladies, if you please, last orders at the bar."

The landlord took the photograph from Louise, frowned and scratched his head. "Now, I have seen him before; not last night though, my night off last night wasn't it? Can't help you there. No, the person who was on duty last night isn't on tonight, sorry. He'll be here tomorrow though," he added helpfully. She was about to turn and go when a balding red-face man lumbered up to the counter and pushed an empty glass forward.

"One for the gutter. Same again please landlord," he said, swaying slightly. The landlord took the empty glass and thought for a moment.

"This fellow might be able to help you, though Miss," he said, "he's in here more often than me or any of my staff. Richard, you seen this fella before?" The photograph was still on the bar counter. The man called Richard looked at the landlord, looked at Louise Templeton, then pulled on his reading glasses and looked at the photograph. He seemed a little the worse for drink and stared at the photograph for what seemed an age before replying.

"Price, that's what he said his name was, Jonathon Price, doctor chappie; been in a couple of times." The advocate's heart missed a beat. Price had mentioned the name Richard and, looking around, she saw that the room was panelled.

"When?" she asked breathlessly. The red-faced man seemed to consider the question for a minute.

45

"Well there'ld be Monday and yesterday."

"He was in last night? Are you sure? What time"

"You don't half ask a lot of questions, young lady," he said, smiling, "'course I'm sure; I'm not drunk you know! Time? It'd be about eleven o'clock until eleven forty-five."

She had found her witness, but no matter how much she pleaded with him to come with her and make a statement there and then at the police station, he refused. He gave her his name, his address and his 'phone number, but that was all. It was a start, however, and she suddenly felt flushed with success. Tomorrow she would work on him.

Chapter Five

Thursday Morning (Practice Week)

"Come on Dr Price, wake up, I've got some good news for you." Price awoke with a start to find the custody sergeant standing over him. He looked up for a moment in bewilderment before the events of the previous day flooded back and he remembered where he was.

"What is it now sergeant?" he asked wearily, "more questions?" The uniformed sergeant smiled; his answer was as welcome as it was unexpected.

"No more questions, doctor; you're free to go."

"What?...Why?....How?..." Price was speechless.

"Chap walked in here at the crack of dawn and made a full statement. Told us how he was in the Queens Hotel with you from eleven o'clock until quarter to twelve on Tuesday night. Quite certain about it he was and he's a respectable, well known local businessman to boot. Witnesses saw the car and the bike go past the Hawthorn at about ten to eleven and the car was seen turning round at the Glen Helen at eleven o'clock. CCTV at your hotel showed the car returning at twenty-past so it stands to reason you couldn't have been driving it. Sorry you've been inconvenienced. Can I get one of our officers to give you a lift anywhere?...back to your hotel, perhaps?"

Price asked the name of the good Samaritan who had volunteered the statement, but graciously declined the lift. He realised that an olive leaf had been held out and was prepared to let bygones be bygones, but felt that he had spent rather enough time in the company of policemen and would value a solitary walk in the fresh air. He collected his belongings, thanked the sergeant and left.

His watch told him that it was a fraction before nine when he arrived at the hotel. He nodded to the daytime receptionist who smiled back at him. If she knew anything of the dramatic events which had taken place then she certainly didn't let it show. He made his way quietly up to his room and sat down on the bed for ten long minutes. Holding his head in his arms, he thought about what had happened over the previous three days. The whole thing was a desperate nightmare. Price recalled, not for the first or probably the last time, what Kinnish had said:

Great holiday, Jonathon; just stand by the roadside and watch the races. You'll love it.

The guy who had talked him into all of this was now lying in a refrigerated drawer

47

in the local hospital mortuary. That, in itself was rather upsetting, but on top of that, it did certainly look like someone, he knew not who, had some sort of personal grudge against him. In normal circumstances, a normal person, who allowed himself normal emotions, would have felt rather upset about that fact, but circumstances were most definitely not *normal* and Price could not allow himself to be *normal*. Once, long ago, he had been involved in a case, not *quite* like this one, but similar enough, he supposed: it had led to a breakdown and had disturbed him for years. Unlike most people, he knew, well enough, the true meaning of Depression. Somewhere on the far off periphery of his conscious mind, those old and worrying thoughts had already begun to intrude. Fortunately, he was still lucid and had insight: he recognised that the thoughts were paranoid delusions. The psychiatrist had told him as much all that time ago and he did not want to sink into that dark abyss again. Price steeled himself and hardened his resolve. He may have known Kinnish; at times he may have liked the man, but he was not going to have a breakdown because of him.

He stood up, peeled off the clothes which he had been wearing for well over forty-eight hours and climbed into a hot deep bath. Bliss. He had been dreaming of this moment for some time. He was just beginning to properly relax when the telephone rang. He groaned. Not again! Who could believe it? He thought for a moment and then wondered if it was his advocate. The police would surely have told Miss Templeton of his release and he certainly owed her his thanks; the custody sergeant had told him how she had found the witness. He climbed out of the bath, pulled on a bath robe and walked over to the 'phone.

"Hello, Price here."

"Jonathon, wonderful to hear about your release; the Chief Constable rang me up himself just a few minutes ago."

Even though he had only met the man once, Price immediately recognised the voice of the Chief Race Doctor. So the Chief Constable himself had been involved, Price thought, some news travelled fast indeed on this little island.

"Thanks for calling, Dr Duffy; much appreciate your concern." Price was about to put the phone down, expecting that to be the end of the conversation, but the other man seemed to want to continue.

"You are feeling alright aren't you Jonathon? I mean you're refreshed, you've had plenty of sleep…"

"Yes I feel fine Dr Duffy, well nothing that a couple of hours…" he was unable to finish the sentence.

"That's great Jonathon," Dr Duffy interrupted, "its just that, well with what happened to poor Steve and there's another chap, young Smith, who came off his Fireblade yesterday afternoon and broke his leg and another fellow you won't know, but was supposed to arrive today…won't be coming…in hospital with suspected appendicitis…well, as I say, its just that we're seriously down on race medics at the moment and I just wondered, well I wondered if you could help us out with the practice session this afternoon. Of course," he continued hurriedly, "given what you've been through I wouldn't normally have asked you and I won't take it at all the wrong way if you give it a miss today, but…" his voice trailed off. It sounded like what indeed it was, a desperate plea for assistance.

"I…I don't have any transport," Price answered lamely. It was true enough, but Dr Duffy had a possible solution.

"Can you ride a motorbike, Jonathon?" Price sighed; his fate was sealed.

"Yes," he had to admit, "I can; used to have a big Suzuki a few years ago, in fact when I was a medical student I used to race. I've even got a national licence. Haven't ridden for a couple of years, but I suppose…"

"Excellent. Now I've got a spare little 600 Yamaha. Wonderful little machine. We'll get you put on our group insurance. I can sort you out with a helmet and gear. I'll drop it off and you can go and have a play with it for a few hours before the practice session. Now, I make it a quarter to ten. I'll have the bike round at your hotel within the hour. Roads close at quarter to two, so you'll have three hours, near as damn it, to get used to it. Right. Now as for the Practice itself, I'd like you at the Creg…that's the Creg Ny Baa hotel," he added, "know how to get there?… and, by the way, Jonathon, the Chief Constable has assured me that the police haven't released your name and have told the local media that the Kinnish thing was probably just a tragic accident."

So that was how Jonathon Price, who had never even sat upon one of the modern 600cc supersport machines, far less ever ridden one, found himself nervously piloting a little rocket-ship around the Isle of Man TT Course that sunny Thursday morning. After a few miles his confidence grew more and more and the wobbles grew fewer and farther between. He had read enough about modern machinery to treat the bike with the utmost respect. Six hundred it may be, but with well over a hundred horse power on tap and weighing in at little more than the two fifty machines of his youth, he knew that the cemetery was potentially only a twist of the wrist away.

Long before he arrived at Ballaugh Bridge, Price decided that he had had enough of the TT course. He had grown sick and tired of bikes overtaking him at breakneck speed, leaving unsettling bursts of noise and buffeting pressure waves of turbulence in their wake. It was time to seek quieter roads.

Indicating well in advance, he rode over the famous hump-backed bridge (his wheels remaining firmly on the ground) and turned left onto a quiet country road. The signpost had suggested that it led to a place called Jurby. The land was flattish, and the green fields spoke of crops and arable farming. It was a sharp contrast to the rugged splendour of the Mountain Course, but a pleasing contrast nevertheless. He seemed to have left the high speed action well behind and for that, at least, he was more than grateful. After meandering along the lanes for fifteen minutes or so, he noticed an incongruous collection of buildings in the distance. As he grew closer, their layout and design began to resemble an old airfield. Sure enough a signpost appeared announcing Jurby Airfield. A short while later, another sign told Price and anyone else who happened to be passing that this was the home of "Jurby Junk", whatever that was. Price was curious; he had never ventured to that part of the Island before and decided to find out more. He turned right and rode slowly past a number of ancient hangars. Some were rusted, empty and decayed, others appeared less dilapidated, others seemed still to be in use. Of aircraft, however, he saw none; from all he could see, the place was now an industrial park of sorts, albeit a seedy, ramshackle and run-down one.

He brought his machine to a halt outside a large newish building, constructed, he guessed, from galvanised steel. A large sign informed him that this was the *Famous Jurby Junk*. He had never heard of the place before, but was minded to investigate so he put the bike on its stand and dismounted.

Walking through the entrance he was instantly struck by the size of the place. A little later he was struck by what it contained:...junk...nothing more, nothing less. He laughed; there could be no claim, at least, against the owner for misrepresentation. He roamed idly up and down the aisles, passing yard after yard of deep shelving filled with what could only be described as an Aladin's cave of the detritus of modern civilisation. Crockery and kitchen paraphanalia, records and CD's from every era, rusting garden tools and unwanted garden gnomes, old paperback books and postcards: the variety of junk seemed to be surpassed only by its volume. After a while he had seen enough. He looked at his watch and mentally calculated that he had just enough time to get back to the Creg Ny Baa before the roads closed, but as he turned to walk out of the building, he caught sight of an odd-looking piece of apparatus sitting on the edge of a shelf which seemed to be filled with ancient electrical equipment. He moved in to make a closer inspection. The contraption was made of a substance called bakelite; it was a forerunner of modern synthetic materials. From its casing to the ancient needle meters, dials and controls, the device looked as though it came straight from the fifties. He looked at the handwritten label and saw what the machine was alleged to be. He wondered. If it was what it said it was and worked, it could be useful. For the giveaway price it was certainly worth the risk. He picked up the machine, took it to the sales counter and paid. It was bulky, certainly far bulkier than modern such devices, but he managed to squeeze it into his rucksack, pulled on his helmet, mounted the bike and left.

He had decided to continue to avoid the TT circuit so he took the old road to

Ramsey. It ran in the same direction as the TT course from Sulby onwards, but was almost straight as a die and, more importantly, was virtually empty of traffic. Price was, after all, still coming to terms with the 600 Yamaha motorcycle. Arriving at Ramsey, he turned right onto the main road in from the north. He rode down the gentle incline, over the bridge and then, at the first roundabout, turned left. Keeping to the narrow road by the quayside, he made his way slowly towards the centre of the little town. It was hard enough, considering the number of vehicles parked on either side of that road, never mind the less than considerate pedestrians who seemed to step out between those vehicles with what seemed like an almost suicidal intent.

He had almost made it to the town square when another maniac stepped straight out into the road in front of him. Price's right hand clenched shut as he banged on the front brake. Swearing beneath his breath he looked up in time to see the little old man step back and fall to the ground. Price was worried now. He stopped the bike, put it on its stand and rushed over to the prostate body. As he ran towards the diminutive figure, his mind had been overcome with thoughts of first aid, emergency resuscitation and the like, but when he reached it the little man jumped up and grinned. Price looked at him in wonder as realisation dawned:

"I know you...you're..."

"Very big in Albania," the old man answered with an even broader grin. It was infectious and Price burst out laughing; this particular old man had that effect.

"Sorry for getting in your way, young man," he continued and with a shake of his head, a wink of his eye, and a clever little contrived tumble he carried on his way along the quayside. Price smiled, got back on his bike and continued.

Price had absolutely no intention of taking the mountain road; he knew his limitations when it came to motorbikes and a hundred mile an hour plus free for all somehow did not fit easily with them. There was a coastal road to Laxey and from there he could cut back to the Creg Ny Baa. He had not been on the road himself, but he had looked at the maps and on this occasion, discretion seemed the better part of valour. He turned left out of the square then right onto Ramsey promenade, passing the swimming pool then filtering left onto the Laxey Road. Thankfully traffic was still light. Hopefully no-one would notice his uncomfortable gear changes, wobbly riding style and less than perfect machine control; he had, after all, not been riding bikes for that long (well recently, at least). He rode up the hill, passed over the tram lines and swung to the left. To the right a track veered off to Ballure reservoir, but Price was not going that way. To the left, side roads dropped off towards Port-e-Chee, Maughold and other villages beside the coast, but the main road climbed ever upwards. Price tipped the Yamaha into a steep left hander past a large old house which bore the unusual name "Rest and be Thankful", climbed another steep hill, nudged the machine to the right then accelerated onto a long straight. He was starting now to get to grips with the machine and at long, long last his face was starting to wear a smile.

After a few more miles, Price slipped the machine into the sharp left-hander before the Dhoon Glen halt of the Manx Electric Railway and wound on the throttle. The confidence was coming, but maybe just a little too fast. At the end of this particular straight the road bent savagely to the right, the road-sign said:

Danger everlasting bends
And another sign very near it announced that:
Roads bite Back

How many degrees did that mean?, he thought to himself. He braked the Yamaha and cranked over to the right, but the bend went on and on and on and on. By the end, his smooth cornering style had degenerated into a graceless wobble, but he managed to hold it. Suddenly there was no time. The tightening bend opened up to reveal an extreme hazard. Price braked heavily and only just managed to avoid a collision with a pile of rocks. He got off the bike and put it on its stand. In front of him lay what the emergency services would have described as a serious incident.

The cliff had collapsed a very short time before: that, at least, was pretty obvious. In front of him lay a monstrous heap of rubble, in places several yards high. A cloud of reddish-brown dust drifted out from the ragged and uneven precipice which rose from the side of the road to his right. The rubble stretched along the road for a hundred yards or more, blocking it completely. It was on the cards that people were injured; if they were, then those injuries could well be serious. Price knew that he was the only medic on the scene and he knew that he would have to do something. It was at times like this that he wished his UK mobile phone worked on the Isle of Man.

"Can anyone hear me? Is anyone trapped?" he shouted.

There was no answer, so he climbed onto the pile of rocks and tried to make his way forward. As he did so, a low whoosh and rattle announced a further rock fall from the cliff to his right. The situation, which at first had not looked good, was now starting to look desperate.

There was a cry: a dim and muted voice called from somewhere beneath the rubble and Price struggled towards it. He shouted again and the voice replied; it was somewhere below him. Price had never been an action man; more of a thinker, but that desperate cry awakened something in his heart, something which had probably never spoken before. He threw himself at the rubble like a man possessed, forcing himself through the rocks and stones as if there were no tomorrow. He dug until his hands were bleeding; eventually, he reached the crumpled roof of a car. After some more effort, he had cleared a way through some of the rocks beside the top of the driver door.

By now he was lying on the roof and he leaned over, wiped the thick layer of dust from the window and looked in. The terrified face of a young woman was looking out.

"Get out of the way," he shouted, "there's no way I can open the door; I'm going to have to smash the window."

"My baby, my baby," she screamed, pointing to the back of the car.

Price peered in through the tiny smeared aperture that the frantic movement of his hand had produced in the window's dirty brown coating. The interior of the car was in darkness: he could see nothing but the wild terror of the woman's eyes. Behind him there was another low rumble and rattle of falling stone. He felt a sudden, sharp blow to his right temple and instinctively put his hand to the source of the pain. There was a warm, wet stickiness and moving his hand before him, he saw that it was stained red with his own blood. He glanced at the cliff above him: it looked desperately unstable and he feared the worst.

"Get back," he shouted. "Try and cover your and your baby's eyes." Something in the tone of his voice had the desired effect and the woman drew back from the window and pulled herself backwards to shield (Price assumed) the small child in the rear passenger seat of her car.

Price seized a jagged piece of rock and, still lying on the crumpled roof of the car, swung it with all the strength he could summon at that foot or so of the driver's window he had managed to expose. The rock hit the toughened glass with a loud bang and the window cracked, but did not shatter. Inside the car the woman screamed. The scream brought Price back to a sort of reality. Something deep inside him remembered what little he had been taught about dealing with emergencies.

"Look love," he said as calmly as he could, "what's your name?"

"Claire." she sobbed.

"And your baby?"

"He's called Juan."

"Well, look Claire, my name's Jonathon. I'm a doctor so you needn't worry. I'm going to have to smash this window with a rock and there might be a little bit more noise, but I'm going to get you and young Juan out of there, I promise you and I'm not going anywhere until I do."

A small voice in the darkness beyond the cracked glass whimpered, but said nothing more and Price brought down the piece of jagged rock with all his might. There was a loud crack. He brought it down again and this time the rock went through and the driver window shattered. Price brought the rock down again and again and again, until the frame had emptied to leave a space big enough for someone to crawl through. Behind him another low rattle announced a slither of rocks; there was precious little time. He stretched his arm through the now-empty window frame.

"Come on, Claire," he said encouragingly, "can you pass Juan out first; don't worry, I'll take him and then I'll pull you out."

"I'm passing him out now," she said and a plump, but uncomplaining baby made its way through the empty window-frame. Price had not thought about what to do next, but he suddenly felt a presence behind him.

"Here, I help you," a voice with an unmistakable Russian accent said, "you pass me baby and you get woman."

In the enlightened times of the Twenty-First Century, passing a baby to an unseen, unknown man behind you, whether or not he was possessed with a Russian accent was most certainly not the correct thing to do, but, once again, Price forgot his training and gratefully passed the baby back, stretched out his arm and helped the young woman to scramble from the car. She emerged, scratched, bloodied, dusty and bruised and he pulled her forcibly back towards the still-unsullied section of road where he had left his motorbike.

They had just enough time to run over the uneven pile of rocks when a roar announced a further cliff-fall; the remaining portion of rocks which had hung there teetering since the initial collapse now descended like an avalanche and buried the whole site below a further ton or more of rubble.

Price looked around. The scene was no longer empty. A few cars and a few more motorbikes stood there in the road, their drivers and riders looking at the cliff-side collapse and wearing expressions of awe. Someone was holding young Juan and the boy's mother was already taking her baby back, but the person who held the baby was a woman. Price ventured a question and discovered that a man had passed her the infant a few seconds before. She could not describe him, save that he was wearing motorcycle leathers. He had passed her the baby, nodded, got onto his motorcycle and then set off back down the road to Ramsey.

Emergency Services were arriving: an ambulance and a police car, but Price suddenly remember that he should have been elsewhere. He looked at his watch: Christ; he should have been elsewhere at least half an hour ago. He looked around: the young woman, Claire and her baby were talking to the paramedics and had no further need for him. It was time to leave; he climbed onto the R6 Yamaha, fired up the engine and rode off back down the road towards Ramsey. He knew, well enough, that he could turn left at Dhoon Glen and get to where he wanted to go.

He found the road, made the turning and followed the little lane back to Laxey. Once he got there, he regained the main road and rode steadily on, keeping the sea to his left and the Great Wheel to his right, carefully obeying the speed limits until he saw the turning and joined the back road to the Creg. Ten more minutes and he had reached the famous pub; he pulled into the car park, killed the engine and got off the bike.

[The large public house at that famous corner of the TT Mountain Course forever known as Creg Ny Baa was called, for many years "The Keppel Hotel". Lying on the mountain descent to Douglas, it sits at the apex of a right hand bend, itself at the bottom of a long, straight, steep drop from a bend known as "Kate's Cottage" (in itself a misnomer: its true name was "Tate's cottage", misquoted once by a radio commentator, the name "Kate's" has stuck). Nowadays "The Keppel Hotel" seems to have been lost and we are left with "The Creg Ny Ba".]

Price had made his way through the busy public house until he stood outside the front door on the very apex of the famous corner. The road had been closed for well over an hour and the practice session had been underway for more than half that time. He put his helmet and his rucksack on one of those convenient straw bales that guarded the building. The fluorescent-jacketed marshals stared at him for a moment, and the Deputy Chief Sector Marshal approached and began a very aggressive and one-sided conversation.

"Are you Price?" he asked. Price nodded. "You were supposed to be here over an hour ago; who do you think you are; what do you think you're doing?"

"Er, sorry," Price replied, " I got a little caught up; have I missed anything?"

"Missed anything," the Marshal continued, "have you missed anything? We're bloody lucky that you haven't missed anything, as you put it, because if we had, then someone could be dead. This is a serious business, Doc, so please treat it seriously. If you're going to do a session, then please turn up on time!"

"Sorry," Price said. "I'll try to do it right next time." The Marshal nodded, the heated atmosphere cooled and they shook hands. As far as both of them were concerned it was the end of the matter.

The practice session was a good one. As far as Price was concerned it was impressive, from the point of view of the sheer spectacle of the thing if nothing else. The bikes (large and small) and the sidecars hurtled down from Kate's Cottage, braked furiously and tipped into to the right hander around the Creg before accelerating away down the longer, straighter road to Brandish Corner. The Creg itself was a sharp corner: more than ninety degrees. Price doubted whether even the top guys could take it at much above sixty, but on the approach they could be doing well over double that before they started to brake and on the exit they could probably get up to something like treble. From what he had seen, it was one of the few places on the Mountain Course where there was some run-off. Machines which had overcooked it on the long approach down the hill could stick by their line and take the Laxey Road to the left hand side of the pub, if they could not make the right hander. One or two of them took such an option, but not many. All in all it was a safe and exciting practice. No-one was hurt, no-one came off and (Price later learned) the absolute lap record was unofficially broken.

After the session had ended, Price made (for him) the bold decision to ride out from the front of the pub and take the TT course back to Douglas. It was a shorter, far quicker route, but, to Price it constituted a significant leap of bravery. He crawled out to the front of the car park, watched patiently for an opening in the fast and heavy traffic and then accelerated cleanly into space. Down the drop to Brandish he, tentatively at first, then with growing confidence opened the throttle and kicked up one, two, three, four then five gears; with speed came exhilaration and those demons from his subconscious slowly receded. At the right hand kink a few hundred yards before Brandish he glanced at the digital speedometer and was horrified to see it reading one hundred and ten miles per hour. He eased off the throttle and squeezed the front brake, cogging down one, two, three gears before the sharp left-hander. There was another fast descent from Brandish to Hillberry, but Price had seen enough action and slowed; there would, he thought, always be time for improvement.

Price trickled into Douglas, crawled along with the heavy traffic on the promenade and turned into his hotel's car-park. He parked the Yamaha and decided to go for a walk. It was Thursday evening and the capital seemed to have filled up since he left the place that morning. The promenade was now awash with bikes. It was nearly two miles long from end to end, but the cars which had formerly occupied most of that space seemed to have mysteriously departed. In their place now, row after row of gleaming, brightly polished two-wheeled machines stood enthusiastically to attention. In the car park near the Sea Terminal (called, for some reason *the Bottle Neck Car Park*) a large marquee had materialised; it seemed to be doing a busy trade. Along the seaward side of the promenade, a number of sideshows, simulators and fast food outlets were now in place and then there was a funfair and what looked to be bungee jumps. Crowds of people thronged the area and the road seethed with traffic as ferry after ferry disgorged its cargo of cars, vans and above all motorbikes into the already overcrowded town.

Chapter Six

Thursday Evening (Practice Week)

Price pulled off the borrowed gloves, boots and leathers, sat down on his hotel bed and uttered a deep sigh. He could have cursed Kinnish, but the poor sod was dead, so cursing did not seem, well, really appropriate. The simple words that his friend had uttered came once again to mind:

"It's great fun, Jonathon, it really is. Come to the lovely Isle of Man and just stand by the side of the road and watch the races…nothing to do, well nothing much during the day and loads of entertainment in the evening."

The promised agenda was, so far at least, proving less than accurate.

Price was dog-tired; he had spent years working his guts out pursuing a hard and seriously time-consuming profession, but the last four days of *holiday* had been the most exhausting he had ever known. If he could have done, he would have gone straight to bed and probably fallen asleep within minutes, but the time for conscious choice seemed to have ended; he had a task before him now and whether he liked it or not, he had to see it through. Kinnish was dead and someone had tried to put Jonathon Price in the frame for the anaesthetist's murder. Price realised that the signs were not good; in reality he knew nothing, but he could well believe that someone thought he knew more. An attack on his own life could be next.

From what he could gather, the story put out by the police was that Kinnish had been involved in a tragic accident. There had been no suggestion of anything else on the local radio stations and, thankfully, his own name had not been mentioned. None of this really made him feel any happier though; it was patently obvious that someone, somewhere had other ideas. The black uncertainty once again allowed other thoughts to start to intrude. And the rock fall that afternoon; was that an accident? Price shook his head, of course it was, it must have been. How could someone, anyone, have known he would be passing? Impossible, but who was the Russian who had suddenly appeared behind him? The Russian had done nothing wrong though, in fact he had helped. And what were those suggestions Kinnish had put to him about gambling syndicates in the Far East? The man had put forward no evidence to support such claims, but he had made them and a short while later he had been killed. Were such syndicates really interested in the Isle of Man TT Races? Price considered the question for a few minutes and realised that he could not think of an answer. If Far-Eastern betting syndicates were involved, how in the hell could he look into that? Once again, he put his head in his hands. It was far, far beyond him: how in the hell had he become involved in this nightmare?

He stood up, shook his head and thought about the way forward. He had spoken to his advocate, the attractive, efficient and resourceful Miss Templeton, by telephone that afternoon. His gratitude had been undying, but he still needed one more *small* favour. He had asked her to meet him at the Queens Hotel that evening at eight. To his surprise she had accepted.

After a long, hot shower, he pulled on a clean set of clothes. His wardrobe was limited; a meeting with an attractive young lady had not been on the agenda when he had packed for the TT, but he made the best of what he had. That old cliché *smart but casual* he hoped probably fitted the bill, but hope was the best he could do. He cast a critical eye again in the full length mirror: *not bad,* he supposed, but worried again about what she would think. After a few more minutes posturing and posing he looked at his watch and decided. It was the *TT* for god's sake, not a fashion parade; he grabbed his jacket, flung it over his shoulders and was gone.

At half-past seven Price walked into the lounge bar of the Queen's Hotel. It was busy, but a little less so than most other establishments he had passed on the way there. It was a large, square room. The walls were lined with wooden panelling and the panelling was in keeping with the general character of the place and his mood: dark and gloomy, but the bar staff were obliging and the locals were friendly enough. Price noticed a familiar face, ordered a pint and moved over to join that face at the table in the corner, furthest from the door.

"Richard," Price began, "what can I say? I'm eternally grateful for what you did, I…"

The red-face balding man interrupted: "Shut it son. You didn't do it. You were here, so all I did was tell the old bill the truth."

"But you didn't have to Richard, I mean…"

"Like I said son, I believe in the truth…and helping out my fellow man. I had a problem with the police once and if someone had just had the balls to tell the truth then, well…" his little speech ended lamely, he got up and made the few steps to the bar. "Same again Landlord. What do you fancy young man, pint of Okells, eh?"

Once drinks had been placed on the table the two men began to talk; well Richard talked and Price listened. The topic was one close to Richard's heart; the TT races.

Outside the pub, a particularly loud motorcycle pulled up; its engine note throbbed, burbled and then stilled.

"…And anyway young fella," Richard continued, "like I said, when my rider won the Senior in….bloody hell, it's her…"

The men sitting in the crowded lounge bar turned, almost as one, towards the door. An apparition had walked in to the room. She was tall and thin apart from certain important feminine curves. Clad all in black, from her three-inch high stiletto boots to her skin tight leather trousers and her figure-hugging leather jacket, the apparition oozed serious, unadulterated sexuality. Conversation, which had flowed loud and unchecked for most of the evening suddenly halted and a strange and dizzy silence fell over the room.

After a second or two the apparition spoke: "Nice to see you Jonathon, Richard, aren't one of you boys going to buy me a drink?"

Jaws dropped and the two men sat there open-mouthed. It was a few moments before Price spoke. "Er yes, of course, Miss Templeton; we, er didn't quite recognise you straight away. What would you like?" The other men in the room resumed their conversations and the silence lifted.

Price purchased a round of drinks and rejoined Miss Templeton and Richard at the corner table. The conversation was one of motorbikes; there could, of course, be no other and it appeared that the lady advocate knew at least as much about the subject as the man, even though he was probably old enough to be her father. Funnily enough, after the initial shock of meeting, Richard and Miss Templeton seemed to get on like a house on fire; it was almost as though they had known each other for years. The language had become technical and Price, who was becoming bored with the subject anyway, allowed his concentration to wander. When it returned he found he was lost, cut off from his companions by an impenetrable forest of complex jargon. He cast his eye casually about the room, catching by surprise the gaze of a man who was standing at the bar. The man turned hurriedly away and walked out of the room, leaving a half-empty glass behind him. He had been watching them, though, watching them and listening to their conversation and Price had seen the man's face before, although he couldn't remember just where or when.

Price turned back to his companions. They were still discussing valves, camshafts, carburettors and the like. He had intended to ask Miss Templeton for a favour. It was the reason why he had invited her out for a drink that night, but then he hadn't counted on bumping into Richard and he didn't really want anyone else to know his plans. Still, he wanted to tell someone something and realised that unless he told them everything, they wouldn't be interested and they wouldn't understand. The time therefore seemed to have come to share his confidences, but not there, not in a crowded public bar with who knows how many other people listening in.

"Can we go somewhere a little more private?" he interrupted. The other two stopped talking and looked at him.

"Time for me to go home, I suppose," Richard said with a knowing smile. Miss Templeton looked embarrassed.

"No, no; don't get the wrong idea, either of you," Price protested. "I want to talk about something, but I don't really want to talk about it in here. It's too important and too sensitive. You can probably guess what I mean. We could go back to my hotel, unless either of you want to suggest somewhere else?"

His companions looked at him and then at each other.

"Come round to my place, if you like, it's just up the road in Onchan," Richard offered, "unless Miss Templeton wants to…"

"No, no," the lady said hurriedly, "Your place is fine; you two order a cab and I'll follow you."

Richard's place turned out to be a large and gloomy property which stood alone, some distance from its neighbours, on a cliff top at the extreme edge of the town. The last house on that road in Onchan, it stood behind a tall privet hedge and was set back some way from the road. Beyond it lay empty countryside, below it the dark and lonely sea. When the taxi dropped them off it was quite late, but the orange ribbon of sodium lights came to an end some distance before the house and in the exaggerated darkness of the unlit road, it seemed later still.

Louise Templeton arrived a few seconds later and parked her Harley Davidson on its side-stand in the driveway. Richard led them over to the front door, took a yale-type key from his pocket and, with a slightly shaky hand, pushed it into the lock and turned. The door swung open and they followed him into the house.

"Watch out for the mat," he said fumbling with a switch on the wall, "oh sorry Jonathon, I did warn you."

Price had caught his foot on something and stumbled forward, but somehow managed to stop himself from falling headlong. The solitary naked light-bulb flicked on, illuminating the hallway with its feeble glow and Price, cursing beneath his breath, looked down to see the edge of a well-worn oblong of faded carpet curling upwards from the tiled floor. They made their way along a shadowy corridor, then through another door. Richard pressed another switch and Price gasped at what he saw.

It was a large square living room; unlike the hall it was brightly lit and comfortably furnished, but also full of, well…..motorbikes. Highly polished and gleaming, they stood around the place like so many well-dressed guests making polite conversation at a party. The walls were a pale shade of blue and Price later discovered that Richard referred to it as his *Blue Room*. Louise Templeton walked from machine to machine, gazing at each with the eye of a connoisseur. It was obvious to Price that the lady had seen some of the bikes before, but she still seemed impressed. Richard followed her, supplying the commentary.

"That one, that's…?" she said.

"Mike Hailwood's Ducati," Richard confirmed proudly, "the one he won on in his comeback year."

"And that?" she asked.

"Honda RVF. Used to be ridden by Joey Dunlop," he replied.

"And that beauty?"

"Ah," he sighed, "that one's really special. That is H Rembrant Fowler's twin-cylinder Norton, the winner of the first ever TT in 1907. People will ask you whether any rider ever won a TT at his first attempt, well Fowler did: the first one!" He laughed quietly to himself..

"I've not seen that one; I thought it was lost, forever," she said quietly.

"Well no, love, it might be lost from general sight, but it's here. In my little collection."

The two of them went on like this for some time. They shared a passion from which Price seemed in some way excluded. It was obvious that Richard was a serious collector; when he saw that Price was interested, he led them to other rooms where they saw more of the same. Price realised that the collection was unique and probably priceless. Of the many machines in that display, there were copies, replicas, elsewhere, but here lay the originals.

They could have gone on all night, but Price, who *quite* liked motorbikes, thought enough was enough and brought the unscheduled meeting to order.

"Louise, Richard, can you please stop looking at the bikes and sit down. I think we need to talk." The advocate and collector looked at him in surprise, but took his advice, found comfortable chairs and were seated.

"Come on then Jonathon," Richard began, "we're all ears, what do you want to talk about?" Miss Templeton nodded her agreement. They knew, of course, what it would be.

"*Murder!*" Price announced in a chill whisper. His companions said nothing, so he continued. "My friend, Steve Kinnish, was murdered. You both know that. He wasn't the victim of some drunken hit and run, despite what the police are now saying. He was targeted in a cold and calculating way. The murderer, whoever he was, planned everything very carefully indeed. He knew where I was staying, stole my car and killed Steve just when he thought I had no alibi. It was all clearly designed to put me in the frame. If someone had just wanted to get rid of him it would have been easy enough, but to steal my car, make sure plenty of people saw it and then put it back in the hotel car-park, no, sorry, that's a carefully planned crime. You agree?" The other two nodded, but said nothing; they could see his line of reasoning.

"Okay, point number one. Steve got killed. Point number two, someone wanted to put me in the frame. That leaves us with two questions. Question number one, why would someone want to kill Steve. Question number two, why then try and implicate me?" The question invoked no answer so Price continued: "I can only say one thing, one name: *Rob Taylor*. Steve Kinnish and I were there, on the mountain, when Taylor crashed. There was something funny about that crash; Steve wasn't happy. Steve started to investigate; he asked a few people a few questions and, then, he died. We spoke a few times and he had certain ideas. I can't say that I was too impressed with most of them at the time, especially his ideas about Far-Eastern betting syndicates, but the fact of the matter is that for some reason he got knocked off his bike and killed. The next thing that happens, I'm arrested for his murder." He paused for a moment. Neither of the others spoke. "I need to look into Rob Taylor's death and I need some help. Will either of you help me?" He looked up at his companions as he made this request. Louise Templeton fidgeted and stirred. She had a small question.

"Thanks Jonathon, we know all of that, but what, *exactly*, do you think happened to Rob Taylor? I mean, the guy crashed his bike at 130mph and he died. What's suspicious about that?"

"He was murdered." Price said. There was a certain degree of grim finality about the statement: from the tone of Price's voice it appeared to be non-negotiable.

"Hold on a minute," Miss Templeton asked, "How can you possibly say that?"

" I have heard things, Miss Templeton," Price replied, "strange little things from all sorts of different people. I, of course, saw the accident. Steve told me about the injuries, or rather lack of them. I had that strange telephone call from the radiographer who didn't think Taylor's injuries were that serious; well, that's what she said before she hung up and then, of course Kinnish told me that the same radiographer had mysteriously been sent home on extended leave. There was no post-mortem on Taylor; I was with Steve when we tried to get access to the mortuary and as far as I'm concerned, the behaviour of the mortuary technician was *most* suspicious. Then, I was at Quarry Bends on Tuesday when the number two Russian rider, Rorletski, came off. I talked to him for ages and he told me plenty of things about Taylor….about how he had become ill a few days before practice began…about how he had been sick…." He stopped in mid-sentence as a face suddenly appeared on the edge of his memory.

"…Hold on a minute….that's where I remember that guy from," he said.

"Who?" Miss Templeton asked.

"The guy I saw in the Queens tonight, the black guy; the one who was watching us. He was at Quarry bends yesterday, sorry on Tuesday evening. He was there when I was talking to Rorletski, come to think of it he was only a few feet away; he can't have missed anything."

"Hold on a minute Jonathon," Miss Templeton demanded, "this is the first time you've mentioned this. Who was watching us?"

Price told them about his eye contact with the man in the Queens and his feeling that the man had been listening to their conversation. Miss Templeton and Richard listened, but shook their heads. They were far from convinced and both privately thought that Price was becoming a little paranoid.

"So," Miss Templeton said, "you've said murder. How? I mean, what do you think happened: did they sabotage Taylor's bike?"

"No," Price responded, slowly and carefully, "it's possible, but I think it's a lot more subtle than that." He seemed unwilling to be drawn further, but the advocate pressed him.

"How?"

He shook his head slowly. "I don't know for certain," he replied, but I suspect..."

"What?" she replied.

"Poison," came the answer.

The conversation carried on for some minutes. The shock disclosure made by Price seemed at least to have had some form of impact on his companions. More importantly, he had told them why he had to see Taylor's body in the mortuary. Louise Templeton gave the usual cautious lawyer's advice:

"Why don't you speak to the police, or the coroner; let them deal with it. If you try anything on your own you'll only get yourself into trouble."

Price looked at her and shook his head. "I don't think the police or the coroner would believe me; you've pointed out yourself that I don't have any evidence and I don't, *yet*. I mean to get some and then I'll go to the authorities."

The advocate had heard what Price had said, but still seemed to want it spelled out in black and white. "How are you going to get evidence," she asked, "you would need a court order for a post-mortem, you know, unless you had some sort of legal interest in Taylor's body and I don't think at the moment you have enough..."

"Miss Templeton," he interrupted, "All I want to do at this stage is examine his body...*externally*...and take a few strategic blood samples. Something I can get to a toxicologist friend I happen to have back in England. Now if we could do all of that *unofficially* between friends, as it were,..." he gave his advocate a wink and her eyes rose upwards to the ceiling.

"It's most irregular Jonathon and probably illegal." she said, "I *might*," she added, looking at Richard "be able to put you in touch with someone who..."

"Is that all you want to do, young man?" Richard cut in. Price looked at him in surprise and he continued "if you just want to get into the mortuary and have a look at one of the bodies, no questions asked, I can arrange that. I happen to be able to get into that place at any time of the day or night. When do you want to go?"

63

Miss Templeton raised her eyes and said nothing, but Price looked at the man in amazement: "How on earth?" he said.

Richard smiled. "I'm an undertaker," he said, "with the biggest practice on the Island!"

Chapter Seven

Friday Morning (Practice Week)

Price had woken well before dawn. He gazed out from his hotel room window across a sodden rain-swept promenade. The crowds of last night were no longer, but the rows of wet motorcycles still stood there forlornly whilst the rain poured down incessantly from a leaden sky. The weather had changed dramatically. He turned on the radio, tuned into the local station and learned, much to his relief, that the Friday morning practice session had been cancelled due to "poor visibility on the mountain", a euphemistic description, if he had ever heard one. He thought about going back to bed, but the thought quickly passed. He had recovered from his experiences of a couple of days before and was now wide awake, so decided to go for a stroll along the seafront before sitting for an early breakfast.

He walked out of the hotel and, for no particular reason, turned right and started along the promenade. The pavement followed the gently curving bay towards the harbour and the sea terminal. The small hotels and boarding houses lay, for the most part in darkness, but the signs in the windows now advised passing custom that there were "No Vacancies". It was a reversal of the message they had conveyed earlier in the week, a subtle change, but one which Price had not noticed.

After a quarter of a mile or so, he turned away from the line of buildings and looked across the roadway out to sea. The rain beat down, bouncing off the tarmac. Few people were out and about, but that was not really surprising given the weather and the hour. Only the men from the Douglas Corporation seemed hard at it. Small groups of them worked their way along the promenade, emptying the overflowing rubbish bins of the detritus of the night before, whilst a large road-sweeping machine passed backwards and forwards, cleaning the street. It was a scene that would be repeated every morning until the races came to an end.

A large and brightly-lit vessel had entered the bay. It was the morning ferry from Heysham, Lancashire, and Price knew that it was called the Ben My Cree. It passed close by the small island with its landmark 'Tower of Refuge' that lay a few hundred yards off the shore and approached the Sea Terminal. Price, who was going in that direction anyway, decided to watch the visitors disembark. He crossed over the road and carried on walking along the broad paved area that bordered the sea wall. For most of the year that area lay empty, but not now. The funfair had arrived and its rides and stalls stood silently in place waiting for the day to break and the crowds to return. He walked on, passing to the seaward side of the blue and white marquee and then close by the Sea Terminal building to reach the outer harbour.

He was just in time to see the large ferry turn and reverse slowly onto its mooring. It moved awkwardly and to Price seemed a little top-heavy, but he knew nothing about boats. Ropes were thrown to the shore and heavy winches took up the slack then pulled the heavy cable taut. There was a harsh metallic rattle as iron chain slid across steel plate and then with a clang the huge sea door at the stern of the vessel opened and the ramp to the harbour began to descend. Somewhere, deep within the blackness of the vessel's interior, motorcycle engines burst into life. The throbbing, pulsating tones echoed across the water and reverberated around the quayside. Price looked on in fascination as the vehicles began to leave. One by one they drove up the ramp, motorcycle after motorcycle. Some bore a single rider and little else, but most were more heavily laden. The ones with the German plates seemed to bear the greatest and most impressive burden. They were large, heavy machines with rider, pillion, panniers and tent. They trickled up the linkspan (a pivoting floating bridge which connected the stationary ferry with the shore), stopped for a second to gather their senses (and in some cases pull on waterproof clothing) and then roared off into the night.

Price counted them in, for a time, but then lost count; there were just too many. The number plates themselves told a story. Not surprisingly, the majority were British, but the Germans came a close second, followed by the Swiss, the French, the Spanish and the Swedes. He knew that the TT was popular, but had had no idea that it was as popular as this. It took a good half an hour to disgorge the vessel and Price watched for every second. When the ferry was empty, a handful of vehicles drove on for the return journey and it departed, on its way back to Heysham to pick up another full cargo of motorbikes and bring them to the road racing capital of the world.

A heady sweet smell of petrol and engine fumes drifted across the water and was gone. Even though it was still pouring with rain, Price smiled; he could *taste* the atmosphere.

When he got back to the hotel, breakfast was beginning to be served. He sat down in the restaurant and started to plan his day.

With no duties to attend, Price had some unexpected free time. He wanted to see Louise Templeton, but he also wanted to speak to an old, old friend. After consuming a hearty breakfast he returned to his room, sat on his bed, pulled over the telephone and dialled. It was a Cardiff number. It rang for a few seconds and then a pleasant female voice answered.

"Hello, Roy Love Investigations; can I help you?"

"Is Roy there?" Price asked. The female voice considered its position for a few seconds and then replied.

"Sorry, Mr Love is out of the office at the moment; can *I* take a message?" The voice was educated, a touch musical and definitely Welsh. Price left his contact number and put the phone down.

It was nine o' clock. Price decided to call on his advocate. He left the hotel, walked through the centre of Douglas and, on reaching Victoria Street, turned right. The road climbed steeply and swung to the right. Price discovered that most streets in this little town renamed themselves every few yards - this particular road had now become Prospect Hill. He made the steep climb and crossed the road. According to the business card she had given him, Miss Templeton worked out of number * Athol Street and was an associate of Mr Bradley Fitzgerald, Principal and owner of the practice. Price located the building and walked through the door. It was an unusual looking reception area for a lawyer's office, Price thought. Posters advertising well known feature films hung from the walls and, as for the usual certificates, diplomas and books, there were none. Price walked over to the receptionist, a pleasant middle-aged lady, and explained why he had come. He was told, apologetically, that Miss Templeton was in Court. He turned and was about to go, but the lady continued.

"Mr Fitzgerald has heard about your case, Mr Price and would like to see you."

Price shrugged his shoulders. He could see no real point, but…

"Up the stairs; then the door right in front of you," she said.

He followed the directions, reached the door and knocked.

"Come in," a voice called from within.

Price opened the door and walked into the room. He looked around: it was a warm but untidy little sanctuary. Like the reception, it seemed empty of the standard trappings of a lawyer's office. The walls in here were adorned with all manner of prints, but there did seem to be a general theme: the royal and ancient sport of golf.

"Fore!" a cry rang out from behind the heavy oak desk, closely followed by a small white ball. A head appeared, closely followed by a body and arm clutching an impressive-looking club. "Sorry," the voice apologised, "nearly got you there; good chip out of the bunker, though, wasn't it?"

Price looked at the owner of the face and smiled. Bradley Fitzgerald, advocate, tended to have that sort of effect on people.

"You wanted to see me," he asked.

"Did I?" Fitzgerald asked.

"Yes, you did. I'm Jonathon Price. Your Miss Templeton has been representing me, and doing an extremely good job, if I may say so."

"Good job?…oh that's good, no complaints then?" the man enquired.

" No, none at all," Price replied.

"Are you getting legal aid, or, er…?" Fitzgerald wondered.

"Well I'm a doctor, Mr Fitzgerald, a consultant surgeon," Price responded, "so I rather suppose I'll be paying your firm privately, don't you?" Bradley Fitzgerald's face immediately lit up with delight.

"A medic, eh. Do you play golf?" he asked.

Price shook his head; it was a funny sort of question, he thought, given the circumstances. He had expected something a little more legal.

"That's a great pity," Mr Fitzgerald said, pulling a face, "got a game this afternoon and need one more player to make up the numbers."

"Sorry," Price said. The funny little man sighed and shrugged his shoulders. He asked no further questions and moved round to Price's side of the desk to position himself for another putt. Price took it as his cue to leave.

He learned from the receptionist that Miss Templeton was representing clients in the magistrates' court, but would be back in the office that afternoon. He made an appointment to see her at two that afternoon, then walked back out into the rain.

So far the morning was proving less than successful. The weather was not conducive to wandering around the town, even if Price had been an avid window-shopper, which he was not. Far less was he attracted by the thought of riding around the Island on a motorcycle.

He had followed the road back down the hill and reached the promenade by the ornate Victorian clock tower. He looked up and could just make out the orange brick tower of the TT Grandstand at the top of Nobles Park, but the grey rain-laden clouds hung ominously low, hugging the skyline. The northern cliffs of Onchan had all but disappeared behind a sombre veil. From time to time the mist cleared for a moment, revealing the rocky headland, but then more cloud descended and it was gone. Of higher ground there was no sign and Price knew that there would be no motorcycle action that day. He lowered his gaze and looked down the promenade. A heavy, rattling horse tram passed by, its steel wheels cutting through the puddles of dirty black water. Price jumped aboard, more for something to do than anything else. The conductor, heavily clad in a bulky yellow jacket, took his pound fare without speaking and the tram drove on, its driver shivering and cursing against the rain. Price rode the full distance to Summerland: the tram was desperately slow and the journey seemed to last forever; he vowed not to bother again. Walking back along the promenade from Summerland, he came across the Queens, a pub he had now visited on a number of occasions. He was cold, wet and hungry and so he walked through the door. A decent bit of lunch was what he was looking for, but as he approached the bar, he discovered it was not to be his day.

Apologies of the Management - No Food today – Chef sick

The notice pinned above the bar said it all, but the landlord still had to spell it out to some of the customers:

"Look," he said to one of them, "can't you read the sign? There's *no* lasagne today and there's *no* scampi either; in fact there's *no* anything. I'm sorry, but I can't help you. If you want something to eat, you're just going to have to go somewhere else."

Price left, walked back along the prom and killed a little time. Eventually the hour grew close to two and he made his way back to the office on Athol Street.

He was directed to Miss Templeton's office and after a sharp tap on the door was invited to enter. The advocate was sitting at her desk with her back to the window. As he walked in she stood up. With a wave of her hand she motioned him to take a seat.

"I've made a few enquiries, Jonathon," she began. "Rob Taylor's body is still in the mortuary. It won't be released until after the Inquest is opened and the Coroner gives permission for the family to take it away. They would normally have done that by now, but there hasn't been any court time and the Coroner's been busy with other matters. The Inquest will be opened next Thursday, that's the day before the Senior TT. The Coroner will probably hear identification evidence, allow the body to be released for burial or cremation then adjourn; the witness evidence and details of what exactly happened will come out when the hearing resumes at a later date. What that means is you're going to have to get some evidence to support your theories before next Thursday. Do you think that's enough time?"

"It's cutting it a little fine," Price said. "It really depends on when I can get into that mortuary and collect some samples. The analyst will probably need a few days to carry out the tests. We can probably do it, but we need to get into that place soon, preferably today or tonight. Have you spoken to our friendly undertaker?"

"I have," the advocate confirmed. "He tells me that his staff have the access code for the security door so that they can get into the place out of hours. The mortuary attendant is only there on a Monday to Friday nine to five basis. Richard says that he can get you in there tonight. Is that what you want?"

Price nodded.

"He says he wants to meet you at the usual place; can you get there before eleven o' clock?" Price nodded again and Miss Templeton continued: "It's most irregular Jonathon; you could get in serious trouble if you got caught. I have to advise you about that. It's almost certainly illegal, but I haven't looked into it too carefully for obvious reasons. Please, please think carefully about what you want to do."

Price knew the risks; he had already been down that route. He responded with passion: "*Miss Templeton*, I have spent some time in a police cell; I *know* about serious trouble. A guy who I knew pretty well was murdered the other day. Now, as you know, that fact hasn't really been publicised yet; the word on the street is still that it was some sort of tragic accident, but you and I know otherwise, *don't we*. Something has happened here that is not *quite* right. I feel that I have a duty to look into it. Now, if you, if anyone, thinks otherwise, then you're quite at liberty to…"

"No, no," Miss Templeton interrupted, "that's not what I meant at all; I believe you Jonathon, but I just have to tell you about the dangers, about the risks."

Price spent most of that afternoon sitting in his hotel room. Eventually the telephone rang. As he had hoped, it was his old friend.

"Jonathon?" he asked. Price warmly confirmed his identity. "I see you're in the Isle of Man, boyo," Love said, "what are you doing there?"

Price told him. Price spoke for several minutes; he told his old friend everything and Roy Love listened. Eventually there was silence and the Welshman replied:

"I *do* have a little inkling about the place… and the event," he said. "I have been to the TT a number of times. In fact I have heard of your chap Rob Taylor and, believe it or not his team, Petromax. I heard of them long before our telephone conversation tonight. What have you got on them?"

Price explained that he had *absolutely nothing* in the way of evidence. Again, his friend, on the other end of the phone was silent. After Price had made his long explanation, Love said one or two interesting words.

"You know I've got a little private investigation business nowadays, Jonathon?" It was a careful question and Price knew it. He muttered something which signified that he knew. Love continued: "I can tell you (off the record) that I did get a call a few weeks ago from someone about Petromax."

"Who?" Price interrupted quickly.

"Can't say, at this moment in time," Love answered quietly.

"Look, Roy," Price protested, "I don't need your half-confidences. Can you help me or not?" Love explained that he would have to speak to his client. He promised to ring back.

Price sat there in the hotel room for an hour, two. Eventually the telephone rang again. Price picked up the receiver: it was Love; he had spoken to his client.

"So Roy, can you help me?" Price asked again. The response was hesitant, it's answer less than clear:

"We don't have a conflict of interest, I think, Jonathon," the Welshman responded cautiously. "My client thinks I should come over to the Island and work with you, *as soon as possible*."

Price asked when. Love told him that he had looked at the ferries and the flights, but there was absolutely no chance of getting over there until the Monday, at least. There was argument, but eventually Price had to accept. Love would fly in on Monday morning, first thing. In the meantime, Price had things to do.

Price was seated in the Queens Hotel. He had entered at about half-past ten and made his way to the usual table. The pub was crowded, but he had managed to find a seat. The conversation around him was loud, and German; he nodded politely at the leather-clad speakers and sat down. He was surprised to find that his friend, the undertaker, was not there. He ordered a pint of the local beer and waited.

Dead on eleven, a man entered the room. He was tall and thin, wore a black, full-tail suit, white shirt and long black tie. A top hat was missing, but that was all.

"Would the friend of Mr Kinnish," the man announced in a soto voice, "please make himself available for the wake and the midnight service; the car is outside." Those drinkers within the pub who heard looked up for a moment, but then resumed their usual conversation. Only Price realised that this was his cue to go.

Chapter Eight

Friday Night (Practice Week)

A full length hearse stood outside the public house. It was black, of course, and its windows bore a dark and heavy tint. Price could just about make out the shape of a coffin in its rear. The man in the black suit invited him to step into the car and Price complied. The vehicle drew off, slowly and decorously. It passed along the promenade and up the hill, following the gentle curve of the bay, before pulling into the dark, gloomy drive that belonged to the last house in Onchan. It cut its engine before the front of the house and stopped.

Out of the house, a figure emerged. Its garb was darker than the night and it walked slowly towards the stationary car. Like the car, it moved slowly. It reached the hearse, opened a door and took a seat beside the doctor.

"Time to go," the figure breathed softly and the vehicle moved off again.

The hearse turned left out of the driveway and Price felt an elbow nudge his arm. He ignored it at first, but the nudge became more persistent. At last he turned to the man sitting beside him; the interior of the car was dark, illuminated only by street lights and the headlights of passing cars, but Price sensed that the man winked: it was Richard, of course and he pushed a silver hip-flask towards the doctor's lips. Price shook his head and turned away; the undertaker shrugged his shoulders and took another swig. The car drove slowly along the promenade for a while, before turning off to the right. It would be a few more minutes before they reached the hospital; plenty of time for Price to think about and plan what he had to do. He carried a small rucksack, but that was all. He alone knew what the rucksack contained and how woefully ill-equipped he would be for the rather gruesome task that lay ahead. The undertaker must have been telepathic: Price was still thinking about the potential problems when he received another nudge. He looked at his companion who passed him a small, grey attaché case. The case was unlocked so he opened it and there in the case lay all that he could possibly require. In the dimly lit gloom of the interior of the car, he could see scalpel, syringes, specimen bottles and needles. Steel and glass glinted in the cold headlights of a passing car and Price closed the case.

They had driven up Ballaquayle and Ballanard Road. The hearse turned left into Jonny Watterson's Lane, moved slowly down the hill, then climbed up the other side. It passed by the old cemetery, crested the brow and then turned right. Price knew that the new hospital was only seconds away. The car reached the roundabout and turned onto the perimeter road. It was very, very dark, but the dipped headlights of the hearse picked out signs indicating a number of turnings to their left: to the helicopter pad, the main hospital car park, the main hospital entrance, the Centre for Nurse Education, The driver of the black car ignored them all and continued. At last, he brought the vehicle to rest in a small and unlit parking lot beside a plain unlabelled door. The engine died and the driver got out.

Price reached for the door handle and was about to get up, but his friend, the undertaker, put a hand on his shoulder and pulled him back down again.

"Wait here for a minute," he whispered, "Ernie has gone to check things out; the staff know him out here so they won't think twice if they see him in the mortuary in the middle of the night. They don't know you so we'd better keep our heads down until the coast is clear. He'll be back in a minute."

Sure enough, a few minutes later, a ghostly figure emerged from the building and drifted silently back towards the car. Price heard a tap on the window; it was soft, gentle, almost imperceptible, but, through the heavily smoked glass, he saw that the figure was motioning them to come with him. Price got out of the car and slowly moved forward; the undertaker made up the rear. The undertaker's assistant led them through an open door and along a darkened corridor. He carried a small pocket torch and its thin, pencil-like beam picked out the way ahead. Price followed its dancing path through another doorway into what felt like a much larger space. The space seemed devoid of windows, its emptiness smothered in a deep and heavy darkness that even the feeble torchlight seemed hardly able to penetrate. A door clicked shut behind them and Price suddenly noticed the low hum of machinery and felt the icy chill air.

"Wait 'till I put the lights on, then we can have a look around," the undertaker's assistant said, moving to the wall. There was a flicker and a flash as a row of fluorescent tubes hanging from the ceiling burst into life and flooded the room with their cold impersonal light.

It was a long, high-ceilinged chamber. The door they had entered by lay behind them. At the far end of the chamber, Price could see another door; what that led to, he could only guess. To his left was a wall of plain white-painted masonry, to his right, a wall of shiny stainless steel, its surface interrupted by three rows of protruding heavy doors. Price could see now the reason for the hum and the reason for the cold. The entire wall was a refrigeration unit of industrial size and scale. It did not take much imagination to work out what it contained.

The undertaker's assistant had picked up a book from somewhere; Price guessed, rightly, that it was a ledger of sorts. After turning a page or two, he paused; his eyes seemed to focus on a particular entry and he read silently for a few seconds, before turning to Price.

"Robert Taylor?" he asked. Price nodded. "Number three," Ernie replied. The men moved along the wall. Price could see that each door bore a number. At number three they stopped. It was on the bottom row. The undertaker's assistant bent forward, pulled a chromium-plated handle and the steel door swung open. Behind, it on a gleaming steel trestle, lay a shape, shrouded in white cloth. Ernie gave the trestle a gentle tug and, with a dull rattle, it slid outwards over its rollers a short way into the room. He drew the white cloth aside to reveal a face.

"This him?" he asked.

Price looked down at the bloodless, lifeless flesh and struggled to recall the face that he had looked at on a mountainside some four, nearly five days before. He nodded.

"That's him," he replied. The undertaker's assistant drew the trestle out to its full extent and pulled back the cloth.

"You'd better get going doc," he muttered, "don't want to rush you, but…"

Price put the case that Richard had given him down on the floor and opened it. He knew that he needed to take some samples: blood, skin, hair, but something stopped him in his tracks; he knew, deep down, that there was something else he had to do first. He turned away from the attaché case, pulled the rucksack from his back and placed it on the floor. With a certain grim intent, he opened the thing and dragged out the instrument inside. He had replaced its batteries, but he had no real idea if it still worked. His companions stared at him; the undertaker scratched his head.

"Aren't you going to start taking samples and things?" he asked.

Price waved his hand dismissively. "In a minute," he replied. Holding his breath he twisted the heavy knob and the old-fashioned meter dial flickered. The small loudspeaker uttered a flat "clack" and the undertaker and his assistant jumped.

"What the hell's that?" the undertaker demanded.

"Shhhh!" Price whispered, holding his finger to his mouth. He moved the machine slowly towards Taylor's body.

"Clack…………clack……..clack……clack…..clack…clack..clack,clackclackclack," announced the little loudspeaker. When he put the machine on the body the clacks blurred into a loud unpleasant rasp. He moved it way again and the rasp broke up into its constituent clacks. He repeated the whole process; the result was the same. A grim smile of satisfaction settled across his face.

"So what…er, what does that mean?" the undertaker asked.

"Radiation," was Price's terse reply. "This is a Geiger counter, and that body," he pointed to Taylor, "is radioactive. Come on, Richard, help me take the samples and let's get out of here."

The samples were taken quickly. It was an unpleasant task, but one that Price knew he had to do. The blood samples were a problem, of course; blood clots after death, but serum separates, as Price knew well enough. Cardiac puncture was the answer, with a long wide bore needle. The procedure was less than pretty and even the undertaker looked the other way. There were certain even less endearing samples, but Price carried them through and eventually his bottles and tubes were full.

"Okay Ernie," he said, "I've done what I need to do; you can push Mr Taylor back and we can all get out of here."

The fluorescent lighting snapped off and the oppressive blackness returned. The three men felt their way out of the inky chamber, through the darkened corridor and into the shadowy car-park beyond. It had been a scary and intimidating experience for all of them. When they reached the comfort and safety of the hearse, Richard reached to his side and pulled the silver flask from its secret resting place. The engine started and his assistant swung the vehicle round. The undertaker looked at Price and raised his eyebrows.

"You're a cool bastard, you are," he said, "do you want a drink?" On this occasion, Price accepted and raised the flask to his lips. The burning spirit trickled down his throat; it was a new and strange sensation.

"What the hell is that?" he asked.

"Canadian Club whisky," the balding undertaker answered with a wry smile, "it's just about all I ever drink."

The hearse moved back towards Douglas and Onchan, retracing its route. The driver spoke even less words than before. Eventually, it reached the last house in Onchan. The undertaker got out.

"Do you fancy a nightcap?" he asked Price. The doctor looked at his watch and shook his head. It was nearly four in the morning, he was tired and he needed to go to bed. The undertaker's assistant turned the hearse around and drove back to Price's hotel. The doctor thanked him, got out of the car and wearily climbed up to his room.

Sleep and silence had been what he had expected, but such was not his lot that night. When he walked into his room he saw the light on the telephone beside his bed winking urgently. He realised the significance and picked up the phone. It was a message of generally poor quality, but Price immediately recognised the source.

"Jonathon," the male voice said, "I tried to contact you earlier this evening, but you were out. Do not, repeat do not, try and make the investigations you suggested. You do not know how dangerous your adversary is. Do not try and look at Rob Taylor's body. **They will be watching you.** I have spoken to my client and I have now been appraised of the risk. You are in serious, serious, danger. I can say nothing more, but stay in your hotel room, repeat stay in your hotel room and keep the door locked until I get there on Monday morning or until you hear from the man from...."

The rest of the message broke down into an unintelligible crackling. Price frowned and played it again. It told him nothing and served little purpose other than to generate alarm. There was a reference to someone; in the garbled recording Price thought he could identify the words "Pink", "Black" and "Smith", but he had no idea of their context. The message raised far more questions than it answered.

Price picked up the phone and rang Love's home number. It was the middle of the night, but this disturbing little message needed a little bit more explanation. The number rang and rang, but there was no reply. He tried Love's mobile, but it was turned off. He frowned, the matter would just have to wait until the morning. Still, he thought, it could all be nothing. He knew from previous experience that Roy Love often looked at matters from their bleakest possible perspective. He sighed and wished he had not bothered to listen to the answerphone; it was late and in a short while he could have one of the busiest days of his life. He crawled into his bed with the intention of getting a few hours sleep. He would have to be up early. Love's suggestion that he remain inside his hotel room behind locked doors until Monday was, of course, ridiculous. It was now a little after four am on Saturday. Price was rostered to be on duty out on the Course from eleven. Practice week may have ended, but the races themselves were about to begin and begin with a big one, the Formula One TT.

Chapter Nine

Saturday Morning (Race Week)

Jonathon Price awoke. He opened his eyes, slowly came to his senses and remembered where he was. Bright sunlight streamed glaring and undiminished through the unfettered window of his hotel room. After a few seconds he remembered the events of the night before. It had been dark when he had returned and he had not closed the curtains. He looked at the clock beside his bed. It was late morning, very late.

He swore.

Hopefully he glanced at his watch and then realised that the bedside clock was right.

He jumped out of bed and rushed over to the bathroom. This time he had absolutely no intention of going out unwashed, no-matter what might be involved or what time it might be. After a very brief shower, he returned and pulled on some clothes. The borrowed leathers followed; they were tight, but given his current mode of transport, he had no real choice. His movements were rapid and after no more than fifteen minutes he left the room. He looked at his watch and swore again. It was five minutes to eleven; he had slept far, far longer then he should. He was supposed to be at his allotted spot (where was it now?) at eleven. He would never make it.

Price ran down the stairs, leaping two at a time where he could, until he reached the car-park at the rear of the hotel. He pulled on his crash helmet and gloves, turned the ignition key and pressed the starter button. To his relief the 600cc motor burst immediately into life. He selected first gear and let out the clutch.

He had no recollection of where he was supposed to go and, in any event, the roads were about to close, so he rode up to the back of the TT Grandstand, parked the motorbike and climbed the tower. He thought he would explain his little oversight to Dr Duffy, the Chief Medical Officer. Dr Duffy would understand (he assumed), but he had only walked up a handful of steps when he heard a voice behind him call his name. He turned in surprise; the voice belonged to a leather-clad figure wearing the yellow jacket of a Travelling Marshal. His face was vaguely familiar.

"Dr Price!" the man exclaimed. What are you doing here? You're supposed to be at Glen Helen."

Price looked at him blankly; it wasn't a contrived expression, it was genuine and the travelling marshal realised that fact straight away.

"We'd better get going Dr Price," the man said. "I take it from what you're wearing that you ride a motorbike?" Price nodded. "Quick one?" the man continued.

"Yamaha R6," Price responded.

The travelling marshal grinned. "I'm on a Honda Fireblade," he said, "follow me, you're going to have some fun!"

On the instructions of the marshal, Price brought his bike round from the back of the paddock. He was waved through the scrutineering bay and suddenly found himself alone in the pit lane off the Glencrutchery Road less than twenty minutes before the start of the Formula One TT. The Grandstand was packed with spectators and the pit-lane was already manned by the racing teams' crews. In the holding area behind him a number of scantily-clad and attractive young ladies stood alongside the riders holding sun-brollies aloft to protect the legendary stars (and lesser mortals) from the dangerous heat of the early June late-morning sun. The competitors were already warming up the engines of their machines. In the background, he could see that generators hummed and thick electric cables ran to the all enveloping warmers wrapping the tyres of the brightly coloured racing motorcycles that stood ready and waiting before the start. A public address system had crackled into life and loudly announced the runners for the first race. Price realised that the time had come for him to leave.

The travelling marshal (whom he later discovered was called Keith) pulled up beside him on his CBR900RR Honda Fireblade. He raised his visor.

"OK Doc; little ride over to Glen Helen. Road's closed. Don't try too hard; just follow me."

They were simple words, but delivered in a comforting, reassuring tone. The marshal pulled down his visor, revved his engine and set off down the pit lane. Price pulled his visor down, gulped, revved his engine and followed.

He accelerated smoothly, but sedately and pulled out onto the Course. The "TM" plates were already pulling far ahead of him, but he knew the man was a professional and would wait. Growing in confidence, Price wound up the 600cc motor and changed up, up and up. He flashed past the filling station and plunged down Bray Hill. From the corner of his eye he glimpsed crowds of spectators: they packed every inch of available space, standing in front gardens and at the entrance to side roads, sitting on walls and on the roofs of bus-shelters. He had ridden down Bray Hill at 30mph and even at that speed it had seemed steep. He glanced at his instruments: the digital speedometer read 90; he felt like he had dropped off a cliff, but he knew that he was travelling far, far slower than the men who would follow him in a few minutes time. He tried to concentrate on following the line of the travelling marshal ahead and swept through the right-hand kink at the bottom of the hill. A half-second later, his front wheel lifted off the ground; he smiled, despite himself, Ago's leap and a wheelie, this **was** going to be fun.

He accelerated up Quarter Bridge Road and then began the descent to the Quarter Bridge. The travelling marshal slowed; the roundabout ahead was tight and could be greasy, given the amount of traffic it bore. Price knew that, but the man ahead was looking after his interests and warning him of the danger. Price took the advice and slowed to what seemed like walking pace. They rounded the corner, passing well to the right of both roundabouts and then accelerated out onto the straight towards Braddan Bridge. Price was beginning to enjoy himself now and the 600cc motor was beginning to sing. He followed the marshal and tucked into the left and then right-hander at Braddan. The field by the church and its rustic grandstand were full and, although he could hear nothing, Price knew that the spectators were waving and cheering him on. He climbed the low hill to Union Mills, notched down a couple of gears, then swept through the right-hander by the pub, down the short hill, through the left-hander by the church hall and then up the long hill to Glen Lough. The travelling marshal ahead of him glanced in his mirrors, grinned to himself and gave a slight, almost imperceptible shake of his head. Another slow one, he thought, but at least Price seemed safe and unlikely to crash. He braked for the right hander at Glen Vine and allowed the race doctor to catch up.

They barrelled down through Glen Vine and Crosby. It was a thirty limit for most people, for most of the year, but not now. The road was almost a dead straight, until you got to the left hander by the mock castle. Price had been pulling an indicated one-thirty before then, but eased off and braked. He had nothing but respect for the course and had no reason to take any risks. He powered past the post office and then up the short hill past the Crosby pub. The front wheel lifted at the brow and then found the tarmac again. The travelling marshal had held himself back and now the two machines swept down the hill and through the fast right-hander past the Highlander restaurant. Price was tucked in behind the fairing, but glanced up and saw his digital speedometer flicker past 140. Once again, a broad and unseemly smile flickered across his face, but only for a second: the mentor in front of him sat up and braked. Price followed his leader and the two machines swept into a left hander past Greeba Castle then a right hander again and along through Appledene to Greeba Bridge. It was fast and furious (Price thought), but it was all a good 40 or 50 mph slower than the racers. Keith, the travelling marshal, had known that all along, of course; an ex-racer himself, he could have gone an awful lot faster, but he had given his escort the ride of his life; a fast, but safe one and what was wrong with that?

The two bikes reached the right-angled corner of Ballacraine. The traffic lights were off, of course, but Price respectfully followed the marshal through the bend and up the short hill to Ballaspur. They rode on through the difficult left-hander (the one where the famous Milky Quayle had crashed, Price seemed to remember) and then cranked to the right and on down through Ballig Bridge, Laurel Bank and the Black Dub.

A few minutes later, the marshal, followed by Price, pulled off the road into the large car park which lay in front of the Glen Helen public house. The pub was set well back from the main road and lay at the mouth of Glen Helen, one of the many thickly wooded Manx National Glens. A fast-running stream tinkled and scurried out of the rocky glen beside the pub and then cascaded into the steep-sided ravine which ran alongside the eastern border of the road from Douglas until it passed beneath it and eventually meandered down to reach the sea at Peel. It was a picturesque, but as Price knew well-enough, extremely dangerous section of the Course. He parked his bike, took off his helmet and gloves and walked over to the Marshal's hut.

"Morning," he said, amicably. There were a handful of men and women standing by the corner. Most of them were wearing fluorescent jackets which identified them as track officials. Price, of course, had been issued with such a garment, but had left it back in his hotel.

"Who the hell are you?" a tall and burly ginger-haired man, with a thick moustache and beard, asked. "Roads are closed, if you don't know and, unless you're a racer, you shouldn't be riding along here like that!"

"Jonathon Price, race doctor," Price answered with (he hoped) a disarming smile. The ginger-haired man was not impressed.

"Where's your ID?" he demanded.

Price had not been asked for ID before, not ID to prove he was a doctor anyway. He frowned, stared at the man and shrugged his shoulders.

"ID?" he began. Luckily the travelling marshal, who had parked his bike beside him, appeared on the scene.

"Dr Price was a little late," he ventured. The ginger-haired bearded man glared at him. "So I made an *executive* decision to give him an escort down here and…" (he looked at his watch) "we've made it just in time!"

The ginger-haired man was about to kick off, but he also looked at his watch and realised that the debate could be postponed until later.

"Christ," he said, "it's eleven thirty; they'll have started. Less than five minutes to here, you know." He abandoned the conversation and ran back to the marshal's hut at the apex of the corner.

Price turned to the travelling marshal and was about to voice his thanks, but the laconic rider had already pulled on his crash helmet, started his bike and made his way to the boundary between the Glen Helen car-park and the edge of the track. He gave Price a quick wave, revved the throttle, dropped the clutch and roared off up the hill on his way to Kirkmichael.

Price looked around and took stock of the place. It was a sharp left-hand bend which came at the end of a steep-sided, narrow, twisting and thickly wooded valley. The approach was on fairly level ground, but the road began to climb as it entered the corner and continued upwards through a succession of corners until it reached the open expanse of the Cronk-y-Voddy Straight. As for danger, there was plenty. The organisers had done their best with straw bales liberally clustered around most of the immovable obstacles and inflatable air-fences positioned for greatest strategic effect, but Price could see that there was no run-off at all on any of the approaching bends, while the boundary of the exit of Glen Helen itself consisted of a rocky cliff which climbed vertically to a pine forest at least thirty feet above.

There was a commentary box at the apex of the corner and large banners claimed it in the name of *Radio TT*. Crowds of spectators seemed to fill every available inch of space. Many clustered behind the rope which divided the large car-park from the road, patiently waiting for the first machine to arrive. Most wore leathers and their motorcycles formed orderly rows behind them. It was a colourful spectacle. The bright sunlight broke through the surrounding trees and glittered off the shiny metal steeds. Loudspeakers hanging overhead barked out the news that the first machines were approaching. The crowds tensed with expectation and necks craned forwards; all eyes focussed on the road. In a minute, the leading bike would surely appear.

Price could hear it now. The engine note whined and throbbed, its pitch rose and fell as the gearbox played its merry tune, but the sound got louder and louder, echoing down the valley. Suddenly the machine appeared into view and shot past them, the rider's left knee sliding against the tarmac, as he negotiated the right-angled bend. It was a tight, neat piece of cornering and the machine maintained its momentum, leapt forward up the steep climb, took the next corner and was gone. It was the number-one plated machine, a Suzuki, but ten seconds had not quite passed and another machine had arrived, a Yamaha and then another, a Honda and then another, the black and gold number-four plated Petromax ridden by the Russian rider Rorletski. Above him, Price heard the flat drone of rotor blades and looked up to see the Greenlight television helicopter sweep by, two hundred feet above them, as always intent on ensuring that their camera crew could keep coming up with the best shots of the action and the manoeveres of the leading bikes below.

The machines started out individually at ten second intervals, so working out who was actually in the lead could be quite difficult; it was obvious to Price, however, that Rorletski was doing quite well. The commentator at Glen Helen was even more impressed, judging by the furious narrative which boomed out from loudspeakers to the watching crowd. The commentary, of course, was not just for their benefit, but was fed live by Manx Radio to spectators all around the Island and beyond.

"Yes and that's number four, Rorletski right behind them on the Petromax machine. Fast, very fast. He's right on the pace…in fact.….are you sure Morris? Yes?…how about that… Rorletski leads by one second…that's one second at Glen Helen on lap one." The commentator continued to give the positions and times, but racing bikes were sweeping past every few seconds now and the deafening engine noise drowned out most of what he was saying.

Price raised his eyebrows: leading on lap one? Still, he thought, it was a long race; six laps at thirty-seven and three-quarter miles per lap. Two hundred and twenty six miles in total. So far they had only done about nine and a half; there was plenty of time for the leader board to change.

It took fifteen minutes or so until the last bike screamed past and silence, of sorts, returned to the glen. By then the leading machines had already flashed past the grandstand and were well on their way back to Glen Helen for their second lap. The frenetic commentary informed Price (and forty thousand others) that Rorletski was still in the lead and had managed to pull out a five second advantage by the end of the first lap. He was lying third on the road, but by the sound of things that position was about to change. Suddenly, the crowd tensed again and moved forward to the rope. A helicopter had re-appeared and was flying towards them as fast as it could go. It was the Greenlight TV chopper and it signalled the imminent arrival of the race leaders. A crescendo of sound funnelled down the valley and then, suddenly, a clutch of racing motorbikes burst into view, piled past the assembled spectators and were gone.

But there was a change from the last time; three bikes flashed past almost in unison, and the black and gold Petromax machine had gained a slight edge and, on the exit from Glen Helen at least, was the leader on the road as well as leader in the race. Suddenly a voice screamed and Price turned his head to look back down the road; he was awarded by the sight of a large, but riderless motorcycle pirouetting end over end towards him. The crowd drew a sharp intake of breath and retreated from the rope barrier. The motorbike flew harmlessly past, sparks flying as it bounced off the tarmac, until it came to rest on its side just before the marshal's box and just below the Radio TT commentary position.

"Medic!" a shout went up; Price grabbed the orange emergency box and started to run. The accident had occurred at the left-hand bend just before Glen Helen itself. It was a notorious corner. It was far, far too dangerous to run along the course, but a narrow footpath, little more than an earthy thread of footworn grass, ran from the car-park between the low stone wall which bordered the road and the deep and rocky ravine which carried the fast-flowing little river. It was a short path and as he ran along it the doctor's heart pounded rapidly and forcibly; he did not know what he would find.

Seconds later, he found the path blocked by a cluster of people in front of him. "Medic, out of my way!" he shouted

The crowd of curious onlookers stood to one side and he managed somehow to squeeze through the tiny gap between them and the wall. As he did so, he saw, to his lasting amazement, a leather clad figure lying on his back in the tiny level space (it could be no more than three feet wide at the most) which existed between the wall and the ravine. The figure was moving, obviously in great pain, but equally obviously still alive. Price fell onto his knees beside him.

"What's your name mate and where does it hurt?" he asked.

The prostrate figure moaned. Someone had already removed his helmet and applied a hard collar.

"John," the man answered, "and f***ing everywhere; you want a list?"

Price took the rider's pulse: it was rapid and thready; a quick glance at the man's limbs suggested major compound fractures, but the doctor knew the doctrine of the golden hour and the fact that minutes spent on careful diagnosis at this time could well be time wasted. He examined the fallen rider rapidly but skillfully and then flipped the orange box open, grasped a pair of heavy duty scissors and opened up one arm of the leathers along the seam. Within seconds a large bore intravenous cannula was in place and haemacell, a plasma substitute, was pouring into the injured man's veins. There was little else he could do at that time, other than reassurance; the air-med chopper had already been summoned and less than five minutes later Price heard the noisy chat of rotor blades as it began its descent. Whilst Price had been working, the marshals had been doing their job; two halves of an aluminium stretcher were carefully slid beneath the casualty and on Price's command the men around lifted. It was difficult, but with a bit of a struggle they managed to carry their charge along the narrow path by the gorge, through the car-park by the pub and into the field beyond. The helicopter had already landed. The noise of its rotors was deafening. Price shouted out a brief handover to the airborne medic and the marshals loaded the casualty in the rear, then with a high-pitched drone the turbojet engine took up the load and the aircraft was gone; it would be at Nobles hospital within three minutes.

"Jesus, he was lucky!" a voice said.

Price turned around to face its owner; they were now back in the car-park and the person he was staring at was that same ginger-haired, moustachioed and bearded chief marshal he had been in some dispute with some thirty or forty minutes earlier. The man had been beside him for most of that time, giving instructions, barking orders, helping, assisting, but more than that, simply being there. It was the first time Price had heard the man give his own opinion.

"What do you mean?" Price asked.

"Didn't you see the crash?" the man answered, responding to a question with a question. Price shook his head, so the man continued. "They clashed fairings, he was thrown off the bike, bounced off the branches of the tree and landed on three foot of grass. He missed the stone wall and missed the ravine, either of those would have killed him. Bloody million to one chance, if you ask me."

Price was going to ask him for more details, but suddenly the crowd jumped forward and the loudspeakers barked; it was lap three and the race leaders were coming past again. The incident by the ravine had only taken sixteen minutes or so from its beginning to its end, but such was the speed these riders were circulating, the leaders were already back again. The black and gold Petromax roared past; this time it was visibly in front of the competition. The loudspeakers shouted out the positions to the men on the ground.

"And it's Rorletski on the Petromax." The commentator screamed, "come on Morris, is that how you see it?" he asked, urgently seeking confirmation. There was a pause of a few seconds before the timekeeper gave his edict:

"Rorletski leads on the road and leads in the race on lap three by eleven seconds," he announced gravely.

Price sat down on the tarmac in the middle of the car-park; the lower leaderboard riders were going past, but the top men would be well on their way to Kirkmichael by now. This particular race had captured his imagination and, entranced, he listened to the Radio TT coverage. He recalled from his youth that once upon a time they used to have a commentary position at Ballaugh Bridge, but that was a long time ago. He remembered the commentary (when was it? 1986 or so?) when the Irish rider Gene somebody or other had hit a horse that had jumped over the fence. The next commentary position nowadays was the Ramsey Hairpin. It was miles away and an awful lot could happen by then. Although he had only met Rorletski once and knew nothing about him, Price had liked the fellow and found himself shouting the Russian on. His feelings were hidden at first, but they became more vocal as the lap and the race developed.

The loudspeakers shouted out the news:

"Thank you Radio TT, this is Fred here at Ramsey Hairpin taking up the commentary. The weather's still good and the crowds are still out in force. Hold on a minute....yes...we can hear an approaching bike. Let's look down the road. Yes, the spectators down at Stella Maris are waving their programmes. Here it comes.....oh, fast, fast Mr Rorletski, but so smooooooth, yes we'll give him the thumbs up and off he goes up towards the Waterworks. Nothing else in sight. Well, I must tell you listeners that our rushing Russian seems to have it well under control; is that how you see it Geoff?" The timekeeper confirmed the placing. The expected favourites were well behind.

"Come on Rorletski!" Price shouted when he heard the news. Most of the spectators in the Glen Helen car-park looked at him as though he was stupid, or at the least a little bit strange, but a black-leather clad man wandered over.

The man was tall and quite old. He sported a greying beard and his clothing was somewhat dated, but he looked, in a curious way rather distinguished.

"You… cheer Rorletski?" he asked tentatively. Price looked at him in surprise.

"Yes, why?" he asked.

"But, Rorletski Russian; you English; why?" Price thought for a moment; it was an unusual question.

"Well," he said, "I met Mr Rorletski a few days ago and I thought he was a decent chap; Russian, of course, but he seemed enthusiastic about the TT and, anyway, he's doing bloody well. We English always like the underdog, you know." The black-leather clad biker grinned.

"Kak vas zavut……what is your name Englishman?…..I like your, er…..way of thinking."

"Jonathon Price," the doctor replied, "what's yours?"

"Mikael," the man replied, "and these," he waved his open hand towards a group of similarly black-leather clad bikers behind him, "are my comrades. We come to TT this first time; you be our friend!" The man held out his hand in friendship and Price, a little embarrassed, clasped the same and shook it. The man walked back to his comrades, but at least he seemed happy.

There was another crash; not desperately serious, but bad enough for the helicopter to be summoned. By the time he had dealt with it, Price had missed the leaders on lap four. A short trip to answer a call of nature took him away from lap five, but he was back by the side of the road for the sixth and final lap.

The bikes were still flying round. By now, of course, the leading machines had already caught up with the trailing ones and had lapped a good few, so there were absolutely no gaps on the mountain circuit. Price stood there, by the side of the road, watching the tail-enders go past. Suddenly, he caught sight of a black and gold machine; it whipped past and was gone. The loudspeakers stuttered and then barked.

"Number Four, Rorletski leads past Glen Helen."

The time difference was twenty seconds; the Russian was leader on the roads and leader in the race. It was a turn up for the books, Price thought, but the second, third and fourth machines roared through the corner and seemed, to his inexpert eye, to be going faster and gaining on the Russian.

At the Ramsey Hairpin, his inexpert opinion seemed to be proving right.

"A bit of a wobble, but it's Rorletski first through; does he have a problem though?

87

He was well clear on the last lap, but there's a cavalcade of machines right on his tail this time. How do you see it, Fred ?" the commentator asked.

"Rorletski leads, but down to three seconds," the timekeeper replied.

"Three seconds!... he's lost an awful lot over that last lap, hasn't he, Fred?" the commentator asked gleefully; "can he keep up the advantage over the mountain climb and drop?" The timekeeper's response was inaudible, and the radio cut back to the Grandstand.

There was a short burst of advertising with a few musical jingles and then the broadcast cut back to the anchorman, big Geoff at the Grandstand.

"The lights are on at Cronk-y-Mona," he announced, "for numbers four, three, five and six; it's time to step out onto the Glenclutchery Road and see who's going to win the Formula One TT." There was a crackle of static and then he continued: "There's a machine into view; out of the dip and onto the road. It's....no sorry it's a back marker who's about to be lapped....Here we go, black machine, number four, takes the checkered flag...now...and number three goes through...now. A nail-biting wait for the next....and its number five now.......and..... number six....now. I make it number four, Rorletski, on the Petromax machine the winner, by about.....two seconds, but we're obviously going to need some confirmation on that one."

The black-leather clad bikers in the Glen Helen car-park burst into an impromptu celebration. Victory shouts (one assumed, not knowing much about the Russian language) burst forth and bottles of an unknown clear liquid seemed to materialise from pockets, rucksacks and panniers. Mikael wandered over to Price.

"Doktor!" he hailed, "you have supported our rider and must be with us in our great celebration. Drink!" It was an order rather than a question, but Price was able to defer it for an hour or two, at least.

"I'd love to," he said, "but I'm on duty. How about tonight? Come to the Beer tent by the Sea Terminal at.....8 o'clock... and we'll have a drink together".

Meanwhile, on the radio, there was a wait for several minutes before big Geoff came back on line.

"Yes, the Russian's done it," he said, "by one second. I'm over with him now....Mr Rorletski you've won the Formula One TT, the first Russian ever to do it and on your first attempt too. No-one's ever done that before; how does it feel?"

Chapter Ten

Saturday Afternoon (Race Week)

It was mid-afternoon on Saturday, the first race day of the Isle of Man TT meeting. The excitement of the earlier Formula One race had left a definite buzz in the air. After an hour's break, just enough time for the spectators to visit the Glen Helen Lodge, grab a bite to eat or take refreshments of a more liquid nature, racing was about to resume. This time it would be three-wheeled action: the first of the two sidecar events. A few dozen radio sets crackled and the overhead loudspeakers boomed. The race had started and the first machines were off.

The sun was still shining brightly through the trees as Price took a seat on the low wall by the marshals' shelter. He had spent much of the intervening hour with his newly acquired Russian friends and had learned a great deal about Rorletski and, of probably more importance, about Rorletski's employer, Petromax. He was now chatting to the Chief Sector Marshal. Price had been accepted, his earlier actions had evidently made the grade and the ginger-haired giant spoke to him as if he were a long lost friend.

"Keep your eyes open for this next lot, Jonathon," he said, " the sidecar boys are a bit wild. They may not go quite as fast as the solos on the straights, but they're a damn sight quicker round corners like this one and some of the lines they take are, well, *interesting*, let's leave it at that."

The overhead loudspeakers crackled and boomed again and the voice from the Grandstand announced that the leading machines would be well on their way to Glen Helen and so he would now hand over to the commentary team there. The men in the Radio TT box above Price's head took their cue.

"Thank you Geoff; well here we are again at Glen Helen and a big thank you from Morris and myself to the Glen Helen Lodge for a delicious bit of lunch. Oh, yes and a message from the marshals here at Glen Helen: it's the old chestnut I'm afraid, flashes under the trees. Can those of you with flash cameras please make sure the flash is turned off or taped over. We don't want the riders distracted, *do* we. Now the first machines should be here any minute and I suppose the question on everyone's lips is will the number one machine of the local legend have pulled away or will any of the following pack have managed to keep up with him. Hold on, I think I can see some movement in the distance…"

A rising wail crept up the valley: crescendo after crescendo of ear-splitting sound bounced and reverberated between the hillsides as racing machinery approached. Suddenly the first sidecar was upon them. The crowd flinched and gasped. The first machine was a bright green affair; wearing the number one plate of the local favourite, it screamed round the corner on a very tight line, the passenger hanging so far out that his bottom scraped along the road. But the favourite had company; over to his right a shocking yellow outfit bearing the number two plate was having a go. It took a far wider line than seemed sensible or safe, but hell, this was racing! The spectators by the rope scuttled backwards. The machine turned into the corner so late that Price tensed expecting a crash. The commentator was having the proverbial kittens.

"Cooperman's through; he's in the lead, but big Stan's taking a wide, wide line; he wants to overtake, but is there room, is he going to make the corner?" he screamed excitedly, "oh Stan, Stan we love you dearly, but that's a little too close for comfort; you can join us in the commentary box any time you want, but we'd prefer you not to bring your outfit with you." The yellow outfit screeched below the foot of the commentary box and passed within inches of the wall. It had made the corner, just, but the manoeuvre had cost a little time and the green outfit held a lead of a dozen yards over the yellow one as the two machines howled up Creg Willey's Hill. The road was silent for what seemed an age before the next machine roared past; this race was already looking like a two horse one. Morris, the timekeeper confirmed what everyone who had been watching already knew.

"Cooperman leads on the road, just, but Stan Turner started 10 seconds behind, so I make it a lead of nine point five seconds to big Stan."

The rest of the field followed through without incident and then the road fell quiet again. The spectators learned that the leaders were identically split at Ramsey Hairpin and Price looked forward apprehensively to the next lap.

Out of the corner of his eye, he noticed some activity down by the footbridge over the little river and he turned to see three individuals carrying bulky equipment enter the large car-park. Their identical jackets announced the arrival of a Greenlight television crew, ready to film the outfits take the corner on the coming lap. They trouped up to the foot of the commentary box and spoke to the Chief Sector Marshal.

"Mind if we get a few shots from here, mate?" the cameraman asked in a cheerful Aussie twang.

"Be my guest," the ginger-haired giant replied.

"How did you get here," Price cut in, puzzled by the small group's sudden appearance, "I mean, the road's closed, isn't it?"

The Aussie smiled. "Working our way right down this section. Started off at Ballacraine this morning, then Ballaspur, Ballig, over the road then down the valley."

"What, is there a footpath?"

"There's a footpath, some of the way," the man laughed, "rest of it we just have to use the river." Price looked down and noticed, for the first time, that the crew were soaking wet from the waist downwards; he shook his head, they certainly took their filming very, very seriously.

Price saw that there were two men and one woman. The tall Aussie was obviously in charge and under his instruction the other two erected a large tripod on the apex of the corner and placed a massive camera on top. It was pointing down the road towards Ballacraine and Price hazarded a question.

"Big lens, that; think you can spot these guys when they come past?" The tall Aussie grinned; he, at least had a sense of humour.

"We'll catch 'em mate and if any of them have pimples, warts, or small growths on their backsides, this camera'll get those as well.

The shrill, excited voice of the commentator in the box above them informed the waiting crowd that the leading machines would be there any minute and everyone dashed to their places. The film crew had settled for the apex of the corner, just below the radio commentary box and they did not seem inclined to move. Price stood a dozen feet to their left. He heard the noise again, at first low-level and far off, but within half a minute pianissimo down the valley had become fortissimo near at hand and a second later two screaming racing outfits burst into view. It was an exact rerun of the first lap: the local hero led, but the bright yellow outfit was only inches behind. The local man was again on the left hand line and the challenger was on the right; they took up all of the road and neither of them seemed prepared to yield an inch. Price stepped back again, but the TV crew kept on filming. The whole thing seemed to happen in slow motion and the doctor distinctly remembered shouting a warning, but to no avail. This time, as before, the Scottish favourite kept on the tight inside line and shot up the hill, but the number two machine ran wide, this time too wide.

There was a scream from the crowd and a loud bang. In an explosion of colour and action pieces of fibreglass, fairing, perspex, wood and metal showered across the road as the racing sidecar impacted with the Greenlight television crew, the marshal's box and then ricocheted into the Radio TT box above. Price was watching from a few yards away and had to agree it was a seriously spectacular collision, probably the best (or worst) he had ever seen. He ran to the impact site, expecting the indescribable. The marshals were already out in the road waving their yellow flags.

"Shit, mate, I think I've broken my leg," the young female member of the TV crew announced. It was another Aussie twang. Price had reached her first, but on a quick cursory examination, he felt that her diagnosis was probably correct. He reassured the girl that she was OK and he would be back and carried on to look at the rest of the casualties. In the back of his mind, he had always dreaded an accident like this.

"Doktor Price, can my friends and I assist?"

It was an unexpected question, at an unexpected time and delivered in an unexpected accent. Price turned without thinking to face Mikael Boroweski and his Russian friends.

"Certainly, you can Mikael, but what can you do?" The Russian smiled.

"I am surgeon, now with hospital in St Petersburg, but formerly with Soviet Army Field Hospital and these comrades my old unit." His friends stood to attention behind him. Price looked at them and, despite the serious nature of the situation, laughed.

"Okay Mikael, you and your friends crack on; we'll worry about the paperwork later."

Price and the Russians went into action. Surprisingly enough, the sidecar driver Stan Turner and his passenger walked away without injury. Big Stan was tense and angry, and shouted at Price, but he did apologise to him later in the week. It was understandable, of course: he really had wanted to win. Price had more important things to deal with, though, at the time. The other member of the TV crew (apart from the cameraman) was English. He was grey and shocked and said very little at the time, but Price discovered that he too, had a broken leg. The big Aussie cameraman (Price never did find out his name) was unhurt and philosophical about the total destruction of his professional equipment and near wiping-out of his crew.

"Aww sheee, just a racing accident, mate, what else can you say," was his commentary on the whole incident.

Mikael and his former Soviet Army field unit had fought their way with commendable bravery into the demolished marshal's hut only to find it empty. Strangely enough, they didn't seem the slightest bit surprised. Someone, Price thought, had obviously learned valuable lessons about scorched earth and the retreat from Moscow, but he let the comment go at that particular moment. The radio commentator and his faithful timekeeper had remained in position to the bitter end, but thankfully their injuries were minor, comprising cuts and bruises only. They too were philosophical and tried to laugh it off. The commentary from Glen Helen had been brought to a premature end, but the box would be rebuilt and the team would return for the Monday race day.

The two casualties were placed on stretchers and carried to a nearby field. In the distance they could all hear the throb of rotor blades as the helicopter approached. The injured Englishman had perked up and his colour was beginning to return. "This isn't as bad as when I had to ditch my Tornado," he muttered. The stretcher-bearers looked puzzled, but the Australian girl tried to sit up and, in pain fell back down again.

"Is there another helicopter?" she demanded, "because I am not flying with him."

The little adventure took a good half-an-hour to sort out and, by the time the helicopter had gone, the local man had been through again. He and his passenger were on their own now and the nearest opposition lay a minute behind. With all of the dramatic developments, most of the spectators at Glen Helen had lost interest in the result. The tail-enders flashed through and the spectators made their way back to their motorbikes and cars and got ready for the roads to reopen. The radio commentary announced that the local man had won and the Roads-Open car had set off. The marshals set about putting away their gear and untying the rope. Price had pulled on his helmet and gloves and was sitting on his bike ready for the off when he felt a tap on his shoulder. He turned.

"You stay in Douglas, Doktor Price?" It was Mikael and the (former) Soviet field hospital. They were all on bikes. Price nodded. Mikael beamed. "Then we follow you, we give you escort!" he said. Price could think of no real answer so he nodded again.

The Roads-Open car flashed past, tyres screeching as it took the left-hand corner, the rope dropped and the bikes at Glen Helen set off.

Price turned left and accelerated down the road back towards Douglas; behind him engines thundered. He glanced in his mirror and what he saw nearly caused him to fall off his bike. One or two of his escort were on modern machinery, but the vast majority were not: black, old fashioned Soviet-era machines poured out from the car-park, holding up the traffic which backed up behind. There were solos, sidecars, but they all moved together in a grim, but determined procession. Price looked in his mirror again and saw the flags: not the flag of the modern Russian Republic, but the old flag, the one that had terrified Hitler; the hammer and the sickle set against the people's blood. Price gulped, wondered for a moment what he had set in motion and turned his attention to the road ahead.

At Ballacraine, the traffic lights were red and he came to a halt. The motorised division of the former Red Army came to a halt behind him. Most of the spectators had left, but those who remained stared in amazement; motorcycle racing heroes travelling at furious speeds would probably not make them turn their heads, but this ....was rather different.

The lights turned green and the procession moved on. Price wondered where they were all staying; he assumed it was a campsite somewhere, but in his conversations with Mikael, the man had said nothing. He glanced in his mirror again and noticed that the cavalcade had got longer. Bikes and sidecars seemed to be joining from every side road.

They rode through Glen Vine and Price got his answer. As the road fell before him down to Union Mills, a cacophony of horns blasted behind him; he glanced in his mirror. Mikael Boroweski saluted and the Red Army escort turned right into the Glen Lough campsite. Price raised his right hand to wave and laughed to himself. He had heard that Glen Lough was a campsite which was very popular with Germans; these guys would have plenty to talk about with them.

Chapter Eleven

Saturday Evening (Race Week)

Unescorted now, Price carried on down the hill to Union Mills; the traffic was extremely heavy, as it always was for an hour or so after the races. Bikes and cars were returning to Douglas, their riders, drivers and passengers tired, but happy after a full day spent spectating by the roadside. The fundamental aim of all concerned would now be to get back to their digs, whether that be hotel, guest house, campsite or private home, abandon the vehicle, freshen up and ready themselves for the second half of any TT race-day, that strange phenomenon that was Douglas promenade by night. If the races themselves were a unique experience, then equally so was the activity and entertainment that the evening provided.

Price shared that common purpose and his frustration grew as his speed fell. Union Mills to Quarter Bridge had become an impenetrable queue of vehicles trickling forward at walking pace. He realised that he should have turned off and made his way back by side roads, but it was too late now so he took a few deep breaths and waited. Eventually he reached the landmark pub by the twin mini- roundabouts which straddled the rivers Dhoo and Glass. It was a natural bottleneck, formed by the junction of roads from all points of the compass. From the south, the main road from Port Erin, Port St Mary, Castletown and the airport joined the road from Peel and the west at one roundabout, then split again into the main road to Ramsey and the north and the road running east into Douglas at the other. The public house known as the Quarter Bridge (for obvious reasons) lay between the south and east points of the compass, separated from the road by a temporary low wall of bulky straw bales. Banners advertising almost every kind of product that could remotely be of interest to motorcyclists bedecked the pub and the bales. The banners formed a visual extravaganza which was repeated throughout the Island and could be seen at almost every corner of the legendary thirty-seven and three-quarter mile Mountain Course.

Price turned into the road which led towards the centre of the town and rode down to the Sea Terminal. This was another mistake. A ferry had just docked and was disgorging its heavy load of motorcycles and cars. The congestion was intense. He crawled past the huge blue and white marquee which proudly guarded the southern entrance to the promenade. Large crowds of revellers were already gathering outside in the warm evening sunshine. Price glanced to his left and caught sight of a massive screen which had been erected on the other side of the road. It stood beside and dwarfed the Victorian clock tower. Metal barriers now ran along the pavements on both sides of the promenade, preventing the crowds from spilling out onto the tarmac. On the broad walkway by the sea wall the funfair was in full swing. Loud music blared from speakers mounted on almost every lamppost. Racing simulators bucked and reared, treating those lucky enough to step inside to a lap of the Mountain Course at 120mph. Bungee jumps bounced those individuals foolish enough to part with their cash up and down on the end of a large piece of heavy duty elastic string, but it was only a few minutes after seven; the evening was not yet in full swing and would not really get going for another couple of hours. At last Price pulled into the car park of his hotel. He turned off the engine, put the bike on its stand and made his way to his room.

On walking into the room, his first action was to move over to the answer-phone, but disappointingly its light was not flashing. Roy Love had not returned his call. Price pulled off his boots, motorcycle leathers and clothes before stepping into the shower. After a few minutes beneath the hot jets of water he began to feel re-invigorated. He stood there for a full ten minutes, then emerged. The day had been productive, he thought and different, but the night could reveal more. Mikael Boroweski and his Russian friends had been interesting companions and had been quite informative, *so far*. He would be meeting them in a few minutes; it was a social call, but he suspected that they could tell him more about Petromax, possibly a great, great deal more. He dried himself, pulled on fresh clothes and looked at his watch: seven thirty, just about enough time to wander back down the road and take a position by the marquee. He walked out of the room, climbed down the stairs and stepped out of the hotel. He took a sharp intake of breath; there had been a metamorphosis: the promenade was now truly alive.

Everything had increased in both volume and tempo. Douglas was a far, far different town to the place it had been earlier. Heavily amplified music cut along and across the road and echoed around the bay. The very pavement itself seemed to be bouncing. Crowds of people flocked every this way and that, smiling, laughing, shouting. The phalanxes of stationary motorcycles had returned to their duties guarding the sidewalks of the road, but the open tarmac was even busier than before. Motorbikes, some large, some larger still (none small) growled, thumped or roared past (depending on their engine configuration, of course) and the heart of Douglas continued to thump and beat as the night moved on. Dusk had not set, but the bright lights of the funfair, the bungee jumps, the simulators, the food stalls, the bars and the sideshows shone out across the bay and dense throngs of people ebbed and flowed as if tomorrow would never come.

He made his way slowly through the crowds towards the Sea Terminal and the large blue and white marquee. It was obvious as he approached that hundreds, if not thousands of people were already there and his chances of meeting the Russians were low, if not nil. He had to try, though, and he fought his way through the crowds to the immensely long bar. The customers were three or four deep and he despaired of success, but a few minutes of perseverance were rewarded by a pint of bitter; it may have been a busy bar, but the staff were efficient, he would give them that.

Price turned away from the bar and moved out of the marquee. He met denser crowds, gathered by the roadside and attracted by the entertainment which the view provided. The promenade itself had by now been sealed off to ordinary traffic and fenced with yet more straw bales. It had become a stadium, of sorts, in which motorcycle stunt-riders and others were to mount a display. Inching himself forwards into the five deep line of spectators he watched the first performance; it was pretty impressive, he acknowledged, but he had something else to do. He moved away from the road into a tiny square of empty space.

Suddenly, he felt a tap on his shoulder. "Doktor Price, we very glad to meet you again!"

He turned. It was Mikael, his friends and others. Mikael sounded a little apologetic, in fact, if anything he sounded a little sheepish:

"Doktor Price,…Jonathon; I must introduce you to our new friends. They stay in campsite with us, Glen Lough, you know it?"

Price nodded.

Mikael continued; it was a stage whisper. "They are *Germans*, but they seem very (how you say) *decent fellows*. We have only discussed TT, and we have *not*" (he muttered as an aside) "said anything about *Stalingrad*."

Price offered his hand and found a multitude of persons wanting to shake it. The Germans and the Russians seemed extremely happy (although already a little worse the wear for drink). They were attired in the usual uniform: black leather from head to toe. The self-elected spokesman for the German contingent was a tall fellow with long grey hair, pulled into a tight pony tail who sported a spectacular handlebar moustache. His age was indeterminate, but it was certainly well in excess of fifty. When he was introduced to Price, he stood stiffly to attention, shook hands and nodded. Price had subconsciously expected the man to click his heels, but he did not.

"*Also*, Herr Price, I am very pleased to meet you. Mein Freund, hier, Herr Boroweski, he tell me that you are Doktor and support this great TT. We…" he indicated his companions with a wave of his hands, "come to TT for many years and we…" (he struggled for a few seconds for the right word) "*applaud* men such as yourself. Ich heisse Stefan und ich…I am sorry I speak too little English. I speak good English mostly, but this beer, this *Bushy's* beer, it cause me to forget my words." Stefan burst into laughter and his friends joined in. Price smiled.

"Danke Stefan; ich spreche ein bistchen Deutshe und ich verstehe was Sie haben gesagt. Ich muss sagen dass ich bleibe das Bushy's ist ein sehr gut wirtshaus."

It was a long sentence for Price and probably, in terms of both grammar and vocabulary, a load of crap, but he had made the attempt and it was appreciated. The black leather clad Germans burst into hearty laughter and clapped him on the back.

"You speak our language, Herr Doctor; for tonight you are one of us!" Someone had obviously been sent to the bar, because Price suddenly found a full pint of foaming Bushy's bitter thrust into his hand. He accepted gratefully and in doing so looked around. He was in the centre of a group of at least fifty people, Germans and Russians all, but that group was small in the context of the massive crowd that was now assembled by the roadside. Price was no good at estimating numbers, but he knew it must have numbered thousands.

The large television screen across the road was showing highlights of the day's racing action. The winner, Rorletski featured heavily, of course, and whenever he appeared the Russian contingent cheered loudly. Price decided it was the time to venture a question to the former soviet army doctor.

"So Mikael, you told me this afternoon that you know Rorletski?" The Russian turned slowly and stared at Price; he looked a little drunk, but his words were unslurred and his speech sounded crystal clear."

"Of course I know him, Doktor Price; Andre Rorletski is my nephew." Price stepped back in surprise; he had not expected this. The Russian continued, "Andre was a great kid; learned to ride bikes off road when he was eight. He has been Russian champion off road and on. If Russia had been great motorcycle-racing country like Italy or Spain or America or Australia or even England, Andre would have been rider for great team like Ducati or Honda, but Russia has no such claim, so Andre never get great ride and he work in factory, racing motorbikes in his spare time for years and years."

"Well at least he got his chance in the end, Mikael," Price added cheerily, expecting the Russian to acknowledge the upturn in his nephew's fortunes, but the former soviet army doctor shook his head gloomily.

"*Petromax*!" he spat out the word in disgust. "It is not an honourable team; it does not leave the same taste in the mouth as the great teams of motorcycle racing. We, my comrades and I know all about Petromax; I am pleased that my nephew has won the great TT motorcycle race, the most famous motorcycle race in the world, but I have no pride in the team that he has chosen to race for." It was a short speech, but one delivered with passion.

Price raised his eyebrows. "What's wrong with Petromax then, Mikael?" he asked.

The former soviet army doctor glared at him. "Criminals; they are all criminals, but the boss man, he is greatest criminal. This company, this man, he get everything he has for nothing; he has oil business, manufacturing business, *nuclear* business (he emphasised the word nuclear) and everything he has, he get for nothing, when old Soviet Union disappear and Yeltsin give everything away to his cronies. All of the rest of us who have worked for the motherland and struggled and fought, we get nothing and these people, who did nothing and were nobodies are now millionaires.....billionaires. We, my friends and I, ask why? Who are these people and why do they have such wealth when the rest of us are so poor?"

Price had no answer; in truth he had wondered the same himself in the past, but two words Mikael had spat out rang some kind of alarm bell deep within him.

"Nuclear business?" he asked.

"Yes, yes, nuclear business," the man replied. "Russian government realised after Chernobyl and other disasters they never told the west about that they could not afford to decommission or even run nuclear power plants, so they decide to get rid of all the nuclear industry. Of course, nuclear industry worth nothing and, indeed, big liability, so they make sure company that get the rich pickings of the state oil deposits have to take with it the burden of the rest. Petromax was lucky winner so they get both." Mikael smiled. " They may have got the good stuff, but at least they will have to deal with the shit."

Price smiled and nodded. Somewhere deep inside his brain a thought had started to take shape.

A screech of brakes made them both to look at the road; a black leather-clad stunt rider had managed to make a thousand cc motorcycle stand vertically upright on its front tyre. The stunt rider was tall, but slim and looked rather feminine. Price stared for a second: something about the rider was vaguely familiar. The massive crowd cheered and whatever thought Price was carrying in his mind disappeared; the whole scene was getting far too big and he was feeling a touch claustrophobic.

The Russians and the Germans had begun to argue, albeit in a friendly, arm-waving manner; after a few beers, they had reverted back to trying to settle old nationalistic scores. Price was feeling tired anyway and couldn't really be bothered to stay and listen. After a while he took his leave and abandoned them. They scarcely noticed his departure and, in truth, neither did the crowd of thousands around him.

It was dark now and the heavy bass of the music thumped as the lights flashed from one end of the promenade to another. Price started to walk away, but somewhere, from the corner of his eye, he noticed a face amongst the crowds. It was a brief glimpse, half a second, no more and when he turned to focus his gaze, the face was gone. There was no way he could be certain, but it looked like the same face he had seen twice before: a tall, thin black man with short black hair. A man he had seen at Quarry Bends and in the Queens public house: the mysterious stranger who seemed to be dogging his footsteps. Price turned and tried to struggle back through the sea of people, but it was hopeless and by the time he had got to what he thought was the right spot, the man had gone. He looked around, but the crowd was growing denser by the minute, the light was fading fast and the face could no longer be seen. He shook his head and made his way slowly back to where he had come from.

After what seemed an age, he reached the pavement outside the Villa Marina and stopped. The volume of music flooding out from the building was now intense, but he recognised the beat: it was a sound from his youth; one of the legendary rock tracks from the Seventies; no doubt it was a tribute band, but Price had to admit that it sounded like a good one. Intrigued, he stepped through the door, paid the admission and moved forward until he reached the hall. He saw that the band was on the stage, was in full flight and sounded brilliant. He stood there and soaked up the atmosphere and the music; the chords were of a song he had heard many, many times before: a rock anthem. He stared at the band and suddenly realised that they weren't any sort of copy; they were the real, genuine and original article. Tomorrow was Mad Sunday; common sense told him that he should have an early night, but the band was playing; in his head he knew he had to go, but his heart told him that he had to stay. In the end, the heart won.

Chapter Twelve

Mad Sunday Morning

A frenetic bleeping brought Price rapidly to his senses; he turned over, leaned across to the bedside table and turned off the alarm. A few seconds later his eyes came into focus and he took on board the time. It was eleven o' clock; gilded rays of sunshine filtered through gaps in the drawn curtains and told him that it was eleven in the morning rather than eleven in the evening. His head felt delicate and his brain a little fragile, recovering, as it was, from an assault by alcohol and heavy rock music. After a minute or two he remembered that it was, it must be Sunday and there was no racing. He let out a deep sigh of relief. A minute or two later he remembered that it was no ordinary Sunday, it was *Mad Sunday* and from what he had heard that particular day had the potential to be the most dangerous of the whole fortnight. Still, he thought, he was not on duty, so he rolled back over and went back to sleep.

Price woke up again an hour or so later. His headache was less intense and his hangover seemed to be fading; he struggled to his feet and peeped through the drawn curtains. Outside, the sun was shining in a cloudless sky; it was time, he thought, to go for a ride on the bike.

Mad Sunday. The name itself gave little of the plot away. If the title "Tourist Trophy" was a subdued misnomer which said little, if anything, about the nature of the event, then how much more so the adjective used to prefix that particular day of the week. Price knew a little; he was about to learn a lot. A quiet voice inside him urged caution, advised against riding a motorbike anywhere and advised most strongly against riding a motorbike on the Course, but he ignored the voice. The six hundred cc Yamaha fired up at the first prod of the starter button, and he made his way out of the hotel car-park and within minutes had joined the heavy throng of two-wheeled traffic which moved with a single unifying purpose towards the track.

He filtered in at the Quarter Bridge. It was a different experience to his one the day before; then it had been an empty road, a guiding marshal and no speed limit. Now he joined a procession of vehicles, mostly of the two-wheeled variety, but the speed failed to rise above a crawl until they had passed Glen Helen, climbed the hill and reached the Cronk-y-Voddy straight.

It was a beautiful day. The sun shone brightly from a cloudless blue sky and the contrasting colours of the surrounding countryside seemed even more intense than anything he had noticed before. The lush green hues of the vegetation, the purple glow of the heather, the bright yellow gorse, the radiant white of the whitewashed Manx cottages and the deep blue of the sea beyond formed an ever changing kaleidoscope in a landscape that was without comparison anywhere on the globe. Unfortunately, Price only managed to catch most of it out of the corner of his eye; by the Cronk-y-Voddy, traffic had started to move quickly and his concentration, by necessity, had become rather focussed on the road ahead and, via his mirrors, on the road behind.

The Cronk-y-Voddy was a long, fast and undulating straight. To its right, empty moorland rose steeply towards the mountainous and empty interior of the Island, to its left, green fields of cultivated farmland dropped lazily towards the sea. The road pointed towards the west coast of the Island and in the dim and far blue distance, hazy mountains rose from somewhere far over the sea – Ireland, or was it Scotland? Price was unsure, but resolved to look at his map and find out later. On any other day, he would have taken his time, looked around and admired the scenery, but this was not any other day. The traffic was mainly two-wheeled, but it was relatively heavy and particularly fast; he was only keeping up with the general flow, but his digital speedometer told him that the flow was averaging between eighty and a hundred miles per hour and the fast boys (of which there were many) were streaking past that flow at speeds thirty or forty miles an hour faster still. It all looked to Price like a major accident, no, correction, a disaster, waiting to happen, so he gritted his teeth, concentrated and held on.

He reached the end of the straight without incident and the road plunged off to the right and then swept up again to the left. A sign indicated that he had passed the Eleventh Milestone of the TT Mountain Course. A thought briefly materialised in his brain *only twenty six and three quarters left to go*, but the thought was swept away by a tide of speed, wind and noise. The road was straight (ish) for a short while, but then a towering wall of masonry appeared, guarding the right hand side of a left then right chicane. A sign announced *Handleys Corner* and Price braked heavily. A trio of bikes shot past him on the wrong side of the road, all travelling at what he considered to be insane speeds, but, he thought, if they wanted to take those sorts of risks, that was their problem. The Course was still two-way until Ramsey Hairpin and he was going to stay firmly on the left until then.

It was half a mile or so later when he came across the first accident. The road had been fast enough after Handleys, but Price had decided that enough was enough and had eased off the throttle. Fortunately, he had already learnt that the best way to survive on this racetrack (sorry road) was to keep eyes focussed on the tarmac several hundred yards ahead. His first indication of trouble was what appeared to be a queue of stationary bikes. He braked heavily and brought his machine to a halt. It was immediately obvious that a serious accident had taken place. He put his bike on its stand by the side of the road and took a few seconds to size up the nature and scale of the incident; it wasn't difficult. The locus was a crossroads which went by the name of Barregarrow. Tiny country lanes joined the main road from left and right and a small car had apparently pulled out from the lane which joined on the left and been hit by a bike. The car was on its side and the road was strewn with debris. Some way further down the course the back end of a bike appeared to be protruding from the hedge on the right hand side of the road. A few bikers were wandering around in the middle of the road; they looked dazed, shocked, but apparently uninjured. Price took charge; got one of the bikers to contact the emergency services and a couple of others to stop the traffic which was still coming from both directions, then he went to look for casualties.

The driver was still in the car; he was conscious and on Price's brief examination seemed okay; he could wait. Price went looking for the biker. He started with the bike in the hedge. It was looking very second hand: the forks had sheared off at the headstock, the fairing was smashed to smithereens, front wheel buckled, tank dented and engine cracked. A growing pool of engine oil had appeared by the side of the road, but there was no sign of the rider. Price looked over the hedge into the field beyond, but he saw no-one. He knew that he would have to reconstruct events and went back to the car. No-one had witnessed the accident. The car-driver had seen nothing; the first he had known about the whole thing had been an extremely loud bang; he had no idea what had happened to the biker. Price looked again at the car and the black streak of rubber left by the bike just before the impact. He wondered. He set off down the road again from the impact site, but this time kept to the left. A few yards later he found the man; he had gone over a hedge and was lying motionless on his back. Price struggled through the foliage and reached the figure; he suspected the worst, but was pleasantly surprised when he found that the man was still breathing and, even better responded to a few gentle prods and a little conversation. Fortunately, the other bikers had done what had been asked of them and a few minutes later, distant screaming sirens announced the imminent arrival of the official emergency services.

By the time the ambulance arrived, the biker was conscious; Price reckoned that he had sustained major fractures to his lower limbs, but the guy would survive. He made a brief handover to the paramedics who thanked him for his assistance, got back on his bike and left before the police arrived. After his recent experiences, he had no real desire to speak to them.

Price rode down through the bottom of Barregarrow and up the other side, past the Thirteenth Milestone and then entered Kirkmichael Village. A thirty mile-an-hour sign appeared and he slowed. The village was narrow and cars were parked on both sides of the road. He glanced in his wing-mirrors and saw the oppressive front end of a large four-wheeled drive vehicle no more than thirty or forty yards behind . He had not seen the vehicle before so it must have come from the Peel Road. He had been through the village before, of course, a number of times, but this time he felt that something was wrong. The vehicle had an English registration, it was black in colour and its windows were of a dark tinted hue. Those facts were not particularly unusual, but something about the vehicle, something about the scene put Price on notice. He obeyed the strict speed limits and crawled through the village, but when he reached the other end, he decided it was time to go. At the end of the village a Forty sign appeared; Price glanced in his mirror: the black, tinted window four wheel drive was still there. He opened his throttle and the bike leapt forward. He took the right-hand bend known to all as Rhencullen without the slightest problem, but as soon as he rounded the next bend, he knew that he had made a mistake.

A marked police car was sitting on the left-hand kerb and a uniformed member of the Isle of Man Constabulary was standing by the side of the road pointing an instrument in what seemed to be the general direction of Price. He braked heavily, but it was too late and the officer with a few unequivocal waves of his arm signalled the doctor to stop. Price parked the bike at the side of the road and put it on its stand.

"Take off your crash helmet please Sir," he was told.

Price obeyed.

The officer continued: "Travelling a little fast, aren't we?" The policeman walked around the bike, took on board the local number-plate, then continued: "Is this your motorcycle, Sir?"

"Well, no, it isn't," Price replied, "but you guys must know that. I'm a race doctor; someone stole my car and wrecked it in Practice week and the Chief Medical Officer for the TT lent me this bike. Don't worry, its taxed and insured and all of that."

The policeman looked at his colleague and raised his eyebrows. It was a knowing look, one of disbelief. "That's right Sir," he said, "now if you could just let me have your driving licence, insurance documents and the vehicle's log book, we can let you get on your way."

"I just told you," Price replied, "I was loaned this bike. I don't have the documents on me at this moment; can't I get them to you later?"

"Not even your driving licence , Sir?" the officer said in tones of disbelief.

"No, not even that. It's back at the hotel. Look, just let me go and I promise I'll get the documents to you by the end of today, or at worst tomorrow. If you don't believe me, just ask your Chief Constable."

The police officer smiled at his colleague; it was a rather smug, arrogant and superior smile. "We don't have a direct line to our Chief Constable Sir and we also have concerns about people stealing motorcycles at this time of year, so, if you don't mind, we'd rather like you to leave the bike here and come on back to Douglas with us."

Price protested, but he knew it was in vain. For the second time in a handful of days, he was nicked!

There was no further point in arguing so he got into the back of the marked police car, sat down and folded his arms. After a few minutes the two officers got into the front of the vehicle and the engine started. The car set off and headed towards Ballaugh. The radio crackled and bleated intermittently, but from its output, Price realised that other things were going on around the course. There were minor accidents here and there, but after a few minutes a disembodied voice advised of a serious accident back in the Glen Helen section.

Price ventured a question. "Aren't you going to turn around and go back?"

"No, Sir, we aren't allowed to travel against the flow of traffic."

"What?" Price asked, "Ever?"

"No, Sir, never. That would be far too dangerous," the policeman replied.

It was the end of the conversation. Price looked out through the rear window: the four wheel drive with the black-tinted windows was still there, keeping a sedate, but solid forty yards behind them. Price could feel old and familiar sensations of paranoia arising yet again, but he kept a grip and said nothing; something told him that his current companions would not even want to know.

The marked police car travelled on past Bishopcourt towards Ballaugh. Price had nothing else to do, so he sat back and took in the scenery. From his vantage point in the rear seat of the car, he had a better than normal view of the road. It was an incredibly fast section of the course: he looked over his captors' shoulders at the speedometer and saw that even the police car was travelling in excess of ninety miles an hour. Motorbikes flashed past the vehicle every few seconds at far greater speeds still.

Price hazarded a question: "Er, guys, you've just booked me for doing what?"

"Fifty-two in a thirty, Sir," the younger officer, replied cheerfully.

"And this?" Price answered, waving his hands around him.

The policemen in the front of the car laughed; they had not seen his arms, but they knew what he was saying. The frosty barrier seemed to be thawing.

"They're not breaking the law, Sir. Where we stopped you, that was a thirty limit. This section is unrestricted."

A large capacity motorcycle shot past the police car missing it by inches; its speed must have been at least one hundred and fifty miles an hour. A shock wave buffeted the police car followed a fraction of second later by a menacing loud roar which spoke of tuned high-performance horse-power and a total absence of silencers. Price shrugged his shoulders. The experience was different, if nothing else.

The police car slowed to take Ballaugh Bridge (all four wheels remaining on the ground), then carried on its way to Sulby. Ominously, the black four- wheeled drive vehicle still followed a constant forty yards behind. Bikes flashed past almost by the minute, but at Sulby, just before the bridge, the car slowed and came to a halt behind another police vehicle. The two officers (whom Price had now learned were called Phil and Ken) got out and walked over to speak to a colleague who was operating another speed trap by the side of the road. The black four-wheeled drive vehicle overtook, but seemed to slow as it turned right and passed over the bridge. After a few minutes the two officers returned to the car and set off again.

"Any more results?" Price asked.

The two policemen looked at each other and grinned. "Davy there got a ninety-five in a thirty," the officer known as Phil replied, "but most were just doing ten or twenty over."

"You know," Price said, "I can't believe you guys; you let blokes come past you at a hundred and fifty miles an hour, then you book them for doing forty…or fifty. Is that sensible?"

"It's the law," came the response.

"Well the law's an ass." Price responded.

"We agree," came the reply.

The police car set off again, rounded Sulby Bridge and moved on towards Ramsey. Price was still looking out of the rear window. They passed the Ginger Hall Hotel and he noticed a black four-wheeled drive vehicle with smoked glass windows start its engine and pull out of the pub car-park. Price recognised the number plate; it had become rather familiar. Again he said nothing; the four-wheeled vehicle was not speeding so he doubted whether his captors were interested.

They drove along the road from Ginger Hall to Ramsey without too much excitement. It was a fast stretch of the course for the TT racers, but for riders on open roads it was a little too bumpy and a little too dangerous. One or two bikers flashed past the police car, but that was all. Price risked a question or two of his captors.

"So, gentlemen, what exactly do you propose to do with me?"

"Well, Sir," the officer known as Phil replied, "if you can provide us with your driving licence, insurance and evidence of your entitlement to ride that motorcycle, then you're in the clear, apart from the speeding offence, that is."

"And if I can't?"

"Then that would be a different matter, Sir."

"What about my bike?" Price demanded, "I mean you've made me leave it back at Rhencullen?"

The officer known as Phil shrugged. "Look, Sir, If you are who you say you are then

I'm sure that you can find someone to drop you off at Rhencullen later this afternoon or tomorrow and pick up the bike. If you aren't, then we can arrange appropriate transport for both you and the bike back to Police Headquarters."

It was the sort of answer Price had expected, so he shut up and sat back in the rear of the police car. They had now reached Ramsey. There was a queue, a mammoth queue of bikes, more bikes and bikes yet again, all waiting to turn right onto the Mountain Road. His captors, Phil and Ken, seemed resigned to it all and used to the wait. After a long while, Price tried another question:

"So, er, is it always like this?"

"Always," the officer known as Ken said with a touch of resignation.

"Don't you, er, ever get sick of it?" Price ventured.

"We're Manxmen, boy," Ken replied lightheartedly, "it's part of our culture, and…..of course, it's very good for overtime!" His companion laughed and the police car turned right, heading for the famous Mountain Road.

The police car moved sedately through the town of Ramsey then began to climb, through the right-hander known as Stella Maris, the severe left-hand switchback of the hairpin then onwards and upwards to the twin right-hand bends of the Waterworks. Whilst he was driving, the older policeman Ken, who seemed to have taken a liking to Price, had begun to relate anecdotes about the road.

"See, this second corner, that's always the one that catches people out; people see the sign *Waterworks* so they slow down for the first one which isn't too bad and once they've got through it they open up the throttle and…"

The police radio cracked and spat: "Be advised, all vehicles, major incident Mountain Road, Windy Corner; possible fatality, over." Ken picked up the microphone.

"Echo Foxtrot Tango, message received and understood; on our way up the Mountain Road, currently approaching Gooseneck. Estimated Time of Arrival five, repeat five, minutes, over."

The crowd sitting on the bank by the side of the road at the Gooseneck was massive. The people there had gathered to watch the *amateur* motorcyclists circulate around the course; to see a *professional* Police driver was an unexpected perk. Ken took the squad car neatly around the sharp right-hand corner; the wheels protested with a loud squeal of rubber and the spectators let out a quiet ripple of applause. The road stretched out ahead of them like a black snaking ripple of tarmac, but still the legions of bikers on their two-wheeled machines flowed past. They drove on past Joeys, Guthries Memorial, the Mountain Mile and the East Mountain Box. Ken was trying hard, but the car just didn't have the horse-power to even try to keep up with the bikes; they were all going so, so much faster. The police car rounded the Verandah at serious speed, taking the four right-hand bends almost as one. Price gave Ken a mental tick for driving ability and the car swept on through the left-hander of Bungalow Bridge. They were approaching the Bungalow at, Price guessed eighty or ninety miles an hour when suddenly lights ahead of them started to flash. Ken stood on the brakes and the car screeched to a halt; it was just in time, for, half a second later, as the occupants of the vehicle began to sniff and taste the pungent aroma of molten rubber which permeated the interior of the car, a quaint "ting ting" heralded the passage of the tram car of the mountain railway across the road.

The two policemen looked at each other.

"That was a close one, Ken," the younger said. The older man nodded and relaxed his white-knuckled grip from the steering wheel.

"Close enough, Phil," was the limit of his expression.

The tram car had passed, the lights had stopped flashing and the police car set off again. It did not have much further to travel. They drove up Hailwood's Rise and reached the Brandywell, but well before then had all noticed a spectacular black plume of smoke spiralling into the sky. It was ominous; it reminded Price of an aircraft crash and his captors seemed worried. The younger policeman was on the radio to base; he knew that the incident was going to be bad and even now was summoning back-up. Ken slowed just before the first bend of the tricky combination that was known as the Thirty Second Milestone. It was a sensible decision; as he rounded the left-hander he feared the worst and banged on the brakes - if he had kept on the throttle, he would have run into stationary traffic.

They were experienced policemen; the line of traffic ahead seemed thick, although not impenetrable, but they pulled the car onto the narrow grass verge by right side of the road, flicked on the hazard lights to warn others of the danger and leapt out, grabbing a fire extinguisher and those items of medical and other equipment which they considered invaluable. Price was about to follow, but he was told, in no uncertain terms, to remain.

"But I'm a doctor," he argued, "I can help you."

"We don't know that, Sir," came the reply, "and, anyway, this is Police business."

Price shrugged his shoulders and sat back in the car, leaving his captors free to run off down the road. From what he could see, and it was still a considerable distance ahead of him, there had been a major crash at the right-hand bend known as Windy Corner. Not his problem then, this time. He sat back and closed his eyes, expecting a long wait.

"BANG"

The gentle doze was rudely awakened; his nose and front teeth smacked against the seat in front of him.

"What the hell…"

"BANG"

He was knocked forward again and the police car moved a foot, a yard, to his right. Fully awake now, he turned to look behind; it was an instinctive, reactive move, but it probably saved his life. He saw the apparition which was trying to kill him: a black, four-wheeled drive vehicle with smoked glass windows and English number plates; it was the one he had seen earlier, he was sure, but now was not the time to hang around and confirm the fact. He tried the door. Fortunately, his captors had not been overly concerned with security. The door was unlocked so he pulled the handle and dived out into the heather. His move came not a moment too soon: a second later there was another bang, the bull-bars of the four-wheeled drive connected with the rear of the police car and sent it off the road, through the flimsy wire fence and down the steep slope into the valley below.

Price turned over from his prone position; he found himself lying in a deep bed of heather and pulled the springy twigs from his face. He was lying on his back, but the purple bracken covered and probably concealed him a few yards below the edge of the tarmac of the Mountain Road. Above him, he could see the Bull Bars of the four-wheeled drive vehicle protruding from the side of the road. He expected some sort of follow-on, but instead he heard raised voices.

"Hey, You, Four-Wheel Drive, what you try to do; you try and kill that man! Yes you, you answer me; I see what you just do; that was no accident."

The voice was a familiar one; Price knew it from somewhere. He struggled to his feet and started to climb back up the steep slope towards the road. He heard an exclamation; it was in an unfamiliar language, but it had the ring of a swear word. The sudden high-pitched sound of a gear-box flung into reverse cut through the air and the bull-bars disappeared. The engine revved in neutral and was then thrown into a forward gear; rubber screeched as it slipped and then bit against tarmac. The engine note rose then dipped as gears were changed and the vehicle accelerated away.

Price pulled himself up the last few feet of heather-sprung hillside, climbed onto the road and looked around. The four-wheeled drive had gone and all he could see was a long line of motorcycles stood in a queue stretching out in the distance towards Windy Corner.

"Hello Doktor Price; you Ok my friend?"

Price looked, took on board the scene and smiled: it was Mikael and behind him the combined motorcycle divisions of the former Soviet Red-Army field hospital and their East German allies.

"Mikael; good to see you and your friends. I think I owe you one, but how could you have possibly…I mean how did you come to be here?" A smile passed across the tall Russian's face; he replied:

"Just coincidence, Doktor Price, we all riding around together enjoying the Mad Sunday." Price looked at Mikael and then at the others; they were all smiling and nodding; they were all lying, but they could well have saved his life so he let it go.

"Where did that four-wheeled drive go?" Price asked.

Mikael pointed down the road towards Windy corner. There was a queue of bikes, but enough room for a car to get past, particularly if the driver wasn't too fussy about using the grassy verge.

"It go down there, but I think it will not get very far. Big accident I think. You see the smoke?"

Price could certainly see the smoke; it was, if anything, even thicker than it had been earlier.

"Anyway Doktor Price, why you in police car? You in trouble?" Price told him and Mikael laughed. "Maybe we have a word with the police; we tell them who you are," he said. Price shook his head.

"I think they have slightly more pressing problems at the moment," he replied.

"Then maybe we help them; come on Doktor."

He turned to walk over to his motorbike. Price hesitated; he looked at Mikael's machine: it was an old, black Soviet era Cossack and appeared thin on passenger facilities. Mikael turned back and saw the expression on Price's face. He laughed again.

"If you not like my motorcycle, maybe you prefer to ride in sidecar?"

He waved his hand at the machine behind his. It was an ancient combination which looked even thinner on modern technology than Mikael's Cossack. In Price's eye it belonged in a museum, but at least it had somewhere he could sit. He was introduced to the proud owner, a bearded giant of a man who went by the name of Peter and climbed on board. The Russians and East Germans kicked their vehicles into life and the convoy set off down the narrow ribbon of available tarmac which lay between the stationary queue of bikes and the grass verge. The bikes they passed were modern and mostly Japanese; their riders had taken off their helmets and were standing by their bikes patiently waiting for the traffic to start moving again. They stared in open-mouthed astonishment at the collection of Eastern bloc machinery; it was from a different era, a different world to what they were used to.

As they rounded the next corner Price saw the extent of the incident. It seemed to have occurred just past the apex of the right-angled, right-hand bend known as Windy corner. At least three bikes seemed to have been involved and wreckage was strewn all over the carriageway. Two bikes were still burning fiercely in the middle of the tarmac, but the two police officers seemed to be paying no attention to the fire and were kneeling by a prostrate figure in the large gravel trap which lay by the left-hand side of the road. Mikael and his friends rode straight up to the burning bikes, seemingly oblivious to the danger. Peter stopped his combination and from somewhere behind Price's seat extracted a huge fire extinguisher. It was at least five times larger than the one the police had taken from their car. Within seconds he had brought it to play on the burning bikes and a sea of white foam rapidly engulfed and then doused the flames. Price was impressed, but he, too, knew he could make a contribution and ran over to the gravel trap.

"Can I help, boys?" he asked. The two policemen looked up at him; he could see from the expression on their faces that they were worried, deeply worried.

"This guy's not breathing too well," Ken said. "We've done everything in the manual, but he doesn't look good; any suggestions?"

Price looked at the casualty; he was a typical biker, wearing the latest multicoloured leathers, but his helmet had been removed and he was now lying on his back. There were signs of serious facial injuries and it was immediately obvious to Price that the man's airway was obstructed.

"Turn him onto his side," Price commanded. The police officers obeyed without question. Price knelt down and briefly examined the casualty; the man's face bore a pale tinge of blue and the signs were extremely bad. Price took his pulse; it was soaring off the scale. He turned to the officers and spoke, urgently:

"Look, Ken, Phil, this guy's in a seriously bad way. Have you called for a back up? For an ambulance?"

The policemen nodded. Ken spoke: "Ambulance and fire engine, both on their way here, but you know what it's like, it's Mad Sunday. Traffic's really bad and they're coming the wrong way up the Mountain. What else can we do?"

"What have you got in the way of a first aid kit?" Price asked. Ken thrust a small green box into the doctor's lap. Price opened it: the contents were, unfortunately, useless.

"I can't do anything with that," he said. Another voice cut in; it was deeper and had a pronounced Russian accent.

"Will these help, Doktor Price?"

Mikael set a huge box down by the side of the road. Price glanced at the box and then at its contents, before nodding to his Russian friend and seizing a handful of surgical instruments. He had no time to speak, but knelt down by the side of the unconscious biker. He knew that time was ebbing away for the guy and that work had to be done. He seized a scalpel and a few gauze swabs and attacked the unconscious biker's neck.

The operation was a cricothyrotomy; the incision being between the thyroid and the cricoid cartilages. It was simpler, easier and safer than a tracheostomy, and, if done properly had the same result. It was, of course, done properly and the unconscious form began to breath and his colour improve as soon as Price had done his work. The doctor turned towards Mikael and thanked him:

"Mikael. This guy owes you a few shots of vodka, I think, if he makes it."

The police decided to speak; Ken was their spokesperson:

"Er, Doctor Price, thanks for bringing your friends along; we think that in the circumstances, maybe we can drop the speeding charge, seeing as how you've been such a good citizen and all."

Price had a question: "Why couldn't you put the fire out?"

"Bloody extinguisher ran out," Phil replied, "we used it all up on the first bike, but then there was no more."

A screaming of sirens interrupted the conversation. Price had already learned that the other casualties were reasonably comfortable and the critical one was now stable. The rest of the cavalry were now coming up the mountain.

He ventured a final question to his late captors. "Ken, did you see that four-wheeled drive come scooting up here? If you did, where did it go?"

The policeman cast a curious gaze at Price. "Black, smoked windows, English plates?" he asked.

"That's the one," Price answered.

"It went down there," Ken replied, pointing to the tiny lane which pulled off the apex of the Windy Corner and dropped down towards Glen Roy and the village of Laxey.

Chapter Thirteen

Mad Sunday (afternoon)

A cavalcade of emergency vehicles with flashing blue lights and screaming sirens had arrived at Windy Corner and, after a short conversation with the first paramedics on the scene, Price decided it was time for him and his irregular crew of Eastern-bloc assistants to leave the medical stuff in the capable hands of others.

"Time to go," he commanded and the group of men mounted and kick-started their bikes. The low-tech machinery fired up and with a loud and minimally-silenced rumble the single and twin-cylinder engines burst into life.

Price was sitting (relatively) comfortably in the chair of Peter's combination. He realised, suddenly, that the outfit stood a few yards in front of the lane he felt they needed to explore and was pointing in the wrong direction. They would have to turn around. He muttered something of the same to Peter and was about to get out, but the giant Russian tapped him on the shoulder and smiled.

"No need to get out, Doktor; this Soviet machine." He pulled a lever on the side of the tank and the outfit flew backwards and spun about. "We have reverse gear!" he laughed. The combination was now facing the tiny lane at the apex of Windy Corner. Price looked around. The former Soviet Army Field Hospital and their East German Allies were right behind him and ready to go forward. Price stood up in the sidecar and waved his arm forward towards the lane.

"Let's go," he said. The combination set off and the cavalcade moved slowly forward crossing over the cattle grid and passing through a narrow gap in the dry-stone wall to enter the single-track moorland lane which led from Windy Corner through a steep cleft in the hills down to Glen Roy.

It was a narrow, tight, bumpy and rutted track which an enduro bike or a four-wheeled drive vehicle might have found just about acceptable. Parts of it looked as though they had once possessed a covering of tarmac, but with the passage of time, such a surface, if it had ever existed, had crumbled, decayed and washed away. The surface which the motorbikes now passed over varied from, at best, an uneven and stony hillside through loose gravel and clay to mud. Price's Alpha, or a modern Superbike would have had absolutely no chance of getting through, but, if the Eastern Bloc bikes had one thing going for them, it was ground clearance. Price laughed as his driver, Peter, bumped and bounced the old-fashioned sidecar combination down the rutted cart track far faster than he thought possible.

They rode on. The view was spectacular: the rolling heather and gorse-clad uplands had a stark and wind-swept beauty all of their own, but as they dropped away the moorland landscape was replaced by a gentler, more pastoral scene of leafy deciduous trees, steep-sided glens and lush green meadows dotted with grazing sheep. Beyond the meadows lay the sea, its colour a deep and inviting blue. Further away still, the mountains of the Lake District rose majestically from the far-off and hazy horizon.

The incline became steeper and the condition of the surface deteriorated steadily. Price began to wonder whether they would get through, but despite these doubts, he had a strange feeling that they were getting closer to something; something intangible, but nevertheless central to the mysteries of the deaths of Taylor and Kinnish. Eventually they came to a junction and on Price's instinctive instructions turned left. They were now on a single-tracked road; it was roughly finished and bumpy but at least it had a surface which bore a passing resemblance to tarmac. The road seemed to follow a particular contour along the foothills of Snaefell Mountain, rising briefly then falling, but moving neither back up towards the Mountain Road nor down towards the Sea. The open moor gave way to thick patches of woodland and the riders' view of the road and countryside ahead was limited. They rode on slowly and cautiously and their route twisted and turned to the left and right. After a mile or two the road descended sharply into a steep-sided hidden valley, one of many which innumerable fast-flowing little streams carved through the countryside in their short journey from the watershed of Snaefell to the sea. They passed through a shallow ford and Price raised his hand, bringing the cavalcade to a halt.

The road they had been following climbed up the other side of the valley and continued on its way, but Price had seen what he had been looking for. To his right an unmade track led off through the trees following the course of the stream. His gaze followed the track until it fixed upon a four-wheeled drive vehicle which was standing in a clearing some fifty yards away beside a small collection of derelict buildings. He could see no sign of life, but beside the four-wheeled drive stood a van emblazoned in the black and gold of Petromax World Racing. He turned to speak to his friends.

"Peter, Mikael; do you have any thoughts about this?"

Mikael shook his head; he replied in a voice which was little more than a whisper. "It is Petromax vehicle, no doubt about that, but why is it here, in this place?"

Peter, the giant had his own ideas. "This is quiet, secret place, Doktor Price; I think Petromax, they have something to hide."

Price looked closely at the surroundings. The deciduous woodland was particularly dense, a canopy of dark green foliage camouflaged the glade from casual passers-by on the road and probably from observation from the air. The track which led from the road to the clearing was unmade, but the rutted and drying mud bore the marks of many recent vehicles. How and why they should have made such a journey was at present a mystery; but Price was determined to find out. He made a decision. "Mikael, Peter, something is going on here. I need to find out what it is. Can, sorry, *will* you help me and, more importantly, will your friends?"

Mikael Boroweski folded his arms in front of him; his face assumed a stern and committed expression. "Doktor Price, this Petromax, and whatever these men are doing concerns us; we have the honour of our country at stake. We follow you and are grateful for you helping us."

"You feel the same, Peter," Price asked the giant.

"Da," came the monosyllabic reply.

"And the other men?"

"They do what I tell them," Mikael responded brusquely.

Price looked around again. The woodland glade seemed empty at present, but the two vehicles parked in the clearing suggested that other people were somewhere in the vicinity. Those other people could return at any time and could, of course, be less than friendly. He shared his thoughts with Mikael. The cavalcade of motorcycles did not blend easily into the background, even in TT week. The machines would have to disperse, lookouts would have to be posted, a communication and command structure would have to be put into place. The tall Russian listened and nodded slowly as Price spoke. Once Price had finished, Mikael addressed the other men rapidly in their own tongue. Price did not understand a word of that particular language so he had no idea of the content of the speech, but the tone and delivery of the words had a certain ring about them and sounded curiously like orders. Whatever the words were, they had an immediate effect and the seemingly languid Eastern-bloc bikers showed a sudden burst of activity. Within a few minutes the collection of bikes and riders had dispersed, leaving Price, Mikael and Peter standing alone by the track. Even Mikael and Peter's machines had been concealed from passers-by and camouflaged with a speed and professionalism which made Price begin to wonder.

It was time, now, to investigate and Price began to walk slowly down the unmade track towards the clearing. His Russian friends followed close behind. They cautiously approached the stationary vehicles and looked inside: as they had suspected, the vehicles were empty.

The four-wheeled drive and the van stood in front of a cluster of buildings; from the road they had seemed totally derelict, but on closer inspection that did not appear to be the case. They were low and constructed of weather-stained local stone. Green moss clung to the mortar and spoke of long ages of disuse. The empty window-frames had long cried out for glazing as the battered roofs had for slates, but the wooden doors were solid enough and most bore well-oiled and modern padlocks. More importantly a number of signs had been securely attached to the doors and walls of each building. The signs were of recent manufacture, Price was certain of that. They carried no visible marks of weathering or the passage of time and the message they bore was clear and unambiguous:

Strictly Private
Trespassers will be prosecuted
Deep mineshafts
Danger of death

Petromax Holdings Limited

Price looked at his friends. "Mineshafts?"

Mikael and Peter looked at each other and then at Price. It may have been his imagination, but they seemed far less surprised than he was. Peter spoke. "Like I said Doktor Price, I think this Petromax, they have something to hide."

Price nodded; it was certainly looking that way.

The three men wandered around the old mine buildings. It was apparent that some had not been in use for many, many years, but others had seen far more recent employment. The sound of a running engine drew Price to one outbuilding where a new diesel generator was hard at work. Its voluminous fuel tank suggested activity on a regular basis. The fact that the engine was running suggested that the activity was going on now. He heard a low whistle and looked up. Peter, who was no more than thirty yards away, was waving for his two companions to join him. It looked as though he had found something. Price walked quickly over and Mikael followed.

It was an open doorway leading to a precipitous stairwell. They had found the entrance to the mine. From the evidence of the open door, they were not alone.

The three men held an impromptu, but urgent counsel of war; the stairwell could reap dividends, but the potential danger was immense. Price was in favour of immediate action, but his two companions urged caution. In the end, the Russians' argument prevailed:

"Look, Doktor," Mikael entreated, "we know there are probably people down there. We do not know how many; we do not know what they are doing; they could be dangerous; they could be armed. We are unarmed, but we know their secret place. We come back later, when they have gone; we explore this mineshaft and then we find what we find. Okay? Agreed?"

Price nodded; he knew that the argument made sense. He turned and walked slowly back down the woodland track with his two companions. As he did, something caused him to look up: it was a flash of bright sunlight reflected on glass. For a moment he thought it could have been a reflection from the window of a passing car, but he realised that the flash came from a point in the woodland above the road. He knew then that it spoke of binoculars at play. He told his companions nothing, but from the corner of his eye he monitored the spot within the woods and his vigilance was rewarded with a further flash and then another. Someone, and Price had no idea who, was watching them.

They got back to the narrow road. It was still empty and Mikael asked Price for further instructions:

"What now Doktor?"

Price shrugged his shoulders before replying. "I think you're right; now we do nothing. Too difficult, too dangerous. I have a friend arriving tomorrow who may be able to help. How do I contact you, Mikael?"

The tall Russian smiled: "Easy. I have mobile. This my number."

He gave Price a card which Price pocketed without even reading.

"You need a lift somewhere, Doktor Price?" he continued. Price thought for a few seconds and then remembered his motorbike, the R6 Yamaha.

"Christ, yes," he replied, "I need to get back to Rhencullen, just past Kirkmichael; I don't suppose one of you guys could give me a lift?"

Mikael smiled again: "Doktor Price, it will be our pleasure."

The journey from Glen Roy had been a convoluted and slow one through a succession of narrow lanes, hamlets and sleepy villages. Price's companions seemed to prefer the quieter, little roads to the busy TT Course. Given the huge difference in speed capability between their machines and the vast majority of those that circulated the Mountain Course, it was probably a sensible decision. They skirted the centre of the Island's capital then rode along winding back roads to Peel, eventually stopping at the famous "Creek" public house on the quayside for welcome refreshments. Price opted for a dressed crab sandwich (which he learned was one of their specialities) and which he consumed whilst sitting in the sidecar on the other side of the road. As he ate, he looked around and was surprised to see the undertaker, Richard, sitting at a trestle table outside the pub. He seemed locked in deep conversation with a blonde-haired lady of indeterminate age. It was possibly a bereaved relative, he thought and decided not to approach.

After a short break, the Russians returned to their machines and continued. They rode along the quayside, turned right along the promenade and then took the coast road to Kirkmichael. Eventually, they joined the TT Course.

It was late in the afternoon when they reached Rhencullen. The sun was still shining brightly from a cloudless blue sky, but was mid-way through its descent to the western horizon. The bike was still there, but Price had never, for a moment feared otherwise: crime, in general and vehicle theft, in particular, did not appear to be major problems on this Island. Price took the borrowed crash helmet from the lock where it hung on the side of the machine and put it on. Pulling on his gloves, he swung his leg over the bike, turned the key and fired up the engine. After his fellow bikers had taken their leave and departed, he waited patiently for another break in the incessant stream of two-wheeled traffic, then accelerated off along the road to Ballaugh. The road was probably a little quieter than it had been earlier, but not much and Price was beginning to feel tired. He certainly had no great desire to keep riding around the Mountain Circuit; he had experienced *quite* enough of that for one day. He passed through Quarry Bends and moved onto the Sulby Straight. At the crossroads by the pub, he turned right and took the road up through the Sulby Glen.

The road wound into a narrow valley which cut a steep gash through the hillside. To his left a shallow river tinkled merrily between rocks and boulders. To his right a shoulder of coniferous forest climbed above the road. After a few miles the road passed over a cattle grid and narrowed; Price slowed, mindful that the beasts of farm and fell were not necessarily acquainted with the fact that it was TT fortnight. Sure enough, a few seconds later, he came across a recently-sheared sheep complete with lamb slowly crossing the road. The long-suffering animal cast him a glance which suggested that she did not entirely approve of the TT Festival.

Price rode on and passed through the pretty little hamlet of Tholt-y-Will; the road then climbed steeply upwards through a tight double hairpin to reach an open expanse of moorland. Finally he came to the Bungalow and the T-Junction meeting the Mountain Road. To his surprise, the TT Course was strangely quiet and Price turned right without problem. He accelerated up Hailwood Rise and flicked the 600 Yamaha around the Brandywell. At the Thirty-Second Milestone he realised that there were problems ahead and slowed.

Red and white cones split the carriageway as men from the Department of Transport laboured furiously. They had pieces of heavy machinery in place and seemed to be relaying the road. Price could see precious little space to get past and one of the yellow-jacketed workmen was waving frantically so he slowed to a walking pace and then stopped. The man ran over to him.

"What d'yer think yer doing fella," he shouted above the noisy background roar, "road's closed from Ramsey Hairpin; didn't the police stop yer?"

Price told the man that he hadn't come through Ramsey, but via Tholt-y-Will. The workman shook his head. He had expected that route to be sealed off as well. Price asked why the road was closed.

"Bad accident earlier on," the man replied, " bikes on fire; a lot of damage and right on the racing line some of it. We're relaying the whole corner: has to be ready for tomorrow's races."

"Any room to get past?" Price asked.

"Shouldn't let yer through really, fella," the man said, "but if the police can't do their job properly, not my place to do it for 'em, is it?"

Price shook his head gratefully. He was shown a narrow, but passable route through the corner, crawled slowly along it and then, on reaching solid tarmac again, opened up the throttle for what was essentially his second closed-roads experience of the weekend. He flew around the thirty-third milestone, slowed for the tight left-hander of Keppel Gate, rounded Kate's cottage and then tucked in behind the fairing for the awesome high speed plunge to the Creg Ny Baa. It had been an exhilarating mile or two, but as he expected it could not continue. A uniformed policeman stood in the middle of the road and held his arm aloft. Price came to a halt. He was getting a little tired of the Isle of Man Constabulary.

Price trotted out explanations and apologies; thankfully the policeman didn't seemed that bothered about the infringement and allowed the doctor on his way. Price turned left by the side of the pub and took the back road to Douglas.

Chapter Fourteen

Mad Sunday (evening)

Price followed his nose back to Douglas and, after a pleasant ride along quiet country lanes, eventually arrived at the north end of the promenade. His journey took him through the tiny hamlet of Groudle and then along a cliff-top road until he reached the outskirts of Onchan, once a village, now more properly described as a suburb of Douglas. He stuck to the coastal road and made his way past the former Summerland leisure complex, scene of a terrible fire in the early 1970s. Suddenly, he hit heavy traffic and after a precious few seconds realised that the continuing journey to his hotel would be a painstakingly slow one. A few hundred yards ahead, he could see a pub. It was large and seemed to have ample parking in front of it so he pulled in, brought the bike to a halt and killed the engine.

Dismounting, he stretched and walked a little stiffly from his 600cc Yamaha to the open door of the Terminus Tavern. It was a large pub, nestling in a natural sun-trap at the foot of the cliffs which bordered the northern end of Douglas Bay. It was set well back from the promenade and the space between the front of the pub and the road held a number of trestle tables and bench seats. Most of the seating was full, as was probably to be expected on a warm Sunday evening in early June, but there were one or two spaces. Price bought a pint of the local brew, found one of the spaces and sat down. He was thirsty and downed half the glass fairly quickly; it was only then that he started to look around. Leather-clad bikers sat to his left and right. In front of him lay the promenade and the sea, but before that stood a little wooden kiosk, the ticket office for the Manx Electric Railway. Trams slowly and merrily clanged and sparked their way up the hill past Summerland on their way to Laxey and all stops beyond. Price looked to his right and noticed the sheds of the Douglas Corporation Horse Tram. It would seem that the Terminus Tavern was aptly named, sitting, as it did at the start and finish of both forms of transport.

It had been a beautiful day and the sun was still shining brightly. Price toyed with the idea of abandoning the motorbike; he felt like he'd been on the thing all day and, to be honest, he'd had enough. The idea of a few more relaxing drinks and then a gentle stroll back to his hotel seemed rather attractive so he mulled it over for a few more minutes. He was already on his second pint and had struck up a conversation with the Dutchman who was sitting next to him. The conversation had started hesitantly enough, but like every biker Price had met on this island, the Dutchman (whose name was Niels) was a friendly soul, had an excellent command of English and took it upon himself to make the relevant introductions. His companions were equally hospitable and further lubrication was inevitably called. The bike would definitely remain in the pub car-park.

The Dutchman was a seasoned and enthusiastic veteran of the TT Races and told Price far more about the event than the Englishman could possibly take on board. Price listened attentively at first, but then his attention began to wander. Some of the stories the Dutchman told him set alight memories of the previous week and Price recalled the crash on the Veranda and the death of Kinnish. He shuddered. The local radio station had reported the anaesthetist's death as a tragic accident; there had been no official comment from the local police, but Price, of course, knew otherwise. He recalled the incident on the mountain, the trip through Glen Roy and the mysterious black stranger who seemed to have dogged his path for several days. Price knew that in the past he had suffered from paranoia, but his recent experiences were certainly not helping.

He tried to keep involved in the conversation with the Dutchman and his friends, but he knew that he was losing touch. After half an-hour or so, they had stopped even trying to include him and at about that time he began to feel that he was being watched. At first he tried to tell himself that it was nothing, that his mind was starting to play tricks on him again: it was just a vague feeling, brought about by the fleeting glimpse of something, someone among the crowd that stirred a vague memory. He shook his head, but the feeling grew stronger. At last, he looked around.

At first he saw nothing, recognised no-one, but after scanning the area for a few seconds, his heart missed a beat. He had spotted a figure who bore a strong resemblance to a man he had seen a number of times before. The figure was standing by the entrance to the Douglas Corporation Horse Tram Sheds. He was fifty yards away, but even at that range Price could see that he was a tall, thin, clean-shaven black man wearing dark glasses and a black suit. Price was sure that this was the same individual he had seen at Quarry Bends, in the Queens Hotel and by the Bottle Neck Beer tent. It was a small island, to be sure, but four times in less than a week could hardly be coincidental, could it? Price was determined to find out. He looked at the man again; this time his glance became a rigid stare and this time his eyes met with the dark tinted glasses. The anonymous stranger lowered his gaze, turned to his right and began to walk away. Price jumped up.

"Hey you," he shouted. The crowd of drinkers around him looked up so he added, almost as an afterthought, "excuse me, Niels I need to speak to that guy." He continued: "hey you! Stop. I want to speak to you."

The black man carried on walking. A horse tram was leaving the sheds and without even changing his stride pattern the man leapt aboard. Price had been walking towards the man; the walk now became a run, but with a sedate "clip-clop" the Douglas Corporation Horse Tram moved off down the promenade. The tram was moving at little more than jogging pace, but it was still hot and had been a long day. Price had no plans to chase on foot so he looked around for a taxi.

He turned back to the Terminus Tavern. A taxi had dropped off a fare and was parked there with its engine running. Price opened the door and jumped in.

"Down the promenade please; and as fast as you possibly can."

The driver laughed. "Have you seen that Prom, mate? Only thing that could possibly move on there right now is a horse tram."

Price looked at the driver; from his expression, the comments were serious. It was only then that he noticed the traffic - the promenade was choked in both directions: movement was nil. He thanked the man and ran back towards the sheds. A ginger-haired little man seemed to be busy harnessing a fresh horse to a brightly painted tram car in front of the building.

"Hey you!" Price shouted. The ginger-haired man looked up.

"Yesssir?" he responded.

"Can you take me down the Prom?" Price demanded.

"Not scheduled to start yet," the little man replied, rather defensively, "last tram just left and that left early 'cause a feller jumped aboard who was in a hurry."

"Never mind that," Price replied, "will you take me?" It was a straight-forward enough question; so was the reply.

"You wanna go now?" The man asked, but he did not say No.

Price uttered the immortal words:

"*Follow that horse tram*," and thrust a twenty-quid note into the hands of the ginger haired driver.

"Sound…" came the reply. The note was inspected and pocketed and Lester (for that was his name) released the handbrake, shook the reins and the one-horse power vehicle took to the road in hot pursuit.

The horse and Victorian carriage rattled and banged across the promenade. The vehicle had a cast iron frame, cast iron wheels and bodywork of brightly painted wood. Suspension was minimal and the engine (Price later learned) went by the name of Daisy. Horse power was, well, horse power, fuelled by an exotic mixture of various types of cellulose derivatives. It was certainly the most complex and unpredictable vehicle Price had been on that day.

The other traffic was stationary, but fortunately the cars and motorbikes were polite enough to respect the iron railway track as some form of urban clearway. Price had perched beside Lester in the cockpit of the antique conveyance and gazed at the road ahead; he could see the other horse tram, but it was now a good three hundred yards in front. His tram seemed to be travelling interminably slowly; its pace borne out by the measured sound of the horses hooves:

"clip-clop, clip-clop, clip-clop," went the audible speedometer. Price knew that they needed to speed up. After a few minutes he could bear it no longer.

"Can't you make this thing go any faster?" he asked, pushing another twenty pound note towards the ginger-haired driver. The little man again carefully inspected the note through his thick-lensed glasses, before thrusting it into his pocket. His response was dramatic; although previously a man of few words, he seemed now to have found the accelerator:

"Sound!!" he said. Rising to the occasion, he stood up, shook the reins and shouted encouragement to his horse. "Giddey-up, girl, cummon Daisy, cummon, cummon, giddey-up."

The transformation was amazing: the powerfully-built cart-horse changed step and moved up into another gear. In an impressive burst of acceleration, the tram shot forward, its speed increasing dramatically for a couple of hundred yards, but then brakes were applied and with a piercing screech and swaying, yawing shudder it slowed and stopped.

The ancient rails of the horse-drawn railway sat in the middle of the road, allowing more modern traffic to pass on either side. That was the general idea, but the planners, when coming up with the scheme a hundred years or so earlier, had unfortunately not reckoned on universal car ownership. The road which had probably been ill-suited to the horse tram for a decade or two, at least, was today, the busiest day of the year, unable to cope: the traffic on Douglas Promenade was gridlocked. In between the stationary cars, vans, buses and horse-trams, motorcycles of every colour, shape and form weaved noisily from side to side trying to gain some position at the head of the field. Price shouted at his driver:

"That guy's getting away, can't you do anything?"

The diminutive ginger-haired driver looked at Price; his face bore just the slightest question of a frown, but his words were forthright enough. "Nothing's moving; what d'you f***ing expect me to do?"

Price looked around and ahead: his carriage stood unmoving outside the Queen's Hotel and the horse-tram he was pursuing appeared stationary outside the Hilton; the gap was no more than four hundred yards, a distance he could easily run provided the traffic didn't start moving again. It was a judgement call.

"Lester," he said, "I need to catch that horse-tram. I'm going to run for it, but if the traffic gets moving make sure you move with it and let me get back on board."

"Sound…." came the inevitable reply.

Price jumped off the tram and started to jog along the pavement. The evening breeze had died - it seemed even hotter and the pavement was crowded with bikers, tourists and locals; everyone seemed to be standing around, admiring the scenery, chatting, eating ice-cream and generally getting in his way. Price was still wearing his motorcycle leathers and after a few seconds he began to sweat profusely.

He ran past the parade of shops which lay to the south side of the Queens. The broad expanse of pavement served as an additional temporary parking place for dozens of motorcycles. These were additional obstacles, as if bikers, tourists and locals had not been enough, but he got through and ran on past the terraced row of hotels which came next. Just as he began to think he was making good time and gaining on his quarry, the traffic began to move again. Somewhere to his left a whistle blew shrilly. Price looked around: it was Lester. The little ginger-haired man waved frantically and Price veered over to his left and jumped back on board the tramcar.

"What's happening?" Price asked, panting and sweating. The diminutive figure shook his head.

"Dunno, but we're moving." Price craned his neck and looked for the horse tram in front, but it was fast disappearing from his sight. Cars, vans and motorbikes seemed to have filled the increasing void between the two horse-drawn vehicles and pursuit seemed futile. Price was determined not to give in so easily.

"When you blew your whistle a minute or two ago," he ventured, "the other traffic moved out of the way. Why was that?"

Lester seemed to consider the question carefully before giving his reply.

"Whistle means we're stopping; they get out of the way so passengers can get off."

"But do they all know that?" Price asked excitedly; he had the beginnings of an idea.

"Dunno," Lester replied, "but I do."

"You do, yes, but don't most of them think it simply means *Get out of the way*?"

Lester thought again for a moment. "Suppose some of them might."

"Ok Lester, that's what you're going to do: blow your whistle for all its worth; start now and keep on at it."

The ginger-haired little man considered the request for a moment. Price supplied an additional twenty pound note to facilitate the thinking process. It had the desired effect. The little man shrugged his shoulders. His response was the one Price had come to expect.

"Sound...."

Lester blew his whistle and shook the reins. "Cummon Daisy girl, giddey-up." The horse tram jerked forward and amazingly, miraculously, the traffic in front of it parted like the Dead Sea in some form of reincarnation of a scene from the Old Testament. They began, at last , to gain on the horse tram in front of them. On Price's request Lester blew his whistle again and again and again; the cars and motorbikes moved to the side and the one-horse power vehicle gained on the one it was pursuing.

The horse-tram was now moving at speed (at least 8 mph) and had passed the Hilton. Ahead of it traffic was heavy, but at the sound of the whistle it moved aside. Price was encouraged:

"We're gaining on him Lester, we're gaining on him. Just get Daisy to pull out all the stops." The leading horse-tram was by now no more than a hundred yards ahead. Price could see the black man with the dark glasses clearly: he seemed agitated and leaned over to speak to his driver before turning back to look at Price.

The black man had obviously given his horse-tram driver instructions. His carriage seemed to gain speed and, within seconds, yards on its pursuer. Price had to speak to his driver again.

"Can't you go any faster Lester? This guy seems to have stepped up the pace; is his horse faster, or what?" Lester seemed unconcerned.

"No worries; his horse there, that's Gladys. She always gets a move on along this section of the Prom, knows she never gets too many fares along here, but she'll slow down for the traffic lights at the end of Broadway." Price looked at the driver in disbelief, but something about the little man's expression seemed to deem question or even comment pointless. Price sat down and said nothing as, punctuated only by the piercing blast of Lester's whistle, his carriage rumbled and rattled along in pursuit.

The traffic lights at the bottom of Broadway were fast approaching, and, yes, the horse tram in front did seem to be showing signs of slowing down. The traffic between the two horse-drawn vehicles had thinned and it was now a straight fight to a finish with a gap of no more than fifty yards to close. Price shouted at his driver:

"Come on Lester; can't you get this bloody horse to go any faster?"

Fifty yards in front the black man with the tinted glasses looked back at them and turned to his driver. He, too would have noticed that the gap was closing.

The lights on the promenade turned to red as the first horse tram hit the bottom of Broadway, but the carriage swept on through the junction forcing traffic coming down the hill from Broadway to brake and swerve. Horns blared and a number of voices shouted angrily, questioning the tram-driver's parentage, sanity and competence, but the tram carried on as before, its speed barely dropping. Ignoring Price's calls to carry on and go straight through Lester had applied the brakes and was now waiting patiently for the lights to change green. Price was fuming.

"We nearly had him, we nearly had him; why in the hell did you stop? We'll never catch him now."

"It's the law," the little man replied calmly. Price looked at his driver and then at the sky and then shook his head. There was no point in further argument. The lights changed and their horse tram lurched forward again, but the gap between the trams was now up to about four hundred yards.

Lester blew his whistle and shouted encouragement to the horse, Price willed the Victorian conveyance forward; he knew that the chase was lost, but prayed for a minor miracle. They were moving quickly again and had just passed the Sefton hotel to join the Loch Promenade when, completely out of the blue, a marked police car, its lights flashing, swept past them and pulled to a halt directly in front of the tram. Two uniformed officers sprung out of the car. Price groaned.

"Not again!"

He realised that someone must have reported a tram breaking a red light; the police had got the wrong tram, but they could go no further without explanation and that, of course, would take time; the chase had been lost.

The two policemen were walking slowly towards them, one with his notebook in hand. In light of his recent experiences, Price was quite surprised to see that they were both unknown to him. He started to mentally rehearse his story when the ear-piercing blast of an air-horn cut through the traffic noise behind him. Startled, he looked around.

A large and powerful black Suzuki motorcycle was approaching at speed; with a squeal of its brakes it pulled up beside them. The rider, who was wearing one-piece black racing leathers and a black helmet with dark visor motioned for Price to get on and pointed up the road at the tram they had been pursuing; a tram which was now disappearing rapidly into the distance. Given his experiences over the previous week, Price could have been forgiven for turning the offer down, but something about the rider seemed vaguely familiar; could this be the minor miracle he was seeking?

"Got to go Lester; sorry for dropping you in it," he said, pulling on the helmet which lay on the seat beside him. He jumped onto the pillion and the rider revved the engine violently, dropped the clutch and screeched away.

When Price later came to recount his adventures on two or four wheels over that memorable TT fortnight, he maintained that if he had had the slightest inkling of what that short trip on the back of that motorcycle was to be like, he would have stayed with Lester in the tram. It was, he said later, simply the scariest thing he had ever experienced.

The police car had pulled across the road about two car lengths in front of the tram, blocking the tramlines and partially blocking the road. On its seaward side, an unbroken line of traffic streamed slowly towards the harbour, snaking, by necessity, around the front of the stationary vehicle. On its landward side, a horse tram, fully laden with holidaymakers was clip-clopping slowly in the opposite direction and an unbroken line of traffic was streaming past that. The black Suzuki which was accelerating hard had simply nowhere to go. Price braced for the inevitable impact. The rider turned for a split second and spoke:

"Hang on." Only two words, but it was a voice Price had heard before, although he could not quite remember where or when. Suddenly, something happened: the engine beneath him crackled and its note changed from a deep and low pitched burble to a piercing, high-pitched whine. An ear-splitting roar burst from the exhaust and the bike leapt forward. It was as though someone had flicked a switch releasing instant power (Price later discovered it was something called nitrous oxide) - the sudden acceleration of the machine was phenomenal. Its front wheel shot into the air and Price's head was flung backward as he struggled desperately to maintain his grip.

The bike flew over the bonnet of the police car. Price felt his heart racing and mentally he thanked his anal sphincter for not letting him down (so far).

There was a loud bang accompanied by the straining creaking sound of buckling metal: they had landed, not on the road, but on the roof of one of the many cars in the queue of grid-locked traffic crawling slowly along the Loch Promenade. Price gulped, but the rider seemed unconcerned. The bike's engine screamed and they were airborne once again.

"Bang," they had landed on the roof of another car.

"Bang," another one.

And so it went on, this roof-top rally down the Loch Promenade.

Fearing a certain, horrible death, Price had closed his eyes sometime shortly after landing on the first car roof. The inevitable accident had not yet materialised so he slowly began to reopen them. The traffic was still grid-locked; there was no available space on the road ahead, so the individual who was controlling this machine had decided on a more straightforward line. Price held on for grim death. The rider of the large and powerful Suzuki had set a special agenda and the doctor cursed whoever it was and then himself for the predicament he had got himself into.

"Bang," the motorbike landed again; the engine whined and roared and the machine took off, but this time it landed on the road. The back tyre of the bike slipped and squealed as it fought for grip; a fraction of a second later the rubber found its mark and the big Suzuki launched itself forward.

Price had no time to collect his thoughts, still less time to consider them. If, for a moment, he had believed his transit along the Loch Promenade would somehow be safer, now that he was on firm land, he was in for a rude surprise. The bike weaved to the right and shot through the smallest of gaps between a long-wheeled base van on one side of the road and a double-decker bus on the other. Price felt his shoulder scrape against the side of the bus; he looked in front of him and was horrified to see the back of a heavy wagon closing off the narrow corridor ahead: once again, he felt he was going to die.

The rider of the bike had other ideas, however, and, seeing some kind of opening, somehow managed to squeeze the bike in front of the van, missing the wagon by inches. The bike shot across the road, mounted the pavement, and weaved through a crowd of pedestrians before rejoining the road. They were now opposite the Admiral's House Hotel and the horse tram lay no more than a couple of dozen yards ahead. It was still travelling along the promenade with its signature clip-clop, clip-clop, but its pace had been slowed by the even heavier traffic passing in front of the Bushy's Marquee at the head of the Prom. Price's heart rate slowed from about two hundred down to about one hundred and twenty when he realised that the chase was all but over. The horse tram came to a halt just before the roundabout by the Sea Terminal building. The tall black man jumped off and hurriedly made his way into the gathering crowd by the large marquee.

A few seconds later, the black Suzuki screeched to a halt. Price jumped off and turned to thank the rider, but by the time he had turned, the bike was gone. The rider had hardly spoken, but Price had one or two ideas as to who it might be.

It was now after seven in the evening and the crowd outside the marquee was already fairly large. The sun had fallen behind the western skyline, but it was still perfectly light: dusk would not fall for at least a couple of hours. Finding a tall black man wearing sunglasses would be a challenge, but it was a challenge Price felt himself up to. Word was already spreading through the crowd about the incredible chase. Someone, somewhere would know something.

Price took off his helmet and gloves; the motorcycle leathers he was wearing did, at least mean that he was more likely to blend in with the crowds than his quarry. His tactics were simple: just gentle questioning, about a close friend he had become separated from in the heat of the busy TT "Mad Sunday". The description was actually an unusual one: tall black men wearing sunglasses and dark suits were surprisingly few on the ground in TT fortnight, although the buoyant financial sector had made such people far less of a rarity than previously.

Enquiries in the marquee had drawn a blank; customers of that particular establishment broadly fell into one of two categories. The first, and by far the largest group were TT bikers who just wanted to tell their friends (and anyone else who cared to listen) wildly exaggerated tales of daring-do concerning the (sometimes imagined) laps they had managed to put in around the TT circuit over the course of the day. They were too full of their own near miss/near death experiences to notice anything other than particularly loud passing motorcycles. This meant that whilst most of them had witnessed Price's arrival, none had seen the man he was following. The second group comprised all the local wasters and alcoholics who simply regarded the beer tent as another bar (and one from which they were not barred) where they could drink from midday until midnight. By this time none of them were really in a condition where they could have noticed anything, even if they had been looking which most of them were not.

There were retail outlets other than the beer tent, however, and at one of these, a nearby fast food stall, Price learned that the man he was seeking had passed by walking briskly back towards the central area of the Promenade. Price carried on in that general direction. Further enquiries confirmed that he was on the right track. The man had been seen by proprietors of a number of rides and sideshows walking up past the funfair which sprawled over a wide expanse of pedestrian walkway between the War Memorial and Bushy's Marquee. As he was passing the rides, Price looked to his left and noticed a couple of police cars by the side of the road. A second later he noticed the row of damaged cars. Each of them bore impressive dents to their roofs. The police were taking statements; the drivers were irate. Price looked away; he felt a strong desire to laugh and controlled it, but couldn't help a flicker of a smile passing across his face.

Price had now reached the War Memorial. A man selling ice cream confirmed that his quarry had passed by only fifteen minutes earlier. The ice cream vendor pointed across the road: he thought that the man Price was following had taken that route, but he couldn't say whether he had entered the grounds of the Villa Marina or not. Price crossed the road, but his enquiries at the Villa drew a blank. Security for the night was tight as a big name rock star had flown in to perform at the Mad Sunday TT Gig. The doormen had instructions to let no-one in without tickets; that included Price and, no, they had not seen a tall black man wearing a black suit and dark glasses. The trail was in danger of going cold. Price reasoned to himself that the man would, in all probability, be returning to his hotel. He had passed the first tranche of hotels which stood along Loch Promenade, he had passed the Sefton; the next row of hotels would be those on Central Promenade. Price determined to make enquiries there.

Traffic was flowing a little easier now as bikes and cars gradually parked up for the night. When the roadside parking space had filled up, the bikes simply parked on the pavement. Price began to think that he had simply swapped on form of congestion for another, but at least, he said to himself, the pavement congestion was a lot safer. It was a quarter of a mile from the Villa Marina to the first of the big hotels that lay along the Central Promenade. Apartments and private houses filled most of the gap. Price kept his eyes peeled in case the man had turned into one of these, but somehow he thought it unlikely. A large hotel would be his best bet. A new excuse would have to be formulated, though; if the man he was searching for was supposed to be his friend, it was hardly likely that Price would not know where he was staying. Price racked his brains: missing property? The man could have dropped something, but what? And anyway the hotel receptionist would only have to take the item and promise to make sure that the man got it. In the end Price decided not to complicate matters by giving a reason. He would simply ask if the man had been seen and take it from there.

The first hotel drew a blank; the staff were polite and cooperative, but they had no guest and had seen no-one fitting the description Price had given. The second hotel likewise. At the third hotel, the staff were far less polite, but the response was essentially the same.

And so it went on until Price reached a large hotel which looked even from the outside as though it had seen better days. He walked though the front entrance and made his way to the reception desk; the sense of former glory now living in reduced means was evidenced by worn and faded carpet, shabby wallpaper and peeling paint. A musty smell which seemed to speak of years of damp, dirt and neglect hung over the place. Even though it was the busiest weekend of the year the place seemed empty. Price rang the bell. No response. He rang again and waited. Eventually, after what seemed an age, he heard footsteps and the door behind the reception desk creaked open.

"Yes?" It was a young girl, no more than eighteen or so; it was obvious from her accent that she was a foreigner. Price thought she sounded eastern European or possibly even Russian; wherever she came from, it was soon apparent that she spoke very little, if any English. He doubted whether she understood his description of the man he was following, or even understood the question he was asking, but of one thing Price was certain: this girl wasn't just afraid, she was terrified of someone or something. Maybe she was an illegal immigrant, maybe something else. Price gave up and left the building.

He moved on down the Promenade, passing from hotel to hotel, but the responses were all the same: the trail had gone cold and Price had had enough. Abandoning the task he had set himself, he turned around and made his way back to his own hotel. It was a good mile or so back the way he had come, but he was tired and needed an early night. Tomorrow was Monday. Another race day and, more importantly, the day when his old friend Roy Love was scheduled to arrive.

Chapter Fifteen

Monday Morning (Race Week)

At six am the prearranged alarm call raised Price from his fitful slumber. For once he was glad to be wakened, for his sleep had been a disturbed one, passing from one chilling nightmare to another. Once upon a time he had been a fairly resilient type - it was necessary in his line of work - but years ago his nerve had been shaken and the last seven days had taken their toll. He pulled himself from the bed, got to his feet and shuffled into the bathroom. He looked at himself in the mirror as he brushed his teeth. Was it his imagination or were his eyes that little bit sunken, the face more creased, the hair starting to show those tell-tale signs of grey?

He turned the shower on full blast and stepped into it. Now was not the time to dwell on past events, he was due at the airport at 8 o' clock to meet his old friend and would need to be fully awake and alert, if he were to be able to bring Roy Love rapidly up to speed on all of the weeks developments. In the light of recent events, the day's racing would be of secondary importance, but Price knew that he was expected at Ramsey Parliament Square when the roads closed at 10.15 so he had a tight schedule to keep.

By six forty-five Price had left the hotel and, clad in his motorcycle leathers, helmet in hand, was walking briskly up the deserted Promenade towards the Terminus Tavern. It was a fair walk, but he was pleased to see that the Yamaha 600 was where he had left it. He swung his leg over the bike, turned the key in the ignition and fired up the engine. It was time now for the airport.

By seven-thirty Price was sitting in the restaurant above the Arrivals Hall scanning the runway and TV monitors for signs of the morning flight from Gatwick. It was listed as on time, but time was precious and Price knew well enough that "on time" could soon become half or an hour's delay. Thankfully that did not happen and, dead on the hour, the British Airways blue and silver bird touched down on the Ronaldsway runway. Ten minutes later Price welcomed his old friend at the Arrivals gate.

Roy Love looked a shade older, but that was only to be expected; the last time they had met was when they had been investigating a series of murders in Manchester and that, after all, had taken place over ten years earlier. Price didn't even want to think how much older he probably looked.

"Good to see you Roy," Price said enthusiastically, shaking his old friend by the hand.

"Likewise, Jonathon," the grizzled-haired Welshman replied. His voice seemed a little flat, but still retained that characteristic musical tone which recalled the Valleys and the Rhonda. "It's a shame that we only ever seem to meet when something bad's going down," he said. The older man looked tired, but he had the spark of a smile on his face.

The two men had known each other long enough: well over twenty years to the best of Price's memory. The friendship could be traced back to a brutal murder in Torquay; days when Price had been a House Officer (a type of very junior doctor) and Detective Sergeant Love had been the investigating officer. The Detective Sergeant had risen to the rank of Chief Inspector and had worked with Price in a complicated and particularly nasty drugs case in Manchester many years later. By that stage Price had been rather more senior, but the case had nearly destroyed him. Now Love had retired from the force, but not from work: from what Price had told him this could be something of a wholly different nature. Love broke the ice.

"So what have you got, boyo? What's this all about?" Price smiled.

"I've told you enough, Roy and anyway, you've got a client, remember? You probably know more about it than I do." The Welshman grinned and shook his head; for once he did seem genuinely perplexed.

"Complex Karma, Jonathon. I've got a few ideas, but we need to sit down and talk; when can we do that?".

"Later today," Price replied. "I've sorted you out with a hire car and booked you into my hotel. I've also made a few notes about what has happened over the last week: here they are. Take the notes, take the car and go back to the hotel. We can talk it all through sometime this afternoon." Love nodded and looked at the notes with interest, but had a question.

"Why can't we do it now?" he asked. Price shook his head.

"TT Racing," he said, "I'm a doctor; I've an appointment to keep by a racetrack in Ramsey and I definitely can't get out of that." Love shook his head in disbelief.

"Motorbike racing!" he exclaimed. "Does that take priority over murder?"

"On this Island," Price replied, "perhaps it does… but anyway, whatever happened is related to the motorbike racing and probably indivisible from it so I think it's probably best if I remained involved, don't you think?" Love thought again and nodded:

"You're probably right."

They arranged to meet at four pm in the hotel bar. Price started to give Love directions back to Douglas, but the older man waved his hand. "No need, Jonathon, I've been here before, remember?"

Price recalled that the retired policeman had been a keen motorcyclist and frequent visitor to the Island in the past. "In fact," Love continued, "I think I'll have a wander up to the Grandstand and watch the races once I've checked into the hotel. See you at four." The two men parted and Price walked back to the car park. It was now eight thirty on Monday morning. Neither men yet knew it, but it was going to be a very long day.

Price chose the scenic route to Ramsey. He wanted to follow country roads and avoid Douglas, partly because he felt like a change of scenery and partly because he knew that the roads into and out of the Island's modern-day capital would be choked for the next hour and a half as most of the Island's working population, to say nothing of the forty thousand visitors, struggled desperately to get to where they wanted to go before the roads closed. He turned left out of the airport and headed for the Island's ancient capital, home of the splendidly preserved medieval Castle Rushen. He bypassed the centre of the town and then turned right at a set of traffic lights taking the road to St Johns via Foxdale and the long and incredibly fast Ballamodha straight.

After a refreshing blast of unrestricted high speed, he slowed and trickled through the single street of terraced houses that made up the old mining village of Foxdale. A few miles further on he arrived at the traffic lights of Ballacraine and joined the TT Course. From now on he was in what he could comfortably describe as familiar territory and, as he had expected, traffic was heavy. Even though the road was open and busy in both directions, people were taking chances; Price kept well in to the left as every few seconds high powered motorcycles shot past in high risk overtaking manoeuvres. It was amazing how quickly you could get used to things, Price thought; only a week before these antics had scared him out of his wits, now he regarded them as just part of the local scenery.

For once his journey around the course was uneventful and he arrived at Ramsey just before half-past nine, parked his bike in a convenient spot and walked over to introduce himself to the marshals.

The racing started on time and, as far as Price was concerned, passed off without incident. By quarter-past three, the Roads Open car had shot past and the day's racing was over. Price climbed aboard his bike and took the mountain road back to Douglas.

The day had started brightly. It had not been cloudless like Sunday, but it had been warm enough and the weather had been extremely promising. A few wisps of pastel white, cotton wool cumulus had drifted lazily across the deep blue sky and conditions had looked good for the rest of the day, if not the rest of the week. As the morning moved into afternoon, however, the wisps were replaced by thicker, heavier cloud. At first the cloud remained high up and far off, but as the afternoon wore on it darkened and descended. By the time Price set off from Ramsey, Snaefell's summit had disappeared and the temperature had started to fall.

As was the usual practice when the roads opened after racing, the Mountain section from Ramsey Hairpin to the Creg Ny Baa Public House was one way only from north to south in the direction of the Course. This policy was applied for an hour or so to allow the traffic, most of which was Douglas bound, to move freely and use the full width of the road without the danger of head on collisions. It was a sensible policy, but did, unfortunately have the effect of turning the latter part of every race day into a mini Mad Sunday, if only for that brief hour. Price rounded the hairpin and, as expected, half a dozen bikes tore past him and roared up the hill to the double right-hander known as Waterworks. The cloud had continued to fall, however and only a few corners and a few hundred yards further on, brake lights were shining as the line of vehicles encountered that peculiar blend of sea and hill fog, found only in the Isle of Man and known as Manannan's cloak (named after Manannan MacLir who once ruled the Island and if legend is to be believed, kept foreigners away by engulfing the island in a shroud of mist). Price, along with a few dozen others, turned on his headlights and eased off the throttle. As he climbed up the mountain, the mist thickened rapidly. It was an eerie experience: the white plumes of fog flowed like liquid from the hillside to cover the road, dulling and muffling sound and sight. Even though Price had ridden over that road a number of times before, he soon lost all sense of direction and would have felt quite lost had he not known to simply follow the road and the other road users in front of him.

He rode on for what seemed miles; by now he had no idea where he was. He had his visor wide open, but visibility was probably down to five yards and he could barely make out the side of the road. Suddenly, red lights in front of him began to flash and a bell began to clang. It gave Price a start and he nearly dropped the bike, but managed to bang on his brakes and come to a standstill. Slowly, the ghostly shape of an electric tramway carriage moved through the grey sea in front of him and crossed the road. It moved slowly from right to left, its bell clanging gloomily like that of some phantom vessel in the fog. Price breathed again: it was only the Snaefell Mountain railway taking passengers back to Laxey. He knew now that he was at the Bungalow and would soon reach the highest point on the Course. Hopefully, once he had begun to descend, conditions would improve, but as the road rounded the Brandywell and gradually began to drop, the fog grew, if anything, thicker.

He travelled slowly on, until a couple of miles further down the road, he rounded a sharp left-hand bend and felt the cold clammy breath of air bearing the strong salty tang of the sea. The road fell steeply before him and confirmed what he had suspected for the last few miles; this fog was rolling in off the Irish Sea and was not going to lift.

Descending the long straight gradient a dull grey building suddenly loomed ahead out of the mist. It was the Creg Ny Baa public house. Greasy yellow light spilled out of the windows throwing up spectral silhouettes and shadows as people passed to and fro within. The light, dulled by the oily sea of fog, served only to accentuate the surrounding gloom. Price trickled round the corner and carried on towards Douglas. He dreaded what that would be like in these conditions.

Approaching the outskirts of the Island's capital, dull red smudges bore testimony to the rear lights of vehicles ahead. They clustered and thickened as the traffic bunched and slowed to walking pace. Hillberry, Cronk-y-Mona and Signpost corner passed painfully slowly. At Governor's Bridge a policeman was thankfully on signal duty and gave overwhelming priority to the deluge of traffic pouring into the town from the Mountain road. Price turned left down Victoria Road, passing the Island's prison before finally reaching the Promenade and at long, long last the car park at the rear of his hotel. The journey back from Ramsey had taken forever and it was now after five; he went straight to the hotel bar. Love was sitting quietly in a corner, but stood up immediately Price appeared.

"Problems, Jonathon?" he asked with a laugh.

"You could say that," the younger man replied. "Have you seen the fog? Took me forever to get back from Ramsey; give me fifteen minutes to get changed."

Chapter Sixteen

Monday Evening (Race Week)

A quarter of an hour later, Price had returned. The bar was empty so the doctor and retired policeman decided to stay there and talk; if potential eavesdroppers appeared they could always go elsewhere. Love had read his friend's handwritten account of the previous week's events and had a barrage of questions prepared. Some of these Price could answer; most he could not. He grilled Price about the accident at the Veranda on the first morning of Practice, about Taylor and his injuries; he asked what tests Price had made on the body and when the results would be available; he asked about the anaesthetist, Steve Kinnish. He wanted to know everything Price could tell him about Petromax, its shadowy owner, its rider Andre Rorletski, his uncle Mikael and the former Soviet Army Field hospital. Price had no secrets and told Love everything that he knew. The older man seemed particularly interested in the mine in the hills above Laxey and in the mysterious black stranger with the dark glasses. It was nearly seven o'clock before Love stood up, bringing the conversation to a close.

"Come on," he said.

"Come on where?" Price asked.

"We need to have a good look at that mineshaft. Can you remember the way?"

"I think so," Price replied a little hesitantly, "but in this fog? Do you think it's wise?"

"Now's as good as time as any, Jonathon and don't forget, the fog works both ways. Chances are that the Petromax crowd won't fancy going down there in these conditions either, particularly not at this time of the day."

Price was still unsure of the merits of his friend's plan. "Don't you think we should get some help, I mean, er, take some people with us?"

"Who do you suggest?" Love asked.

"Well, I suppose we could ask Mikael and his friends," Price suggested.

"We could," Love conceded, "but do you **actually** know who they are? Do you know whether we can really trust them?"

Price agreed, reluctantly, that the answer to both of these questions had to be no. "What about Richard, the undertaker, or Miss Templeton, the advocate?" he asked brightly.

Love seemed to consider the suggestions carefully.

"We could at least tell them where we're going," Price continued, seeing that the older man had not rejected the idea out of hand, "in case, er, we...." His voice trailed off, but his implications were obvious.

"In case we don't come back, you mean," Love said, finishing his friend's sentence for him. "Not a bad idea at all; can you contact them, here, now?"

Price nodded. "I've got their mobile numbers; what do you think I should say?"

The two men discussed the matter for a few minutes, before deciding that the truth would probably be best. Price then returned to his room to make the calls (on his first day on the Island he had discovered that the Isle of Man was counted as "overseas" by his cell-phone network provider and as he had neglected to request 'overseas roaming' before making the crossing, his cell-phone was useless). As luck would have it, Miss Templeton's phone was switched off and Richard's phone rang out. All Price heard was the irritating recorded message telling him to try again later. There was no facility to leave voice mail so he put down the receiver and returned to the bar. Price said nothing about that particular news; he reasoned that his friend would not have been interested.

"We're going to need some equipment," he advised instead, when he returned, thinking practically, "torches, ropes..."

"I know," the retired policeman cut in. "Don't worry, whilst you've been out there enjoying yourself watching motorcycle racing, I've been busy; come on, everything we need is in the car."

"Everything?" Price asked.

"Well everything I could think of," Love replied, "but if you can think of something I wouldn't have thought of, then you're welcome to suggest..." the older man's comments sounded a little tetchy and Price held up his arms to diffuse any potential argument.

"Just one small thing," Price said, suddenly remembering a particular item of kit, "I'll get it from my room."

He returned a few minutes later with a rucksack and the two men made their way out of the back of the hotel to the car park. The dense shroud of fog which now hung heavily over the Island had brought with it a premature dusk. The hotel car park lights were programmed to turn on an hour or two later, but for now, the open space at the rear of the building seemed dark and scary. The hire car, a standard Ford saloon, stood in the worst-lit quarter. Love found the vehicle and opened the boot. The boot light failed to illuminate (pretty well par for a hire car, Price thought) and the rucksack took its place in the gloomy void. The two men climbed into the car, the engine started and the Ford slowly edged its way on to Douglas Promenade. Some way far over to their right the deep and dismal boom of a foghorn , repeated every few seconds, told those denizens of the sea that the port of Douglas was cloaked in a deep and murky veil of dense cloud and shadow.

Love had taken the wheel and turned onto a Promenade which was now almost deserted. Cars and motorbikes still passed along it, but their numbers were a fraction of what could be considered normal. The sudden arrival of a particularly dense fog had driven all but the committed or insane back to the safety of home or hotel; only those who really had to be were abroad.

Their hire car crawled along at little more than walking pace. Every so often dim and blurry beams of headlights appeared and then passed by. Once, a large, dark and unlit shape suddenly materialised out of the gloom; Price's heart missed a beat, but then steadied when he heard the reassuring clip-clop of the horse tram. Love seemed unperturbed.

"*Not* the best of nights to be out, Jonathon, and these horse trams are a bloody menace - they certainly should have riding lights or something."

Price said nothing. Not for the first time, he was having serious doubts about the evening's proposed adventure.

They passed the Queen's Hotel, the Terminus Tavern, Summerland and then climbed up onto the cliff-top road which cut through the eastern fringes of Onchan. The fog thickened and their speed fell again. Somewhere towards the end of the parish, a red-faced balding man was puffing on a small cigar outside the front door of his expansive house. He noticed the headlights of a car approach and then pass by. A second later the red tail lights disappeared slowly along the coastal road towards Groudle. He shook his head at the stupidity of anyone who would even consider driving in such conditions. His mobile phone lay on a table top somewhere inside the house. It was on silent and would remain so until tomorrow.

Price and Love passed Groudle and reached the Laxey Road. They crawled through the village of Baldrine and on Price's directions turned left into the black emptiness of the Manx countryside. The roads got narrower, twistier and, if such were possible, even darker and foggier. After what seemed an age, they found the turning Price had been looking for; the road narrowed yet again and a blacker darkness supervened as they entered the woods.

Price had harboured grave concerns about this mission from the very beginning. Now these began to surface.

"This is ridiculous, Roy," he suddenly said. "It's pitch dark and we're driving along in dense fog in the middle of a forest looking for a tiny glade which, to be perfectly honest, was hard enough to find in broad daylight. I think we should pack it in and go back to the hotel."

His companion laughed. "Not bottling out, are we Jonathon?"

"Certainly not, but we're never going to find the place in this," came the reply.

"Let's just keep on going for a mile or two," the retired policeman pleaded. "I, for one, have a little more confidence in your directions than you seem to have."

Price said no more and a short while later the road began to descend. They were travelling at little more than a brisk walking pace when suddenly they heard water splashing around the wheels of the car. It was a ford. Could this be the one? Love stopped the car on the other side of the stream, got out and turned on a powerful torch. Most of the light was reflected by the fog, but some of it managed to cut through. Price followed the beam with his eyes until it picked out what he had been looking for.

"That's the place," he exclaimed excitedly.

The track was scarcely visible, but it was the one they had been looking for. Love started the engine and they continued cautiously to crawl along it. It was slow, tedious stuff, but a few minutes later he brought the car to a halt in an opening in the darkness. The two men got out; the blackness was stuffy and oppressive, but they could see no other vehicles: it would seem that they were alone.

A sudden, piercing screech cut through the darkness; Price flinched, but his companion placed a reassuring hand on his shoulder.

"Just an owl," he whispered. "You sure this is the place?"

Price nodded.

Love opened the boot and rummaged for a moment or two.

"You take these," he whispered fiercely. Price held out his hands and took hold of a bulky coil of rope and a heavy-duty torch. His companion kept the rest of the equipment, whatever that comprised, to himself.

"Which way?" the older man whispered. Price pointed and started forward. It was late and the fog was dense, but Price had regained his bearings. They walked slowly past the shadowy collection of derelict buildings. A few seconds later Price threw the beam of his torch at a sign:

Strictly Private
Trespassers will be prosecuted
Deep mineshafts
Danger of death

Petromax Holdings Limited

"We're definitely in the right place, Roy," he whispered. His companion nodded.

This time there was no rumble of diesel generators; the silence was far, far more oppressive and far, far scarier. They arrived at a padlocked doorway which the last time Price had been here had been opened. It was the entrance to the mine.

Price turned towards his companion. "This is the place," he said, "what do you want to do?"

Love dropped the holdall he had been carrying and pulled out a long and cumbersome tool.

"Put some light on that padlock, will you, Jonathon," he muttered.

Price swung the beam of his torch around: his friend applied a heavy duty bolt cutter to the lock. There was a sharp snap and the padlock fell to the ground. Love pushed the door open and took a step inside. His companion still had reservations.

"Do you really think this is wise, Roy?" he asked. "This is a serious step into the unknown."

The older man smiled. "He who risks nothing, gains nothing, achieves nothing, is nothing; haven't you heard that before, young man?"

"I have," Price replied, "that's what worries me."

"Come on," the retired policeman said and with the gravest of misgivings the younger man followed his friend through the open door and down the steps into the old mine.

Slowly and with a degree of caution the two men edged forward past a bulky diesel generator and then down a precipitously steep stairway; behind them the door creaked shut. There was no light apart from that provided by their torches, but there was no fog and the two powerful beams provided surprisingly good illumination in the confined space that was the way ahead. Price could see that they were at the top of an old shaft; above them blackened timbers bore pulleys and winding gear from which a thick rope dropped into the inky blackness below. It was drawn as taut as a bowstring. Once, no doubt, long ago, a mechanism had been in place to raise and lower a cage taking miners to their shifts in the far off levels deep beneath them. There was no sign of the cage at the top of the shaft, quite possibly it was at the bottom, but Price was surprised to see that the wheels bore no traces of rust and appeared clean and well-oiled. In addition, a heavy duty insulated electric cable, no doubt fed by the generator, snaked down the shaft: tell tale signs of twenty-first century activity in a nineteenth century museum piece.

The staircase they had started to descend was narrow and clung to the walls of the shaft, heading ever downwards in a clockwise spiral. They took care to stay as close to the wall as possible for to their right lay an inky void with no handrail to prevent a fall into certain oblivion. The staircase was made of cast iron and was attached to the wall by ancient rusty brackets; it looked desperately unsafe, but Price took some comfort when Love pointed out that the centre of each step was far less rusty than the periphery. The staircase had been in use recently and could probably be trusted to bear the two men's weight. They tried to move quietly, but in the silence of the old shaft even the gentlest footfall seemed amplified by the darkness; there was nothing for it, but to press on and reach whatever it was that lay at the bottom.

Fortunately, neither of the men suffered from any of the usual phobias which the darkness, confined space, terrifying drop or general fear of the unknown could trigger, but the angle of descent of the stair was probably about sixty degrees and that descent that was beginning to seem endless. With no handhold on either side, the danger of dropping off the edge of the stair or tumbling headfirst down it was ever present so they had no option, but to proceed desperately slowly. There was no opportunity to rest or relax and after twenty minutes or so their legs began to ache and they began to tire. From time to time they pointed their torch beams down the dark chasm which was the centre of the shaft, but to no avail. The rope dropped down straight as a ruler, but the blackness seemed to go on forever. Eventually Love stopped for a rest and spoke over his shoulder to the man behind him.

"Know anything about these mines?"

"Nothing," his friend replied, "do you?"

"Bought a book on them this afternoon; some of them are two thousand feet deep."

"*How deep*?" Price replied, horrified at the prospect of climbing down a stair twice the height of the Empire State building.

"The miners used to take about two hours to climb down, work a twelve hour shift and then another four hours to climb back up again."

"Don't jest, Roy," Price warned, "we'll have to climb back up as well so you'd better pray this shaft is one of the shallower ones."

"Don't worry," the older man said, "we won't be able to go beyond five hundred feet, no matter how deep the shaft was originally. I reckon we've done over two hundred now so that still leaves us quite a long way to go."

"Why do you say that? I mean, five hundred maximum?" Price asked.

"Simple," Love replied, "water. The top of this shaft is about five hundred feet above sea level. When these mines were running, they were constantly being pumped out; that's why they built the big water wheel down in the village. It's a wet, wet place and unless you keep the shafts pumped dry they just fill up until they reach a sort of equilibrium. This shaft might well go down a couple of thousand feet, but the last fifteen hundred feet of it will be under water. Come on, two hundred feet, three hundred maximum to go."

Price sighed and the two men continued their descent, but a short while later Price began to hear the faintest of noises. At first he thought that his ears were playing tricks on him, but the noise got louder and clearer, a sure sign that its source was getting closer. It was the *drip, drip, drip* of water splashing onto something.

"Hear that?" he whispered loudly to the man in front of him.

"Yes," Love muttered, "sounds like we're getting near something; I'm not quite sure what."

Suddenly a strangely contrasting feeling of space enveloped them. A cold, refreshing breath of air met their faces, drifting up or out from somewhere and shattering the stuffy stillness of the shaft. The spiral staircase carried on down, but to their left the wall ended, replaced by another dark and empty void. Love stopped and played the beam of his torch slowly around. It was a good job that he did. The spiral stairway ended inches below his feet: the torch revealed a rusting sheared-off break in the continuity of the cast iron steps. To their right a short gantry jutted out into the shaft and beside it hung an empty steel cage. A narrow gauge railway track led from the gantry through the opening which lay to the side of the shaft.

"I think we've found what we were looking for, Jonathon," Love said. "Stay quiet, keep your torch beam low and follow me."

The two men turned to their left and moved slowly into the tunnel which led horizontally out from the side of the shaft. It was narrow and low, but they were guided by the railway tracks and the electric cable which snaked above their heads.

After little more than half a dozen yards the tunnel opened up into a wide cavern. The two men stopped and played the beams of their torches about the walls, the ceiling and the floor of the chamber. It was a large, large space, chiselled out, no doubt, under the spluttering candle-light of a generation of miners working for poverty wages a hundred and fifty years or more before. They had done a remarkable job, probably something which modern day workers with pneumatic tools and hard hats would have been unable to match. Price and Love looked around searching for something, neither of them were quite sure quite what. It was difficult and took some time for the chamber was as big as a large warehouse. One of the first things Price found was a large wooden box fixed to the wall. It was marked with a skull and crossbones and labelled "Explosives". Price looked briefly inside: he saw sticks of what looked liked dynamite, but they looked old, desperately old and had probably been there since the working days of the mine. He moved away and then saw railway tracks which led into the centre of the chamber. Following them carefully with his torch he soon came across a simple squat truck sitting at what appeared to be the end of the line, by the side of the truck stood a collection of machinery. Price was not an engineer; most of the machinery was outside his experience, but he certainly recognised what could only be a lathe. Stacked beside the machinery stood a collection of stout wooden boxes. They looked as though they contained something: Price looked inside to see what.

Love moved across to join his friend.

"Found anything?" he asked.

Price nodded and pointed the beam of his torch at the wooden boxes on the floor.

"What's in those?" the older man asked, bending down to examine the items more closely. They seemed to be machined parts, but for some strange reason were individually wrapped in sealed plastic bags. Price recognised a camshaft, a set of valves, clutch plates, that sort of thing; none of the items seemed unusual, although when he picked up the bags they did seem remarkably heavy. That heaviness and the distribution of the parts within the wooden boxes set a train of thought in motion.

Love reached inside his coat pocket and fumbled for a moment before producing his glasses. He pushed them onto his head and then looked again at the objects in the wooden boxes.

"Look like bits from a motorbike engine to me," he said. "Petromax is a motorbike racing team; maybe these are special parts?"

"Special parts?" Price answered in a derisory tone; "so special that they need to keep them at the bottom of a lead mine? Come off it Roy, why do you think anyone would do that?"

"I dunno; maybe they're stolen."

"They might be, but looking at them now, what do you notice?"

Love looked again into the wooden boxes. "Well, there aren't very many of them."

"Correct," his friend answered. "One wooden box; size approximately one metre long, half a metre wide, thirty centimetres deep. Contents: one camshaft size approximately forty centimetres long, one centimetre wide and one centimetre deep. The rest of the box is fully of polystyrene packing. The next box is about the same size and had exactly the same contents. The next box is the same size and had even less in it: just a couple of clutch plates. Why use so much space for a few engine parts and why, for god's sake, go to the trouble of keeping them at the bottom of a bloody lead mine?"

"I haven't the faintest idea, Jonathon," the older man said slowly, "have you?".

"Very clever, Doctor Price, you seem to have caught me out!"

Suddenly the cavern was illuminated with a cold, bright light.

"It is good to see you, Doctor. At last we meet!" the voice continued.

"Who are you?" Price ventured. The voice laughed.

"I am the man you have been chasing, Doctor Price. I have been watching you; you are a clever man...maybe too clever for your own good. Sadly, by finding your way here, you have determined that you must die....Sergei, please deal with the good doctor and his friend!"

A man appeared out of the light. He was pointing a machine gun at the two men. Price looked at his friend; the former policeman shook his head.

The machine gun remained silent and Price and Love submitted to their captors' bonds. At least that gave them a chance of eventual freedom. Anyway, Price knew a thing or two about being tied up: a thing or two more than his captor.

A few minutes later Price and Love found themselves tightly bound and lying on the cold stone floor of the cavern. The megalomaniac responsible decided to try and tease his victims.

"You think we are stupid, do you not doctor? You come here and do not think we keep this place guarded?"

Price ventured a question. "You're the guy who owns Petromax, aren't you, the Russian billionaire?"

"Maybe, doctor, maybe. You know who you are?" the man replied laughing.

"No," came the response.

"You are the guy who died at the bottom of a mine; some guy, some nobody. Hey, maybe in a million years time some archaeologist will discover you and put your body in a museum…then you will be famous, Doctor Price…Ha, ha, ha. Come on Sergei, we have wasted enough time with these people; it is time to move our stock out of here. Please call the rest of the men."

"So who are you then?" Price persisted. "If you're going to kill us don't we even deserve to know that? I thought you Russians had enough guts to kill people face to face, not by a bullet in the back of the head when they weren't looking!"

Something in that sentence touched a raw nerve with their captor.

"I am Vladivir Illosovich, the richest man in Russia and I will not put a bullet in the back of your pathetic little heads. You will stay here, in this mine. Eventually, perhaps, this place will fill with water and you will drown, but maybe you will die of cold, or thirst or hunger before even that happens. Goodbye, Doctor Price."

Illosovich turned to leave the chamber and from nowhere a dozen men appeared. The wooden crates were loaded onto the railway truck which, once full, was pushed along the line. It left the lofty chamber and Price and Love heard a rumble and clang as it moved into the cage.

The light snapped off and Price and Love were left alone in the pitch cold darkness.

It was a good few minutes before either man spoke. Price was first.

"Roy, at the risk of stating the obvious, this isn't looking too promising. We're several hundred feet below the ground, tied up and no one knows we're here apart from a deranged Russian psychopath."

Love thought about the problem for a moment, before replying. "Those people you told: the advocate and the undertaker?"

"Sorry Roy, I forgot to tell you; their phones were not responding."

"Voice mail?" Love ventured.

"No."

"Oh."

Chapter Seventeen

also Monday Evening (Race Week)

Louise Templeton peeled the skin-tight leathers from her athletic body and flopped into her favourite armchair. She took a great deal of pleasure in her stunt-riding exploits, but sometimes found the double life a little bit too much. Today had been particularly tiring. Eight hours at the office, with three of those in court and then a half hour set piece outside Bushy's . She loved the TT, but thanked God that it would be over in little more than four days time. She pressed the remote and her television burst into life; it was after eleven o' clock and she knew that probably nothing showing would be of interest to her, but the screen was at least an ever changing background in the corner of the room. Her mobile phone lay on the coffee table before her, but she decided not to turn it on. In Miss Templeton's experience, the only people who ever rang at that late hour of the night were amorous would-be suitors from the Isle of Man Constabulary, wrong numbers or her boss: she had no need or desire for any of them. After an hour or so she had seen enough of the television and went to bed, falling almost immediately into a deep sleep.

The doorbell rang, a shrill, piercing and relentless sound. Miss Templeton stirred in her bed. The doorbell rang again. This time she opened her eyes and looked at her bedside clock: six am, a good hour before she normally awoke. Rubbing the sleep from her eyes, she rolled out of her bed, pulled a dressing gown over her nightdress and slowly wandered downstairs. The bell had rung twice more before she opened the door.

"Yes?"

"Miss Templeton?"

"Yes? Oh sorry Richard, it's you. Come in. What can I do for you?" The undertaker looked at the flimsy dressing gown which barely concealed the almost non-existent nightdress beneath and smiled, but said nothing and walked in.

"I'm worried about Jonathon."

"Worried, Richard?" the advocate said. "Why?"

"Did he ring you last night?" the man demanded. Miss Templeton shook her head; her phone had been switched off, but that was her own, private business.

"Rang me at about seven o'clock," Richard said, " I had my phone on silent at the time; always do in the evening. I was taking a little brandy with a small cigar, outside on the terrace as it happens. Anyway I looked at my phone at about six this morning and a number came up on the "missed calls" list. I rang it and found it was Jonathon's hotel. They checked their register and found that it was Jonathon who rang me." Miss Templeton listened to the story patiently; she had heard nothing yet that concerned her. "So I got them to check his room and...get this, he left the place at shortly after seven last night and hasn't returned."

"Well, that could be anything," she reasoned, "he might have met some friends and stayed the night at their place. Why are you so worried?"

"Miss Templeton, you agreed to look after him. You know who we're up against; why did you let him disappear?"

"Listen, Richard," she replied, "you and your friends asked me to keep an eye on him and I have done. I followed him on Sunday right up until he went back to his hotel. I even helped him: have you heard about that?"

The red-faced bald-headed man chuckled. "You mean the roof top rally?"

Louise Templeton glared, then nodded "Well, yes, it was difficult, but after your instructions what else was I supposed to do?"

The undertaker waved his hands. "I don't really care about that: what happened yesterday?"

"Well, I had him followed as you asked; he went to the airport, met his friend, went on to Ramsey, watched the race and then came back over the mountain to Douglas."

"Anything unusual?" The undertaker asked.

"No, not really, but it was foggy, you know, last night. He came back, parked his bike up and went into the hotel."

"Did he go out again last night?" Richard asked.

"I doubt it very much, did you see the fog?" Miss Templeton replied.

"Well he did. I've spoken to the staff and he left the hotel at around seven last night with that friend of his." "Love?"

"That's the one."

"Where did they go?"

"Dunno, but I saw a car go past my house sometime after seven. The fog was unbelievably thick, the visibility was atrocious, but I've got a feeling it was them. If it was, they were on their way north. Laxey or Ramsey?"

"Why should they want to go there, Richard," Miss Templeton asked, "particularly at night in the fog?"

"Like I said, I don't know," the undertaker answered, "but they haven't come back and I think we should do something about it."

"Okay," the advocate replied, "give me half an hour. I'll see you at their hotel."

It was over two hours later by the time they had questioned staff and found out all they could about the movements of Price and Love the previous evening. They learned that the two men had left the place in a blue Ford hire car at or around seven. No-one had seen the direction they had taken, but they had not returned. The scent seemed to have gone cold.

Miss Templeton apologised to Richard, but she had to go. An Advocate had her practice and she could not spare the time to indulge in further investigation, not then anyway. She tried to reassure Richard that the two men would probably resurface later in the day with a simple and innocent explanation for their disappearance, but the undertaker shook his head, unconvinced. He felt that the matter was a little more serious than that and resolved to try and get to the bottom of it himself.

A few miles away, deep underground, Price and Love sat back to back in a cold, damp chamber. They had been tied tightly together and there was absolutely no light, but Price refused to allow those factors deter him from the task that lay ahead. The man who had tied the ropes had fortunately no idea at all about the basic principles of binding captives. He had tied his prisoners far too quickly without giving them the slightest chance to relax. When the bonds had been tightened around Price's arms and legs, the doctor's muscles had been pumped up and swollen; artificially, perhaps, for Price had been tied up like this once long ago and had known enough then about the relevant physiology expand his muscles when being tied and later to relax his muscles and allow the ropes to go slack. He had escaped then and was confident of repeating the achievement.

It took him more than half an hour, but eventually the ropes fell to the ground beside him.

"Come on Roy," he said, jumping to his feet. His friend rose stiffly from the ground. "We need to get out of here."

The older man nodded without speaking. Fortunately the Russians had not bothered to take away their torches or any of the other tools they had brought with them down the mine: they were still lying on the floor of the cave beside them. Price picked up the torches, turned them on and passed one to his friend. Guided by the reassuring beam, Price then began to follow the railway tracks back in the direction from which they had come. Love followed him. They were just about to enter the short tunnel which led from the cavern to the shaft when a far off rumble met their ears. Price stopped.

"Hear that?" he said to his friend. The noise grew louder and louder and then suddenly was upon them. Almost simultaneously, the two men dived to either side and pressed themselves against the wall; they were just in time. They had not started along the short tunnel to the shaft: if they had, then they would have been dead. The harsh, splintering crack of breaking timber, followed a split second later by the deafening thunder of an avalanche announced the arrival of tons of rock and rubble at the bottom of the mineshaft; the rubble spilled into the access tunnel. The ground and the walls shook and both men felt that the roof was going to cave in. From the sounds outside, the short connecting tunnel had already succumbed to such a fate. After a few minutes the rumbling stopped and silence was restored. A thick cloud of dust filled the air; one which the torch beams could barely even begin to penetrate, but as the dust began to settle they began to see the pile of rock and rubble, the shattered timbers and the buckled and twisted roof supports. Their worst fears had been realised; the tunnel had collapsed and in doing so had closed off the cavern from the outside world.

The two men stood for a moment or two in silence, but the silence did not last for long. Somewhere close by they heard the unmistakable sound of water. At first it was a thin and thready trickle, but the trickle increased by the second and soon became a roar: the deep roar of water pouring down a two-hundred foot waterfall into the boulder-filled chasm that lay beside them. Illosovich had blown something above them without even having the decency to wait for them to starve or freeze to death first.

The access tunnel was blocked, or as good as. No man could get through it, but unfortunately water had rather better skills of penetration. Price and Love pulled themselves to their feet. A stream of black water splashed and cascaded over the boulders and rubble which lay at the mouth of the tunnel. It was pouring into the cavern to form a rapidly widening pool and there was no other way out.

Chapter Eighteen

Tuesday Morning (Race Week)

Richard sat in the Blue room beside his favourite motorcycles. It was already late morning on the Tuesday of Race Week and he felt, no knew, that all was not right in the world. For once, his mobile phone was switched on and lay conveniently to hand. The mobile rang, he picked it up and answered.

"Hello....yes, you got my message. It's a blue Ford Mondeo: hire car. Last seen leaving Douglas and heading towards Laxey along the coast road at about seven o'clock last night...yes in that fog....yes I know they're probably idiots, but that's the way it goes...just find them, okay?"

There was usually no racing on the Tuesday of TT week, unless, of course, inclement weather had forced postponement and changes to the programme. It was a day for the mechanics to sweat and swear as they struggled desperately to rebuild blown or misfiring engines in readiness for the morrow, a day for the racers to take it easy and relax and a day for the rest of the Island to head north for Ramsey, the Sprint and the Red Arrows.

The Ramsey Sprint had become an institution. No-one could really recall when it first started or why and few visitors actually bothered to watch it from beginning to end, but nearly everyone who had the slightest interest in the races took the time to turn up and wander around for an hour or three, usually sometime in the mid-afternoon when the famous Red Arrows flying display team made their annual appearance above Ramsey Bay.

The Sprint itself was an amateur drag race for motorbikes; it was held up and down an eighth of a mile of the usually quiet promenade which ran alongside the town's Mooragh Park. The race was a low-key friendly affair, taking part was far more important than winning. Anyone with a bike could have a go. There were no race teams, no professional riders and no prize money. As the bikes roared up and down the short stretch of tarmac, crowds of people ambled between the stalls and sideshows which were dotted around the park. It was a lazy sort of place and a lazy sort of day, for most people, that was. If you were looking for somebody on the Tuesday of race week, chances are that Ramsey would be the place you would choose to start your hunt.

Mikael Boroweski and his comrades arrived in Ramsey shortly after one pm. They had no idea that Price was missing and had come to the town because it was somewhere else to go. They had no plans to enter their low-performance machinery in any kind of race, but the drably-painted Soviet-era bikes stood out from the common herd of modern Japanese machinery and attracted their own crowd of curious spectators when Mikael and the Russians pulled up and dismounted. The utilitarian motorcycle clothing favoured by the former Soviet Army field hospital also seemed to raise a stare.

A tall black man wearing darkened glasses was walking through the park. He was wearing casual clothes, rather than a formal black suit, but something about his manner still made him look a little out of place. Not that anyone really noticed; the crowd was far too busy enjoying the sunshine and the bikes and was now eagerly looking forward to the spectacular aerial display of the Red Arrows.

One other man was making his way through the crowds. Unlike everyone else he was walking rapidly, purposely and searching for something or someone. He was a local man who many other locals recognised. Every now and again one of them would fire off a cheery greeting.

"Afternoon Ernie,"

The man concerned would then wave a friendly reply, but his boss, the undertaker had given him his instructions and he stuck to them. A blue Ford Mondeo of a particular registration number was a rather large needle and the Isle of Man not too big a haystack, but the task would be a difficult one nevertheless.

At three o'clock all eyes looked skywards as, right on time, the Red Arrows roared into view and began their display.

Price and Love had been in the chamber for over thirteen hours. They were cold, tired and hungry. The pool of icy black water covered the floor and was gradually rising. They had made use of the time to complete a detailed examination of the chamber and had found ledges, workings and assorted diggings cutting into the walls at all sorts of angles, some well above the floor. It was in one of these workings, a short blind-ending tunnel, hewn out of solid rock, where they were now resting; it had a low roof, was narrow and uncomfortable, but its floor was dry, for now at least. Love had brought several spare sets of batteries, but it was prudent to rest the torches when not in use all the same. By his calculations the water was still rising at the rate of an inch per hour; not too rapidly, perhaps, but fast enough to fill the entire chamber, drowning them both in a few days, unless, of course, the water stopped rising or they found a way out.

Price had slept for a couple of hours; he woke up, stirred and nudged his friend. "What time do you make it, Roy," he asked.

Love was awake. He looked at his watch. "Three o' clock on Tuesday afternoon. Why?"

"No-one will even have noticed that we're missing yet. We're going to have to get out of this place ourselves… any ideas?"

Love thought for a moment, but then shook his head.

"We've had a pretty good look around this chamber; we might have missed something, but I doubt it. We could look at the tunnel from the shaft again, but I couldn't see any way through, could you?"

"I couldn't," Price replied, "but I'm going to have another look. You wait here and keep your torch on, so I can find my way back."

Price climbed down the rough, slippery slope from the mouth of the tunnel and gingerly lowered his feet into the freezing black water. It went up to his knees and was gnawingly, desperately cold. Gritting his teeth, he pointed the torch beam ahead of him and made his way slowly across the cavern towards the place where the access tunnel had entered from the shaft. The cavern had been pitch, pitch black before, but the thin beam of his torchlight was now reflected and scattered from the pool of dark water, dimly illuminating those parts of the chamber ahead of him whilst allowing the remainder to lurk in menacingly deep and inky shadow. The overall effect was now far more helpful, because it enabled Price to find his way around. Even better, it allowed him to notice the roof. He had never looked at it before, assuming it to be far off, uniform and devoid of possibilities, but under the reflected light from the pool of water below, he spotted nooks, crannies, variations and openings such as he had never seen before. He took note of them, but carried on his way to the tunnel which led from the shaft.

The tunnel was passable, but only for half a dozen yards. Beyond that point it was blocked from floor to roof with a compacted plug of rubble. A powerful jet of water streamed from the only gap he could see: it was above him, a narrow channel between the rubble and what was left of the roof. Price had a feeling that a heavy head of water lay on the other side of that wall of rubble. It was no more than a feeling, but it formed the spark of a new idea.

He waded back towards his friend. He had the guiding light of his friend's torch beam to aim for; his own was directed at the cavern's roof. About half way along his journey he found what he had been looking for. He stopped, shone his torch upwards, then switched the light off and strained his eyes looking deep into the darkness.

It had only been the wildest of hopes; something he could not have dared to suppose he would find, but, unless his eyes were playing tricks on him, that hope had materialised into reality.

155

All he needed was to find a few things he had seen floating around earlier. The plan was a risky one, but at least it was a plan: he would now have to sell it to his friend.

Ernie, the undertaker's assistant had thought that Price might have gone to Ramsey and had looked everywhere in town for the blue car and the doctor. He was a conscientious sort of guy, but he was getting tired of the search and was taking a quiet breather and a cup of tea in the café by the boating lake in the middle of Mooragh Park. An old friend had joined him and Ernie was explaining the arduous task he had been set and would probably have little chance of completing.

"Well, you know what Richard's like," he said. His friend nodded. "He's a right old woman sometimes, and today is a case in point. Rang me up, at the crack of dawn, would you believe it?" His friend sympathised, "and told me that this mate of his, this doctor chap, Price, had disappeared the night before. Well I said to him…"

Coincidences are strange and wonderful things, but on that particular afternoon, a number of other people were sitting in the Mooragh Park tea rooms taking a little break and thinking about the way forward. Their ears pricked up, as one, at Ernie's conversation and you could have heard a pin drop in the silence as they listened to what he had to say.

When Ernie walked out of the tea room he was followed by a number of people and a few yards further along the footpath, one of those people spoke.

"Hey, my friend," he asked the undertaker's assistant, "you are looking for my friend Doktor Jonathon Price?"

Ernie looked at the scary collection of Eastern European bikers who had gathered behind the man and then looked around for an escape: there was none.

"Er, yes, yes," he replied. "He's gone missing, do you know where he is?"

"Missing?" Mikael Boroweski demanded, "how, when and why?"

Ernie began to tell the Russians the story, but they weren't the only ones listening. Someone else, standing in the background heard the details and, a few minutes later, was speaking on his mobile and reporting back to his masters, far, far away.

After Ernie had finished his story, Mikael looked at the undertaker's assistant and then back at his team.

"Interesting," he remarked.

"You got any idea where he is?" Ernie asked.

"Maybe, well I think, yes," Mikael replied.

"Where… can we go there now?' the undertaker's assistant asked.

Mikael Boroweski looked at his men and barked a few orders in Russian. They didn't quite stand to attention, but they gave that general impression. Mikael turned to the undertaker's assistant.

"This is very, very bad. Your boss, he is undertaker?"

"Yes, he is; what do you think I should tell him?"

"You should tell him to make ready for business." On that grim note, Boroweski turned and, followed by his comrades from the former Soviet Army field hospital, strode rapidly back towards their waiting motorcycles. The undertaker's assistant stood there for a moment as if trying to come to a decision then trotted after them.

"You coming with us?" Boroweski asked in tones of some surprise.

"I'll follow in my car," the man replied. Boroweski shook his head

"Not where we are going; if you come, Peter will take you in his sidecar."

Price had patiently explained the plan to his friend; it was risky, he conceded, but slightly less so than doing nothing.

Love was unimpressed. "Dynamite, that's probably been here a hundred years, *sweaty* dynamite; blow the rubble from that tunnel !! Come off it Jonathon, do you really think that's a good idea?"

"Well, have you got any better ones?"

"Yes, we sit here and wait to be rescued. Look, like I told you, we've got days before this place fills with water. Someone will find us before then."

"Do you really think so?" Price asked.

"Yes," his friend replied.

Mikael Boroweski and his comrades had left the mountain road at Windy Corner and were now descending along the same bumpy unmetalled track they had followed two days earlier. They stopped and studied the large scale Ordinance Survey sheet which covered the area lying around and below them. Mikael frowned and pointed to a feature on the map which seemed to confuse him.

"According to this map, there should be small lake over there," he said pointing at the steep-sided valley which lay to their left.

The undertaker's assistant looked at the map and agreed. "It's a dub," he said, "a reservoir; would have been built to keep up a head of water for one of the wheels that drove the mines."

"Then where is it?" the Russian asked.

The undertaker's assistant peered into the valley, following the stream as it cut a narrow cleft through the hillside and disappeared into the woods. Of the dub, lake, reservoir, whatever you wished to call it there was no sign. Ernie shrugged his shoulders. It seemed a point of little, if any importance.

"I dunno, dried up; who cares?"

The Russian shook his head. "It was there two days ago, I am sure of it. Let us continue."

The men remounted and continued down the hill.

Eventually they came to a junction and turned left, moving from open moor into thick woodland before dropping into the steep-sided valley they had looked down upon earlier. It was reasonably familiar territory to the Russians, although not to the undertaker's assistant. Born and bred on the Island, he had lived there all his life, but had never been this way before.

Suddenly the procession came to a halt. They had stopped by the ford, but it had changed markedly from the shallow trickle they had crossed two days earlier. The banks were deeply scoured, and bereft of vegetation. Trees had been uprooted and lay at crazy angles across the valley. The trickle of crystal clear water was now a churning foam-flecked torrent; not inches, but several feet deep. From the signs around them it had been far deeper and more powerful some time earlier and was now easing, but it was still too strong and deep to cross. The Russians got off their bikes. Something had happened to the water. Instinctively, Mikael felt it was important to find out what and set off up the valley. In the meantime he set the rest of his men the task of crossing the stream. He was gone some fifteen, twenty minutes, but by his return the men had built a rough bridge from fallen trees. It was not strong enough for the bikes, but it could be crossed on foot, with care.

Boroweski explained the cause of the sudden flood. "The reservoir up there," he pointed upstream, "has gone; there is big hole in dam. Looks like explosives, sabotage. Must have been millions of litres go through here. Reservoir is nearly empty now."

"Why would anyone want to do that?" the undertaker's assistant asked.

"Only one possible reason," Boroweski answered, "someone wanted to flood something, perhaps a mine. Come, let us cross the stream and see what we can find."

Price, unfortunately, found himself unable to share his friend's optimism. They had told no-one where they were going and so, apart from Vladivir Illosovich and his henchmen, no-one would have the slightest idea that they were at the bottom of a mineshaft somewhere in the hills above Laxey. Someone might find the car, but if

Illosovich had any sense that would now be far away. The thick fog would have ensured that no-one saw them arrive and unless they did something about the situation themselves, it was nigh on certain that no-one would see them leave, ever. Price therefore took it upon himself to act.

Price had managed to find the box labelled 'Explosives' and gingerly removed a stick of dynamite. He knew that the explosive was a mixture of nitroglycerin and an inert substance such as china clay and that it could decompose or 'sweat', exuding the very sensitive and highly explosive active ingredient. Whether this had happened, he was unable to tell, but he was taking no chances. In another box, he found what appeared to be detonators and fuses. He had no idea whether any of this stuff still worked, but he felt it was a risk worth taking and slowly waded back across the cavern to the mouth of the access tunnel. Taking great care not to dislodge any rock and cause a further roof fall or drop the dynamite or detonator, he fashioned a narrow hole in the middle of the plug of rubble and slid the explosive into place. He pulled the fuse to one side, keeping it out of the stream of water. He kept a cigarette lighter in his pocket for emergencies, this was certainly one of them. The gas hissed for a second and then burst into a steady flame. Trembling, Price held the flame to the end of the fuse. For a second, nothing happened, then with a spark and fizzle, the fuse began to burn. Price had no idea how long it would burn for and had no plans to hang around and find out. Breathing heavily and with his heart pounding he waded quickly across the flooded floor of the chamber to the relative (he hoped) safety of the blind ending tunnel where his friend was sleeping. It was time to wake up Love and break the news.

Mikael, his comrades and the undertaker's assistant had crossed the makeshift bridge and made their way down the track which led from the road. Well before they arrived in the clearing, they came across more signs of flooding. Flotsam and jetsam were strewn across the path. As they approached the derelict outbuildings, the damage was worse.

One of the men shouted for Boroweski and waved him over to the side of the stream. An abandoned mechanical digger was lying on its side in the water. The man spoke rapidly in Russian and pointed out what the machine had obviously been used to do. A barrier, of sorts, had been placed across the stream and a trench dug leading directly to the building which had stood at the head of the mine. Even though the waters were now receding, a slimy pool of dirty brown liquid still surrounded the small collection of ruined buildings. Boroweski nodded. It was as he had thought, the stream had been diverted and water used to flood the mine. Maybe it had been done just to destroy the evidence, but if Price and his friend had gone down there it was unlikely that they would have got out with their lives.

The cluster of buildings stood in a saucer-shaped depression in the ground. When Boroweski and his men had first seen the site a couple of days before this aspect of the local geography had not been apparent, but water has a particular way of highlighting things. Here it had turned the depression into a lake centred on the building which stood above the mineshaft. The lake was no more than an inch or two deep at its periphery, but rose to the tops of the doorways of the ruined buildings in its centre. Boroweski stood there for a moment, trying to decide what to do; a few seconds later he called to one of his companions and spoke to the man rapidly in Russian. After issuing his instructions, he turned to the undertaker's assistant.

"I have asked my comrades to make a search of the area, but I have little hope that they will find Docktor Price or his friend. I fear that they were at the bottom of the mine and that now they are drowned. I am sorry, but...."

At that moment, a sudden, dull thump shook the ground and interrupted Boroweski's sombre little speech. The Russian frowned and looked up. Two or three of the men were shouting in their native tongue and pointing towards the woods which stood above the water on one side of the clearing. Boroweski barked a terse thread of words at the Manxman who was standing beside him.

"Look, over there; smoke: an explosion. Come."

The dynamite ignited, firing a white sheet of flame back into the cavern which lit up for a moment as if subject to the full blown light of day. Half a second later the shock wave hit the two men and they heard and felt the deafening roar of the blast. They held their breath waiting for the roar to end, but it did not. The explosion had punched a large hole through the plug of rubble and now a torrent of water was pouring through the hole, widening and enlarging it with every passing second. The water level within the cavern was rising rapidly; it had gone up a foot in under a minute.

"Come *on*, Roy," Price shouted, trying to make himself heard above the background noise, "time to go. Follow me and try to keep your torch in the air."

The men slid down from their resting place and into the water which was now waist high. The flow was against them and was strong, but Price had secured a rope to a bracket on the other side of the chamber before he blew the charge. It was a wise precaution, for the current frequently swept their feet from under them and only the rope kept them from being carried away.

They had not gone far before both torches were soaked; a few minutes later one bulb flickered, its white light faded to a dull red spark and then was gone. Love fought desperately to keep the other beam alive, but it was a battle he could not win. The bulb faded and died leaving them in total darkness. The water was freezing cold and now up to their chests. The men carried on, part walking, part swimming until they reached the knot Price had placed in the rope.

"Thi…thi…this is the place," Price stuttered, his teeth chattering with the intense cold. "L…l….look up at the roof."

The roof of the cavern was, perhaps twelve feet from the ground, the place was in pitch darkness, but there was the faintest glimmer of something, far, far above them. They waited and as their eyes grew accustomed to the darkness they gradually began to make out the outlines of what looked like the bottom of a shaft. It was about four feet wide. Price had his own theory as to what it was.

"V…v…ventilation shaft," he tried to explain, but the intense cold made it painful even to speak.

They were soon off their feet and treading water as the cavern filled rapidly to its roof. Price tried not to think how long it would be before they died of hypothermia, but minutes later their heads were in the bottom of the shaft, then their shoulders, then suddenly they shot upwards like bullets firing along the barrel of a gun. The cavern was full of water and the torrent pouring into the place forced an equal volume of water into the vertical shaft. It was a narrow shaft and, by an argument of pure hydraulics was now filling rapidly, extremely rapidly, something the two men discovered to their cost as they shot upwards, bumping and banging themselves against the rough and uneven sides on the way.

The glimmer of light in the distance above them grew steadily larger. It marked the outside world, of that there could be no doubt, but something about it still left nagging doubts and worries in Price's mind. If it was simply the outside, then surely it would be even larger, much brighter and would have cast more light into the mine. As it grew nearer, he realised that the top of the shaft had been sealed by some sort of cap. Whatever it was, he prayed that they would be able to break through it.

The group of Russian motorcyclists looked on in open-mouthed surprise as the shores of the lake began to recede. A current seemed to be flowing towards its centre, then there was a low rumble and the building which stood at the top of the central mineshaft collapsed and was no more. In its place a whirlpool of water circled and spiralled downwards into the ground, carrying with it fallen branches, tree trunks, timbers and the assorted flotsam and jetsam which had lazily floated on the surface only a few minutes before. The level of the lake was definitely falling. Mikael Boroweski shook his head and tried to work out what, exactly, was happening. The water was pouring away, like bath water down a plug-hole, but where and why, he could not guess.

Boroweski stared at the diminishing pool for several minutes until shouts from his companions pulled his attention away. The shouts were in Russian, but they were earnestly given; something just as dramatic was happening on the periphery of the clearing.

Followed by the undertaker's assistant, Boroweski rushed along the edge of the ever-decreasing pool of water and up through the forest to the source of the shouts. A number of his comrades stood expectantly around a low stone wall which formed a perfect circle and rose three feet from the ground. It looked like a small chimney and was capped by a lid of warped timbers. Clouds of acrid smoke drifted from gaping holes between the woodwork and drifted slowly away in the breeze.

Boroweski sniffed the air like a connoisseur.

"Nitroglycerin," was his judgement; the men around him nodded.

He bent his ear to the timbers; the sounds below were a strange mixture, and not only the sound of water rising. He barked instructions to his comrades. The undertaker's assistant could not understand, but their meaning was clear enough.

"Take off the cap."

It was an easy enough instruction, but despite their age the timbers were solid and rot had not taken hold. The ancient lid seemed bound to the stone parapet by rusted and corroded bolts and fastenings, secured and made certain by the long passage of time. The men struggled valiantly, but to no avail.

Beneath them the sound of rising and rushing water forced a rapid decision, and yet again Mikael Boroweski shouted a command; one of the men put something on top of the parapet and they all dived to the ground. A second later, a sudden low thump cut through the air and the wooden cap was gone, replaced in a moment by empty, sweet, thin air. The Russians peered over the edge of the low wall.

Richard, the undertaker, listened carefully to what his assistant had to report. He was grateful, of course, for the update, but found the story hard, if not impossible to believe.

"Just get them back to my house, he said, we can talk about the details later."

An hour or so later, noisy Russian bikes began to arrive; he was glad that for years now he had been shunned by his neighbours.

Price and Love staggered into the house swathed in blankets, with Boroweski and his companions following closely. The time had come for a conference of war. Half an hour later, the Englishman and Welshman appeared in fresh dry clothes; outside the powerful note of a large capacity motorcycle throbbed, burbled and was still. The doorbell rang, was answered and a few seconds later the black, leather clad figure of Louise Templeton strode into the room. The clock struck midnight and Tuesday moved into Wednesday.

Two miles away in a certain hotel in Douglas, Vladivir Illosovich was berating his men. His words were in Russian and the English translation loses something of the anger and the venom of the man.

"Stupid, stupid, stupid," he hissed and spat, "You are all brainless and stupid, I cannot conceive why I allow you to live, far less employ you all. We have had for two years a good safe place to store our merchandise. Now it is gone. Why? Because you have been careless enough to let this man Price find out our secret. Yes, he and his friend are dead now, but this problem should never have arisen. This problem started months ago. You chose the wrong rider; then, when you found out he was unsuitable, what did you do? Stupid and dangerous. There were other ways you could have dealt with this problem, which would not have drawn attention to Petromax or our business. It is a good job that I arrived here on Sunday to take charge of this operation myself. If I had not, who knows what might have happened? We have three more days before we leave this Island. We have destroyed Price and all traces of our activity. We have our merchandise; we must leave with it, so," he finished menacingly, "there will be no more mistakes.......".

☆   ☆   ☆   ☆   ☆   ☆

The Blue room in the undertaker's rambling old house was full and the sweet aroma of hand-rolled Russian tobacco filled the air. Richard stood up and began to speak, but he soon realised that he should bide his time and sat down, leaving the talking to the people who were really in charge in the present circumstances.

Price had now recovered from his spell of enforced immersion in the freezing cold water. Perhaps not surprisingly, he felt that they should inform the authorities, have Illosovich and his men arrested and all the Petromax assets seized and searched, *now*. He looked around for support, but only the undertaker cast his vote that way. Against them were Love, Boroweski, his companions and, somewhat surprisingly, Miss Templeton. Why?

"No, no, no, Jonathon," she argued, "we have absolutely nothing against Illosovich; nothing that the police would even consider."

"What about the mineshaft," Price asked, "what about what happened to Roy and me today?"

"Where's your evidence," the advocate replied. "He'll just deny everything and have half a dozen witnesses to say he was in Douglas all day. Whatever you two found at the bottom of that mineshaft, it's gone, it's history. Illosovich is a powerful guy and he wields a hell of a lot of influence. You'll need a lot more than that to take him down."

"But those engine parts?" Price asked, "they must have something to do with it."

Boroweski cut in:

"Do you have any idea what those engine parts are or mean?"

"No," the doctor conceded.

"So, then I think that Miss Templeton is right," Boroweski replied, "we keep our thoughts to ourselves. We keep, as you English say, our powder dry. We wait, we listen and we learn. If we do that, then sometime soon we will find the evidence to hang this Illosovich and all of his men."

"Okay," Price said, "then what do we do?"

"You, I think, Jonathon, do nothing," Love answered. "Illosovich thinks you are dead; best let him continue in that happy frame of mind. You need to stay out of sight. He'll think that the person who was with you is dead too, but he doesn't know who I am. He's only seen me the once, remember, and that was by torchlight at the bottom of the mine. I think I'll be able to move around fairly safely, but neither of us had better go to back to the hotel; it may be watched. If we could perhaps find somewhere else to stay...." he looked at the undertaker.

The man nodded. "I've got room enough for you both here."

"Excellent, thanks," Love continued, "its quiet and out of the way of prying eyes. When will your forensic results be available, Jonathon?"

"Sometime today, if we're lucky, tomorrow at the latest," Price replied.

"Then I suggest you lie low and wait for those. In the meantime, we need to find out where Illosovich is staying. I can't really see him camping out in a transporter up at the grandstand, so he's probably in a hotel, somewhere. Mikael, can you look into that and when you find him, keep him under surveillance?"

"I think I might be able to help you there," Price said, before Boroweski had time to answer. The others looked at him and he told them briefly about the rundown hotel and frightened receptionist he had discovered on Sunday night.

Love frowned. "Doesn't really sound like the sort of establishment Illosovich would patronize – we've all heard that he likes his luxuries. Still, I suppose it could be worth looking into. Mikael, can you check it out?"

The Russian nodded.

Love then turned to the advocate. "Miss Templeton, you're our official eyes and ears on this Island. I'd like you to find out everything you can about Petromax and Illosovich. We need to know what it is they're doing here. It must be a little deeper than just trying to win a motorbike race, even if it is the TT. Do they own property, do they have money salted away on the Island? Can you do that?"

"I'll use unofficial channels," the advocate replied, "they're quicker and involve far less paperwork."

"Good," the retired policeman said, "then, as it's getting late and we all have plenty to do in the morning, I suggest we all turn in and get some sleep. Wednesday could be another very long day."

"What about you, Roy?" Price asked, "What are your plans for tomorrow?"

Roy Love smiled. "I have a client, remember?" he answered, "one who brought Mr Illosovich and his company to my notice long before you contacted me. My client is now on the Island and tomorrow I plan to meet him and find out what he has to say."

Chapter Nineteen

Wednesday Morning (Race Week)

The Wednesday of race week turned out to be another day of unrelenting sunshine. The handful of clouds which had floated overhead at dawn hung around for an hour or two and then evaporated. The Island braced itself for another day of blue skies and soaring temperatures.

Price was confined to barracks, well at least the rather luxurious barracks of the undertaker's house in Onchan, but he had full access to everything he could possibly require, including phone, fax, internet and e-mail. He had woken up shortly before eight. Love had still been in the house for an hour or so after then, but had been busy: on the computer, making and receiving 'phone calls. Finally, just before ten o' clock, without telling Price where he was going, he abruptly left. The undertaker had made his way out of the house about half-an-hour earlier, so by ten in the morning Price was alone.

First he decided to call the forensic pathologist he had sent samples to a few days earlier. The call took no more than a few seconds, but unfortunately the Professor was out. His secretary took the call, but advised that her boss was giving evidence in a Court some miles away and might be away for the whole day. Price left the undertaker's phone and fax number. There was nothing more he could do, so, after wandering admiringly around the Blue room for a while, he found a radio, turned it on and sat down to listen to the commentary of the day's bike racing.

The radio itself was a beautiful piece, worthy of any collector or museum, nineteen fifties decorated in thirties art déco style. The undertaker would, of course, have described it as a wireless, but its booming crackling sound fitted into place perfectly among the silent Nortons and Velocettes which stood respectfully to attention around the room. Price reclined in the chaise longue, half closed his eyes and began to listen to the commentary of the race. As usual, the commentary was good and within minutes the doctor found himself transported to the Grandstand, Glen Helen, Ramsey Hairpin and all points in between.

Meanwhile, Roy Love was sitting in a coffee shop close to the old harbour. It was now late morning, he was still alone and the shop was empty apart from the pleasant lady behind the counter who had served him. He looked at the door and then at his watch; the faintest cloud of anxiety seemed to pass over his face, but then the door opened and a tall dark stranger walked in. The man walked over to the counter and ordered a latte; as he was waiting for the drink to be poured he looked around the room, his eyes meeting those of the retired policeman. Shortly afterwards, latte in hand, he walked across the room.

"Mr Love?" he enquired.

Love nodded.

"Mind if I join you?"

The accent was an American one, eastern seaboard, Love thought.

"Be my guest," Love replied, "I take it that you are Mr Smith?" It was an alias, of course, Love knew that and the man probably knew that he knew it, but he smiled and nodded.

"Sure am."

"Let's talk."

A quarter of a mile away in Athol Street, Miss Templeton, the advocate, was also engaged in conversation, although in her case it was over the telephone. She had been on the 'phone nearly all morning, but her enquiries had been productive and she had learned a great deal about Petromax , its various subsidiaries and their activities on the Island. Some of those activities made little, if any, sense to her, but she continued to collect and log the information. Maybe when it was all put together everything would seem clearer.

She had discovered that Petromax had been buying property on the Island for several years. That their portfolio included commercial and residential property, she found unsurprising: many others had found the Island's property boom of the latter years of the twentieth and first few years of the twenty-first century a convenient and highly profitably offshore investment. She discovered, however, that the company had also been buying up plots of land in open countryside in various parts of the Island. It did not appear to have made any planning applications, but from what the advocate could see and what she knew about the local planning and development policy, the plots of land Petromax had bought would never have been granted planning permission for anything anyway and the purchases made no commercial sense. Petromax had been paying inflated prices for plots of land: prices which normally only urban sites with planning approval would attract. It looked as if the company had been so eager to acquire the land that it had paid the first asking price, no matter how ridiculous. Curiously all of the portions of land had one thing in common: they contained derelict old mine workings, but what Petromax intended to do with them, goodness knows. The advocate made a note of the plots and marked them on a map of the Island.

Vladimir Illosovich, the mysterious owner of Petromax personally owned a large house in the north of the Island and, from what she had been able to prise out of her confidential sources, was the beneficiary of a number of private trusts administered from the Isle of Man. The trusts were worth billions of dollars. Miss Templeton had discovered that the eighty foot motor vessel currently moored in Douglas Bay belonged to Illosovich. It was an impressive piece of kit: a typical billionaire's bauble, more at home in Monaco or any other Mediterranean port than the cold and breezy Irish Sea, but like a number of other vessels which Illosovich owned, it too was registered in the Isle of Man. It had arrived at the beginning of Practice week; no-one knew from where it had come or when it would depart and no-one knew whether the reclusive Russian was on board or not. He had certainly not been seen.

The more she looked into the matter, the more places it would seem that Illosovich could be staying. She thought herself that the house north of Ramsey would be the best bet. Out in the countryside and far enough away from neighbours and prying eyes for the man to come and go as he pleased. The ship would be too public; Illosovich would go there, no doubt, when he wanted to be seen, but he would not want to stay there, not if he was up to no good anyway. As for the hotel Price had suggested, well she agreed with Love. The place was a non-runner and not therefore worth looking into.

She continued her conversation with Mikael Boroweski. "The house or the boat, Mikael, that's where you need to look. And, another thing, there are more mines, yes, mines like the one where you found Jonathon and Roy. I don't know why they have mines, but maybe you should check them out. Do you have an Ordinance Survey Map? You do…good, then these are the coordinates…"

A few minutes later the conversation came to a close. The advocate put down the receiver and got back to her real work.

Mikael Boroweski and his small band of comrades rode north along the coast road. It was busy, for the Mountain Road was closed for racing and the routine traffic had no option but to use the only alternative route between Ramsey and Douglas. They passed through the village of Laxey and admired the great wheel from afar. It had no involvement in their business so they did not take the time or trouble to stop and inspect it more closely. Continuing along the road, they negotiated the everlasting bends, rode through a number of tiny, but quaint villages and then dropped down the steep hill and crossed the tramlines to enter the sunny northern town of Ramsey.

The centre of the town was busy, of course, for the motorcycle race went right through it, but the Russians followed the promenade past the swimming pool, turned left and then made their way along the quayside before reaching the road to the north. To the north of Ramsey lay a broad plain. It was countryside unlike that seen in the rest of the Island: broad fields of steadily ripening grain, lush green water meadows, narrow unspoilt lanes and hedgerows that any fervent naturalist would die for. Houses sat in glorious seclusion well back from the road and were massive and beautiful. The Russians were suitably impressed. The problem would be identifying the one owned by Illosovich. Eventually Boroweski brought his machine to a halt beside the gates of a large country house and the riders behind him stopped. A little old man was pottering around in the garden; when he heard the noise of the old-fashioned bikes he stopped what he was doing and walked over. He could see that Boroweski had already unfolded a large map and was studying it carefully.

"Hello," he said cheerfully, "are you lost?"

Boroweski looked up, the old man appeared friendly enough; maybe he could help them.

The Russian got off his bike and passed the map to the man.

"We are trying to find a house near here which is owned by one of our countrymen; Vladimir Illosovich: you have maybe heard of him?"

"I know who he is, all right," the old man said, "lives over there," he pointed to a house some distance behind him. "Got a helicopter, noisy thing it is too. Not a very sociable sort of chap, well, that is, I've never met him, but his people go to and fro every day. Is he a particular friend of yours?"

"Well, not exactly," Boroweski replied. He began to tell the little man a little bit about his mission; not too much, of course, but enough to persuade the man that he might want to help them.

The old man listened to what the Russian had to say; he thought for a moment or two, then he made his decision:

"Never really had good feelings about that man. I don't think he's been there for months, but you let me have your number, young man and I'll ring you if I ever see him turn up."

Numbers were exchanged, hands were shaken and the former Soviet Army Field Hospital took to the road once again. As Boroweski rode back towards the south of the Island, he frowned. He knew the old man's face from somewhere, but he couldn't for the life of him remember where.

They had checked out the house - now it was time to look at those other mines which Petromax appeared to own. The first of them was at a map reference near Laxey and quite close to the mine, now flooded, where they had found Price and Love. They followed a succession of winding single track lanes back into the hills above Laxey village, but the plot of land they discovered was deserted. There were no tyre tracks to suggest vehicles or recent visitors and the rusted and decaying mine buildings were overgrown with nettles and long abandoned. If Petromax intended to do anything with this site, then it was obvious that work had not yet begun. Boroweski and his men spent half-an-hour or so looking around, but found nothing and decided to move on. They had other mines to visit; they had to find a way to take a look at the billionaire's luxury yacht and the afternoon was already moving on.

Jonathon Price had dozed off into a lazy slumber. The motorcycle races had finished and the commentary had ended. Andre Rorletski, on this occasion, had retired at the pits after a single lap with engine trouble, leaving the way for the pre-race favourite, a previous multiple TT winner from Ireland to take the chequered flag a full minute ahead of his nearest challenger. Suddenly, the fax machine in the corner of the room began to bleep. Price, long conditioned to life in a hospital on-call room with only a radio-pager for company, awoke instantly. A few seconds later he was standing by the machine, eagerly reading each page even before it had been spat out of the printer.

At seven that evening the undertaker returned. He looked tired and despite a courteous greeting, was in no mood to speak at length to Price.

"We'll talk when the others arrive," he said and retired to one of his rooms.

An hour later the doorbell rang and Price went to the door to answer it. Louise Templeton had arrived and behind her Mikael Boroweski and the combined forces of his former Soviet Army Field Hospital. They all nodded silently and made their way through the hall into the undertaker's Blue Room. Price had just offered Louise a seat, taking another beside her, and, in the continued absence of his host, was wondering whether to begin exchanging the usual conversational social pleasantries when the doorbell rang yet again.

"Can someone else please answer that?" he asked and one of the Russians got up to provide the required service.

The door opened and Roy Love walked into the room followed by a tall black man in a dark suit. Jonathon Price recognised the stranger and jumped to his feet immediately.

"Who the hell *are you*?" he demanded.

"Calm down, Jonathon," Love said, "this is Mr Smith from the famous Pinkerton Detective Agency and I think he has something rather important to tell us."

Mr Smith walked into the room, casting a glance at all of those around him. He took a seat in one of the few remaining empty chairs and quietly lit a cigarette.

The Blue Room in the undertaker's house was a large one, but it was full and the atmosphere within it was now electric. Mikael Boroweski was accompanied by half a dozen of his men; they sat silently around the periphery of the room, but their faces all bore the same question. That question was repeated on the faces of Jonathon Price and Louise Templeton. They had seen this man before, but who was he and, more importantly, what was he going to say?

"Well guys," he began, "I think I recognise quite a few of you, but you don't know me, so I'd probably better introduce myself. I'm Mike Smith, out of the London office of Pinkertons. Some of you might have heard of us, probably most of you haven't. We specialise in investigation, and we're independent. 'No job too small and no job too big'. This is a *big* one. We were instructed by a number of families who lost loved-ones on 9/11 and we've been on the case ever since. You remember 9/11? Silly question, of course you do! Well, everyone thinks it was all down to Bin Laden and maybe they're right, but we don't take anything for granted. We investigate and, being non-political, we don't take easy options. Someone had to put the money up; there are a few people in the world who make plenty of money out of perpetual warfare and they're the ones we need to find. Suicide bombers, extremists, fanatics. They are the enemy, hard to find, impossible to stop, but they can't do anything without funds. Solution: trace the source of the funds and trace where the money gets spent. You guys all with me so far?" He looked around the room and a number of his audience slowly nodded.

"Anyway," he continued, "we've been working pretty hard for the last few years. Good ol' US of A Government was more keen on invading Afghanistan and Iraq, but our intelligence didn't lead us there. We didn't think that Saddam gave a damn about Al-Qaeda, Jihad or any of that stuff, so we didn't really spend too much time on him. We went for the money: where it came in from and where it went. Found a few players, but one was particularly worrying: massive wealth; extreme power and, by all accounts, extremely dubious morals. Any guesses?"

"Illosovich." Mikael Boroweski answered.

"Correct," Smith replied. "He bankrolled Bin Laden and paid for 9/11, but that was only the beginning. His people fed information to the CIA, and the Brits; he led them into Iraq and he's bankrolling the insurgents now."

"But why?" Price asked.

"Destabilisation," the black American answered. "You all know that Illosovich is pretty rich, but you don't know how rich: he owns most of Russia's oil and he has options on just about all of the rest. If he gets what he wants, then the price of oil can only go up. He can't possibly lose."

"What do you think.... this guy actually wants?" Price asked slowly.

"Not a lot," Smith replied, smiling, "maybe just perpetual Jihad in the Middle East and total panic in the rest of the world. That would push up the price of oil, wouldn't it?"

"So that's what it's all about," Price said, "the price of oil?"

Smith grinned and shook his head. "No, I'm afraid that's only the beginning."

"What do you mean?" Another voice spoke; this time it was Miss Templeton's turn to ask a question.

"Illosovich has more than enough money," Smith replied, "what he wants now is power: total, global, power."

Mikael Boroweski cleared his throat. "We Russians know this, Mr Smith, but tell me what this has to do with Isle of Man and TT Races?"

The black American cast Boroweski a curious glance, in itself little more than the briefest flicker of an eye which no-one, except Price, noticed, before continuing:

"Illosovich owns Petromax, a massive international company. Petromax owns a lot more than just the Russian state oil reserves, but, of course, you know that?"

Boroweski nodded, but said nothing.

Smith continued: "when Petromax took over the oil reserves, it agreed to take over responsibility for running the Russian nuclear power industry. As you're all probably aware, that particular industry hasn't been doing too well since Chernobyl so Illosovich offered to decommission it, for free! The offer was, needless to say, extremely well received in the Kremlin, so *bang* Illosovich gets a few power stations and with them a few hundred pounds of plutonium, free, gratis and for nothing. Not much demand for plutonium in the world, is there nowadays? But it's hard stuff to move around; you can't really just shove it in your suitcase and hawk it around the globe, can you? So what does Illosovich do?"

Miss Templeton glanced at their host Richard, the undertaker, who had quietly entered the room when Love and Smith had arrived; he made eye contact, but then looked away.

Mike Smith continued, surer now of the attention of his listeners :

"He goes motor racing: Formula One cars, Grand Prix bikes, World Superbikes, the lot. Expensive, yes, but he gets to travel the world, no questions asked and, more importantly, he gets to take lots of machined parts with him. It's a big thing now in the developing world, motorsport, particularly now that cigarette advertising is banned everywhere else. An expensive hobby, oh yes, but you get the chance to travel the world and take all sorts of expensive toys with you and when your team flies into an airport somewhere, how carefully do you think the local customs check those toys?"

"Are you seriously suggesting..." Price began.

"Yes," the American answered. "What did you find at the bottom of that mine?"

"Well, bike or car engine parts," Price replied, "they looked like a camshaft and..."

"Did you handle them?" the American asked. Price shook his head.

"I picked them up, but I didn't take them out of the plastic bags they were in," he said.

"Good," Smith replied, "if you had done you probably would have picked up a lethal dose of radiation, but I take it you found them heavy, heavier than lead."

"But, how...how...?" Price began.

"Plutonium's a metal," Smith answered, "not a natural metal, it's produced in nuclear reactors and it's heavy, with a density of about 20 tonnes per cubic metre, but it's a metal so it can be machined into any shape you want. They have to machine it to make the hollow sphere they implode in the fission bomb. So long as they don't make the bulk of metal too much, they won't have a problem. The critical mass of a basic sphere of plutonium is only 16 kg. Any of those bits of metal you saw at the bottom of the mine bigger than say, that big?" he held out his hands demonstrating a shape about as big as a large grapefruit.

"No," Price said, "there weren't, but I still don't understand. If this guy is moving pieces of plutonium around the planet, why put them at the bottom of a mine in the Isle of Man?"

"Good question," the black man replied, "answer: its about the last place anyone would ever look; its safe and its convenient. Illosovich moves the stuff around in his bike transporters and stores it here, probably alloyed with gallium and suitably machined, as a motorcycle part. The Island is the Road Racing Capital of the World, for Gods sake; plenty of top riders live here so why shouldn't he base his team here. When he gets an order for the plutonium, he fits a very special part into one of his motorcycles and has it shipped across the world.

"But why," Price persisted, "I mean he's got all that money; why should he want more?"

"For some people there can never be enough," Smith answered, "but with Illosovich, I think it's more than that. He wants to destabilise the world, create a climate of mayhem and fear and then, he thinks, he will have total power."

"Why have you been following me?" Price asked, changing the tack of the conversation. The American smiled.

"I didn't know what your angle was, Dr Price, not until Mr Love here filled me in this morning. I have been following the Petromax motorcycle racing team's tracks for the best part of a year; that's what brought me here. I heard that you had been up there on the mountain when their rider crashed, then I saw you by the Petromax transporter in the paddock, then I saw you talking to their other rider when he crashed by the wildlife park. I started to think that you might be involved when I saw you with these characters", - he indicated Boroweski and his men with a brush of his hand, -" up by that mine I was sure that you were involved and on the wrong side, so when you chased after me on Sunday afternoon, I decided not to hang around".

"Talking about their riders, Jonathon," Love interjected, "have you heard anything from your expert?" Price nodded.

"Fax came in late this afternoon; want to see it?"

"Yes, Jonathon, we might as well, but if I know anything about experts it'll be full of technical stuff. First and foremost, does it take us anywhere?"

Price nodded slowly; his face wore just the slightest trace of a smile. "Oh yes it certainly does," he replied.

"Please tell us more then," Love asked and Price began to speak.

"Seeing as we didn't have the facilities for any sort of post mortem and time, in any event, was rather limited, I was pretty restricted in the range of specimens I was able to take, but I got a sample of blood, some skin and some hair. I took these a few days after Taylor died, don't forget, so there were the inevitable changes that always occur after death. The report is pretty clear, though: pattern of cellular damage in all the tissues submitted for examination highly suggestive of prolonged exposure to ionising radiation."

Love nodded. "So that's what he died of then," he said.

Much to everyone's surprise Price shook his head. "No, he didn't. He may well have been dying of radiation exposure, but something much more simple actually killed him. The report states that the blood level of opiates was way into the toxic zone. He wouldn't have been able to breathe, far less ride his bike with such a level on board, but that explains why he lost control. He would have simply fallen asleep and ridden off the road. It also explains why he wasn't breathing and why he had he had pin-point pupils when we found him."

"So how could he possibly....?" Love voiced the question everyone was thinking.

"Only one possible explanation," Price replied. "Taylor's sitting on his motorbike at the start line waiting for the off; someone comes along, claps their hand on his shoulder to wish him well, but they're holding a syringe of diamorphine, the pure pharmaceutical grade stuff, in their hand. The needle goes straight through Taylor's leathers and into his deltoid muscle. You could dissolve enough diamorphine to do the trick in under a millilitre of water and Taylor would be so pumped up with adrenaline waiting for the off that he probably wouldn't even notice. An intramuscular injection takes a bit of time to get into the bloodstream. So, he would have been fine as far as Ramsey, but then the drug would have started to take effect. I'm sure we'll be able to find witnesses who'll tell us that his riding deteriorated as he climbed up the mountain. Deteriorated up to the point where he lost consciousness and came off right in front of me."

"Incredible," Love said, "so you're sure that was what killed him?"

"No," Price said, "the diamorphine made him crash, but it didn't kill him. It can make you go to sleep and it can make you stop breathing, but, if you remember, we'd taken over the breathing for him well before he got to the helicopter. He would have survived, but unfortunately when the people who wanted him out of the way discovered that he was still alive, they somehow managed to get a large dose of potassium into his intravenous drip at the hospital and that's what caused him to have a fatal cardiac arrest."

175

"So someone did get to him at the hospital?" Love asked.

"Looks that way," Price replied. "Poor bloke didn't stand a chance…"

Mikael Boroweski stood up and looked straight at Jonathon Price.

"So, Doktor Price, we have heard so much; you are a clever man. What, in your opinion, should we do now?"

Price looked Boroweski square in the face and then allowed his eyes to move around the room. Every pair of eyes seemed to be asking the same question. Why he should have been singled out, he did not know. There were decisions to make, but neither the Pinkerton detective, the advocate, nor even his old friend Roy Love jumped up to come to his aid. The room was silent as he considered the question for a long few minutes. At last he spoke:

"Miss Templeton, when is the Inquest on Taylor?"

"Tomorrow morning at ten o' clock," she replied.

"Can you act?" he asked.

"Difficult," she said, "I don't see who I could possibly be representing. I can't just stand up and start speaking; the Coroner would tell me to sit down. Can't we just pass your medical evidence to the police and leave it to them?"

"But I was the doctor on the scene; I was a witness. Can't I give evidence?" Price demanded.

"Have you given a statement? Have you been summonsed?" she asked.

"No," he replied.

"Then you can't," she replied, "not unless…has anyone been in contact with Taylor's family?…I mean they have the right…they could instruct me."

Someone, a balding man with a red face, who until now had taken no part in the conversation, now cleared his throat.

"I…er…have been asked to make the necessary arrangements and I am…er… in contact with the family of the late Mr Taylor," the undertaker confirmed.

Louise Templeton shot a glance at the man; it conveyed pure, genuine surprise.

"Why didn't you tell us, Richard?"

"Well, nobody asked me…nobody tells me anything…"

"Never mind; can you get in touch with them now?"

A telephone call was made; the undertaker displayed all his considerable skills of tact, empathy and understanding, and conveyed to the family the news that the inquest was to be held the following morning and that he had found them a lawyer, a Manx Advocate, who was highly respected and who would represent them at the hearing free of charge. Price got on the 'phone to his pathologist. The Professor was not particularly happy about the short notice, but when he heard a little more of the detail he agreed to come. He would catch the first flight in from Manchester in the morning and arrangements would be made to pick him up from Ronaldsway Airport at eight o' clock. Pinkertons would, of course, pick up the bill.

After arrangements for the inquest had been made, Miss Templeton told them all she had discovered about Petromax and Illosovich. She briefed them about the house in the north, the deserted mine workings and the luxury yacht.

Mikael Boroweski listened to what the advocate had to say, then shook his head. "We visited all of these places," he said, "apart from one, this place near Foxdale. We did not have time to go there; we will try tomorrow, but all the other places, they are empty, deserted, abandoned. We hired small boat and went out into bay to see Illosovich vessel: very large; very impressive, but I think Illosovich not there."

"What made you think that?" Price asked, his curiosity aroused.

Boroweski smiled. "We circle around it and the captain he invite us on board. When he discover we are Russian, he show us all around and he entertain us. Very good Russian vodka. No, Illosovich not there."

At last the council of war came to an end. Miss Templeton had already left, but as Mikael Boroweski followed his companions to the door, Smith, the tall American called after him:

"Mr Boroweski, or should I say *Comrade* Boroweski; I must thank you for the work you have put in on this case."

Boroweski nodded curtly, but the American continued:

"May I ask *why* you have shown so much interest?"

"As I have said, Mr Smith, if that is your *real* name," the Russian replied, "I am uncle of Andre Rorletski, I am friend of Doktor Price and I am Russian Patriot. I feel it my duty to help, for family, friend and country and also, I despise this man Illosovich. Does that answer your question?"

Smith held his hands out palms upwards in a gesture of surrender.

"Okay, okay, man, no offence meant."

"Not offended, niet" Boroweski replied brusquely before striding out of the door.

Chapter Twenty

Thursday Morning (Race Week)

The flight from Manchester was on time and touched down at Ronaldsway Airport at exactly eight am. It was one of the few flights to the Island that had not been fully booked long months before, but the fortnight of motorcycle racing was now drawing to a close and empty seats had started to appear on some of the inbound planes. In contrast, the outbound flights were beginning to fill up as the trickle of visitors leaving the Island fast became a flood.

Professor Clarke stepped down from the aircraft and with the help of smiling ground crew negiotiated his way across the tarmac to the luggage reclaim hall; he was given the usual verbal Manx language welcome to the Isle of Man by a pretty ground hostess and nodded a peremptory thank you. It was a journey he had not expected to make and, if truth be told, he was more than a little cross. Normally he would have demanded rather more notice to prepare for an inquest and, from what Price had told him, this one could be a little controversial. There was even a distinct possibility that he might not get paid his usual fee. He had only agreed to attend because his friend Price had said that it was a matter of national importance. He knew Price well enough to know that he should ignore such warnings at his own peril.

Minutes later, he was standing by the conveyor belt, waiting impatiently for the contraption to start moving. Fortunately, the aircraft was relatively small and was quickly unloaded – a very few more minutes after he had entered the arrivals and baggage claim section of the airport the belt jumped into life. He had planned to spend no more than a day on the Island and had booked a seat on the five pm flight back to Manchester. His luggage was therefore minimal, containing one small case containing his papers and a couple of reference books. The case was just a little too big and heavy to be counted as hand luggage and so, to his annoyance, it had gone into the hold. He looked at his watch anxiously. The inquest was due to open at ten, but he had never been to the Isle of Man before and had no real idea how long it would take him to get to the courthouse from the airport. Fortunately his was one of the first pieces of luggage that the conveyor belt carried into the room. Pulling it free fom the other pieces of baggage threatening to engulf it, he turned and made his way quickly through the double automatic doors to enter the main Ronaldway Airport arrivals hall.

The Professor had been told that someone would meet him, but Price had neglected to tell him who. He looked around, noticing a collection of taxi drivers bearing little cardboard signs with the names of their intended fares. His name did not seem to figure. Thinking that Price had forgotten to send someone, the pathologist decided to take a cab from the rank outside and walked towards the door. As he stepped outside a balding red-faced man in a dark suit approached him.

"Professor Clarke?" the man asked.

"Yes?" the pathologist replied.

"I'm Richard," the man said, "and I'm your lift into Douglas; pleased to meet you. Follow me."

They shook hands and Professor Clarke accompanied the man across a road flanked by colourful well-tended flowerbeds and refreshing looking green slopes of manicured grass and – could those be palm trees - into the airport car park which, the pathologist was pleased to discover, was only a very short walk from the main airport buildings.

Their transport was a black Mercedes diesel saloon. It normally saw service transporting the bereaved to and from a funeral; as far as Richard could remember, this was the first time it had been used for what was essentially a far earlier stage in the whole process, but it was a good comfortable car, had heavily tinted windows to keep out prying eyes and was, on balance, a great deal more suitable for the job in hand than Richard's powder blue Jaguar convertible.

Professor Clarke opted for the front passenger seat, as opposed to a more haughty position in the rear of the car, and relaxed slightly. The cheery Manx welcomes and airport ambience and efficiency were beginning to have their effect. The undertaker turned his key in the ignition and the engine started almost noiselessly. The car drove smoothly to the exit where the driver stopped to place his pre-paid ticket in a slot. The barrier in front of them lifted and they moved off down the road.

It was now a little after eight-fifteen. Richard explained that normally the journey into Douglas would take little more than twenty minutes, but this was the rush hour and with the heavy additional TT traffic, up to half-an-hour longer could be expected. The Mercedes passed through Ballasalla and crossed over the famous Fairy Bridge. Richard made a wish, as did all of the locals when passing that particular landmark. The wish was of course a secret one and the Professor was not informed.

Professor Clarke said little to the driver of the black Mercedes; he probably thought that the balding red-face man knew nothing about the case, but after ten minutes, or so Richard spoke.

"Believe you're going to give evidence at the inquest on Taylor?"

There was an uncomfortable silence for a few seconds before the pathologist replied. "I am," he said, "but I can't really say much about it, I'm afraid. Did you know the man?"

Richard shook his head. "Didn't know him personally, but I'll be dealing with the arrangements. I've seen the body. He didn't die from a motorbike crash."

The undertaker's words had an air of finality to them and the pathologist voiced a question.

"Have you seen many, then, Richard?…I mean, bodies of men who've been killed in motorcycle accidents?"

"Reckon I have, Prof. I've been an undertaker on this island for forty-odd years. I took over the business from my father and him from his father before him, so between us all we've been arranging funerals since the motorcycle races began. That fellow Taylor didn't die as a result of an accident. Someone killed him."

They had hit the expected heavy traffic and, in an attempt to avoid the worst of it, the undertaker turned right at a large roundabout just before the outskirts of Douglas. He followed the road down past the Okells brewery to the quayside on the south side of the old harbour. The road was still busy with traffic, but eventually Richard pulled the Mercedes to a halt beside a certain address in Athol Street. He pointed out the office to the Professor and then drove off.

Professor Clarke walked through the door and into the small reception area. Jonathon Price, Roy Love and Louise Templeton were waiting for him. He recognised his friend, shook his hand and was quickly introduced to the others. It was now ten past nine and the Inquest was due to start in fifty minutes. There was precious little time to give instructions or discuss the case, so Miss Templeton began immediately.

"Thank you for coming, Professor," she said, "how much do you know about the case?"

"Not a lot," the pathologist replied, "only what Jonathon has told me on the phone. I've seen the samples he's sent me and I assume you've seen my report. Can you tell me a little more?"

She replied hurriedly but confidently. "We can tell you an awful lot more, Professor, but it's going to have to be quick and we need a signed statement from you about your findings which we can disclose to the Coroner and any other interested parties when we go into court. Can you do that?"

The Professor of Pathology nodded. It was normal to disclose statements before an inquest, although they were not usually drafted at the last minute as was evidently going to be the case here. His previous experiences with Price, however, had taught him that nothing with that particular man could ever be regarded as totally unexpected.

"I can try, Miss Templeton; do you want to begin?" The advocate began speaking, but the Professor waved his hand.

"I think," he said, "given the time constraints, that we need someone who can take this down; you must have someone who can take shorthand?"

The advocate nodded and picked up a phone. A few minutes were wasted before an experienced-looking older secretary appeared. Miss Templeton, assisted by Price quickly gave the pathologist the background information he needed and, like the fast-thinking expert he was, he, by return dictated his expert report. The dictation had been finished by quarter to ten. The secretary retired to type up the documents and the others left the office for the short walk up Prospect Hill to the Court.

The Isle of Man Court of Justice was a relatively new building which had only been opened in 2000. It stood at the top of Prospect Hill in the centre of Douglas. The eastern wall of the courthouse was glazed and commanded spectacular views of the outer harbour and bay. Before it lay a large paved square, connected to Prospect Hill by a pedestrian walkway, named, appropriately enough "Deemster's Walk" (a Deemster being the local term for a High Court Judge). Miss Templeton led Price, Love and the Professor along the walkway into the square and then, without pausing, on through the glass doors into the foyer of the courthouse. After passing through the obligatory security checks, the advocate spoke to the usher.

"The Taylor Inquest," she asked, "which Court?"

"Number three, Miss Templeton," came the reply.

"Come on, this way," she told her companions, "it's almost ten and the High Bailiff doesn't like to be kept waiting."

A flight of steps led from the foyer to the first floor and opened onto a large, well lit and lofty concourse. Miss Templeton hurried up the stairs and the others followed. The concourse boasted spectacular views through the glazed eastern wall, but the advocate had seen them many times before. She stopped before Court Number Three.

"Jonathon," she said to Price, "you're a witness of fact so you can't come in until it's your turn to give evidence; you'll have to wait out here until you're called. Professor, you're an expert witness so you can come in now. Please sit behind me. Roy, take a seat in the public gallery, if you can find one: these inquests are usually pretty popular. Jonathon, when Frances, my secretary, turns up with the statements please send her straight in."

Miss Templeton had given her orders, quickly and efficiently; she now turned and without further ado pulled the heavy door opened and strode into the Court.

It was a large courtroom, by far the largest in the Island. The entrance from the concourse was at the rear of the room close to the Dock. The public gallery stood by the left hand wall with the Jury (when present) over to the right. Advocates were provided with three rows of seats which took up most of the space in the centre of the court and in the front left hand corner the witness box stood meekly below the Bench. The public gallery, as Miss Templeton had warned, was packed; inquests often were, appealing as they do to those feelings of morbid curiosity that linger, often submerged, within us all. As the hearing was not a criminal trial, the usher decided, after consultation with the Clerk, that the Dock could be used as additional seating for the public and when that, too became full to the point of overflowing, further members of the public were denied entry. Roy Love was one of the last people allowed into the room and thankfully squeezed himself into a seat in the corner of the Dock. It was the first and, he hoped, the last time he would find himself sitting in such a position.

Miss Templeton took her seat in the front row of the advocates' benches and told the Professor to sit behind her. She was not in the least surprised to find another of her profession already in place at the other end of the front row. He was an oily and disreputable man, unpopular with the rest of the Bar and the subject of many whispered rumours; there could be absolutely no doubt whom he would be acting for.

An electric bell rang somewhere in the background.

"All rise!" the usher called and the High Bailiff, acting in his capacity as Her Majesty's Coroner of Inquests entered the Court.

The Coroner sat down, followed by the rest of the court. He began with the formalities which were always required when opening an Inquest. He slowly and patiently explained the purpose of an inquest and what his role would be, namely to determined who had died, where, when, establish a cause of death and give a verdict. It was not his job, he told the Court, to apportion blame. He would be calling witnesses, he said, who would give evidence as to the facts surrounding the accident, but first he required appearances. He looked at Miss Templeton. She stood up.

"I appear for the family of the Deceased, Your Worship," she said.

The other advocate stood up. "I appear for Petromax Motorsport, Your Worship, employer of the Deceased." He sat down, but Louise Templeton remained on her feet.

"Thank you, Mr Gruber," the Coroner said, "Miss Templeton, do you have something else that you wish to say?"

"Yes, Your Worship," she replied, "some additional facts have come to light, Sir, in the last twenty-four hours. In light of these facts, I would like to call two additional witnesses to give evidence. Witness statements are currently being typed up and I should be in a position to present these to the Court in the next half an hour."

"This is rather irregular," the Coroner observed, "are you requesting an adjournment?"

"No, Sir," Miss Templeton replied, "for reasons which will become apparent, I think it important that the hearing proceed today, at least as far as hearing the evidence of the witnesses I propose to call."

The other advocate, Gruber, shot out of his seat.

"I must protest, Your Worship," he squeaked in an irritating, high pitched voice, "whatever the source or substance of this new, so-called evidence, it would appear that My Learned Friend proposes to spring it on us, in, if I may say so, a most unprofessional manner. I insist on an adjournment so that I may consider these statements when I receive them and take instructions from my client."

A barely concealed frown crossed the Coroner's face. Gruber was already beginning to annoy him.

"Mr Gruber," he said, "I am in charge of this Inquiry; you have no right to insist on anything. In addition, I consider your remarks concerning Miss Templeton's conduct most unseemly. Kindly withdraw them."

Gruber flushed and muttered an apology.

"Good," the Coroner continued, "I will take a short adjournment to consider this matter." He got up.

"All rise," the usher commanded, and the Coroner left the room.

The Coroner returned a few minutes later; he had considered the law and felt it perfectly proper to proceed.

"This is, after all, an Inquest," he told the Court, "an inquiry of fact, rather than a tribunal in which to apportion blame. I feel therefore that any evidence which could be submitted which may help in some way to elucidate or in some way make clear the circumstances of this tragic accident would be positively beneficial and I can see no obvious reason for excluding or deferring the same."

It was a rather convoluted way of saying it, but the Coroner was on Miss Templeton's side. She mentally punched the air before gently and submissively responding:

"I am grateful, Your Worship, for your considered and most reasonable Judgement."

A dark cloud of fury passed over Gruber's face; he turned to whisper to the man sitting behind him, a representative of his client, Miss Templeton assumed, before standing up again.

"Let us see, Your Worship, what this new evidence is!"

The Coroner scowled at Gruber's impertinence, but made no comment.

"Resuming the inquest into the death of the late Robert Taylor, I would like, first of all, to call some evidence of identity….."

The first witness was called and the inquest began.

Price sat outside the courtroom and watched with interest and more than a touch of impatience as at first one then another witness was called. He recognised a couple of them: marshals at the Veranda, who in turn recognised him and gave him a wave, having nothing at all to hide.

Half an hour or more had gone by before Price heard the pitter-patter of someone running up the stair. Miss Templeton's faithful secretary, Frances, glanced around the concourse and seeing Price ran over to join him.

"I've got them, Dr Price," she announced triumphantly, brandishing a bundle of papers in her hand. Price took the statements, read them carefully and then signed the ones which bore his name.

"Take them through and give them to Miss Templeton," he directed, "I'm afraid I can't go in there, not yet anyway."

Frances nodded, took the signed and unsigned documents and disappeared into the courtroom.

The Inquest was progressing slowly. Evidence as to the identity of the deceased had been heard as well as some evidence as to the circumstances of the accident when Miss Templeton stood up.

"Your Worship," she said, "I do now have the witness statements I referred to earlier. May I pass them forward?"

The Coroner nodded. "Of course you may, Miss Templeton, just pass them to the usher."

The documents were soon before him. He read them and then re-read them, scratched his head and then scowled.

"Miss Templeton," he said, "are your witnesses here?"

"Yes, Your Worship," she replied.

"And ready to give this evidence?" he continued.

"Of course," she said.

"Then I think, Miss Templeton, Mr Gruber, a little chat is called for in my chambers. I'm going to adjourn now for half an hour."

The Coroner rose and the rest of the room obeyed the usher's command to stand. Gruber hissed at Miss Templeton.

"What the hell's all this about? Am I going to see these statements?"

Louise Templeton smiled. "Let's just see what the Coroner has to say about it, shall we?"

At that moment the usher approached them.

"Miss Templeton, Mr Gruber, could you both come with me; his Worship would like a few words, privately."

The two advocates were led to the High Bailiff's chambers. A knock on the door was followed by an invitation for them both to enter. His Worship was seated at the end of a long table some distance from the door; he indicated that they should both sit down. A number of papers which Miss Templeton presumed to be the statements of Price and Professor Clarke, lay on the table before him. He picked them up and read them again, as if somehow unable to believe the evidence of his own eyes. After a few minutes, he put them down and addressed the female advocate.

"Miss Templeton, do you believe these; are they true?"

Louise Templeton replied immediatedly. "They are signed, Your Worship and the witnesses are here and prepared to give evidence on oath. I don't believe that it is my place to comment any further."

Gruber could contain himself no more. "I must see these statements," he insisted. "Rules of Court are being broken and my client is being denied access to what he should have as of right."

"Rules of Court?" the Coroner asked, raising his eyebrows. "This is an inquest, Mr Gruber, and no-one is on trial. I alone am entitled to determine what evidence this inquiry may hear, for the purposes of justice and to assist me in coming to a proper verdict. Now, I would like to hear your submissions before I decide whether or not to carry on with the inquiry."

"May I at least be afforded the courtesy of seeing this new evidence?" Gruber said stiffly.

The Coroner looked at Louise Templeton who shook her head. She pulled a heavy textbook out of her briefcase and slammed it on the table. "I'm sure that you're more than familiar with *Jervis on Coroners*, Sir, but as you have quite rightly said, this is an inquiry and not a trial and therefore the normal rules of an adversarial contest do not apply. You have seen the evidence which I hope to adduce. I would ask that I be allowed to adduce it now in open court."

"This is wrong; you cannot decide to do this," Gruber protested.

The Coroner smiled. "I already have," he said.

The inquest resumed and the Coroner called for Dr Jonathon Price to take the stand. The usher left the room and a short while later returned with Price who was led to the witness box. Price took the oath, gave his name and occupation and the inquisition began.

"Dr Price," the Coroner began, "I have now seen your statement; I would like to take you through its contents. Are you happy with that?"

"Yes, Your Worship," Price replied. "What would you like to know?"

The Coroner started to read out Price's statement: he started with the Monday early morning practice; occasionally he asked questions.

"So, Doctor, when you ran down the hillside and found Mr Taylor, were his injuries, in your opinion, severe?"

"They were severe, Sir, but in my opinion, as a surgeon, survivable."

"Can you clarify that?" the Coroner asked, "I mean, what were his injuries?"

"Compound limb fractures and multiple rib fractures, but we got to him pretty quickly, stabilised him and the helicopter arrived within a few minutes. When Taylor left, he was intubated, had an intravenous line in place and I had every expectation that he would survive."

"But he didn't, Dr Price, did he?" the Coroner responded. "Do you have any explanation for that?" Price stood there for a moment and then slowly replied.

"I think I do, yes."

Before Price could even begin to continue, Gruber again jumped to his feet.

"I object, Your Worship, this witness is about to give opinion evidence which should, of course, be disallowed."

The Coroner scowled again.

"Mr Gruber," he said, "I have told you before, but you seem incapable of taking the fact on board: this is an Inquest, not a contested action in a Court of Law. There is no Defendant and I alone have the right to decide what evidence I shall hear. In any event, Dr Price is a professional person and I am more than happy to hear what he has to say. Now please sit down and unless you have something more constructive to say, please hold your tongue. Dr Price, please continue."

"As I was about to say," Price continued, "Taylor wasn't really that badly injured; I really expected him to survive so when he died I was really surprised. Steve Kinnish told me…"

"Objection," Gruber almost shouted, already on his feet, "this may only be an inquest, Your Worship, but I do not think that we should be subject to hearsay evidence like this."

The Coroner slowly and, Price thought, rather sadly, nodded his agreement.

"I'm sorry, Dr Price, could you please confine your comments to what you actually saw yourself?"

The inquest continued in a similar vein for a few more minutes before Price dropped the bombshell.

"And so," he said, "I entered the mortuary and decided to take some samples from the deceased.".

"You did what?" this time Gruber actually shouted.

Even the Coroner looked a little perturbed. "Mr Gruber," he said sharply, "there is no need to shout; none of us are deaf." He turned to Price.

"Doctor Price," he said, "I'd like you to elaborate on what you have just told us. When precisely did you attend the mortuary?" Price told him. "I take it that you had obtained permission from the relevant authorities, before you embarked upon this nocturnal adventure?" the Coroner asked.

"Not exactly," Price replied.

"Then how did you gain admission to the mortuary? I take it that the place is normally locked up at night?"

"I'd rather not reveal those details, Sir," Price replied, "let's just say that I obtained certain samples and sent these off to the forensic pathologist Professor Clarke. I'll leave to the professor to tell you what he found."

"Indeed," the Coroner remarked, looking over his glasses at Price in a   most disapproving way, "rather irregular conduct; I would have thought that more orthodox channels would have been open to you, but never mind for now, what was done, was done. You can step down. Let us see what your Professor has to say."

Gruber was on his feet again. "I must protest, Your Worship; These samples have been obtained illegally and this man Price could well have committed the crime of burglary. Consequently any evidence from this professor must be disallowed."

"Mr Gruber," the Coroner said, "I am growing a little tired of your protests. The Professor is here and is willing to give evidence. I think that the interests of justice are best served by hearing what he has to say. Could Professor Clarke please take the stand."

The Professor walked over to the witness box and took the oath.

The evidence that the pathologist gave was devastating. Gruber jumped up and down in ever increasing desperation, but his protests fell on deaf ears. The Coroner was increasingly perturbed to hear what Professor Clarke had to say. He was not alone - as the pathologist continued to speak, the press reporter scribbled furiously thinking that for once her copy was destined for a wider readership than could possibly be offered by Isle of Man Newspapers. Audible gasps of astonishment rose from the public gallery as the Professor revealed, in matter of fact tones, details of his analyses and their implications. When his evidence came to an end he stopped, expecting questions from the Coroner or one of the two advocates; there were none.

The Coroner spoke. "Thank you Professor. You can step down now, but I'm afraid that after what you and Dr Price have told me, I cannot continue with this inquest. Neither can I release the body. I am going to pass the file to the Isle of Man Constabulary; no doubt they will wish to have the body examined by one of their own experts. In the meantime I'm going to adjourn this inquest. Thank you Miss Templeton, Mr Gruber." He stood up, the Court rose and the Coroner made his exit.

Gruber dashed out of the room before even the public had left their seats. He was closely followed by the man who had been sitting behind him. Miss Templeton, Price, Love and the Professor were a little slower and found their exit impeded by a human traffic jam of people trying to leave the room. By the time they emerged from the building, Gruber and his client were nowhere to be seen.

Miss Templeton spoke. "We need to get in touch with the police...now. The Coroner will pass that file to them, but he won't do it today. In the meantime, Petromax and Illosovich will escape. That advocate they had, Gruber, he's corrupt and greedy, but he's devious and he's certainly not stupid. Illosovich'll be paying him one hell of a retainer and you can bet that's who he's gone to see. We *must* find Illosovich. Does anyone have any ideas?"

Professor Clarke coughed politely. Louise Templeton flushed a little. "Sorry, Professor; I know you'll have to catch your flight. What time does it leave?"

"Five o' clock," the pathologist replied, his voice showing just a tinge of regret; he was starting to become more than interested in the case.

The advocate looked at her watch: it was now a quarter-past two.

"Look Professor; we are really most grateful for your help so far. I know that I'm being presumptuous, but would you come with me and repeat what you've just said in Court to the police. I'll make sure that you catch that flight, I promise."

"Certainly," Professor Clarke replied, "glad to be of any assistance."

They decided to split into two separate teams. Miss Templeton would speak to the Coroner's Officer and would make sure that the Coroner's file of papers was passed to the appropriate police officers that afternoon. Then she would accompany Professor Clarke to Police Headquarters where he would tell them what he knew. Price and Love would try and locate Illosovich.

The surgeon and the private detective walked back down Prospect Hill towards Athol Street. Love had recovered his hire car which had been found abandoned the previous day in a quiet tree-lined square in the centre of Douglas. It was now standing in a car park at the rear of Miss Templeton's office ready for use and Love was eager to get going.

"I suggest," he said, "that we start at the Grandstand. Illosovich *might* be there with the rest of his team. I think it's unlikely, but we should start somewhere and the Grandstand is the nearest place."

"If that fails, then where?" Price asked.

"Well there's the boat and the house. We can ask the Harbour Master if anyone's gone out to the boat. If he says no, then we'll drive up north and have a look around. If nothing's doing up there then we'll have another think; agreed?"

"No," Price replied, "I don't think we'll find Illosovich in any of those places and we could waste a lot of time proving me right. I agree that we'll have to get them checked, but we'll get Boroweski and his Russians to do that. I think Illosovich is still in Douglas and I don't think he'll skip the Island tonight. I don't know why he's here…"

"The plutonium in the mine," Love cut in, "if you ask me, it's pretty obvious why he's here and more obvious, now he knows we're onto him, that he'll try and get off the Island with the stuff at the earliest possible opportunity."

"But why should the main man himself come here?" Price asked. "He must have plenty of people he can rely on to distribute the stuff. More importantly, why destroy the place he was storing it; he'll either have to find somewhere else to hide it or he'll have to take if off Island with him. It doesn't make sense at all. Why bring it here if he's going to take it away with him again?"

"Well, he does have other mines," Love suggested; "he could have simply moved the plutonium into one of those." Price shook his head.

"No, Illosovich is here in person for a reason."

"Maybe he just wants to see his rider win the Senior TT" Love said light-heartedly.

Price turned sharply to look at his friend. "His rider win the Senior TT..." he repeated slowly, echoing his friend's words. A strange light seemed to have come into his eyes.

"You had an idea?" Love asked.

"Maybe," Price replied, "but I need to find out a few things before I'm even prepared to discuss it. First of all I need to speak to your Mr Smith and then I need to speak to Mikael Boroweski. Can you get hold of them?"

Love nodded. He was running a mobile phone on the local pay-as-you go

tariff. "I can ring them both now," he said, "but I thought you wanted Mikael to check the house up north." Price shook his head.

"Forget that idea," he said, "if I'm right, what's going to happen is going to happen here and it going to happen tomorrow, after the Senior Race."

"I'll give them both a call," Love said.

Chapter Twenty-One

Thursday Evening (Race Week)

Price and Love had returned to the undertaker's house in Onchan. The undertaker himself was not there, and they presumed that he was going about his usual business. After all life, or in his case, death, still went on and had to be attended to. Price had found a copy of the Race Programme and was reading through it carefully. Love was sitting in a corner of the room, waiting impatiently for Boroweski and Smith to arrive. After half-an-hour or so Love spoke.

"I'm impressed by your ability to remain so detached, Jonathon; to be able to switch off like that and relax and read the programme after all that's happened." There was a trace of sarcasm in the man's voice, but Price ignored him and carried on reading. Eventually the door bell rang. The two men they had been waiting for had arrived, Love led them into the room and they both sat down. Price was still reading the programme.

"Can you put that down now, Jonathon," Love said curtly; more than a little irritated by his friend's behaviour. "We need to talk." Price looked up and smiled.

"Have any of you gentlemen read this?" he said, flourishing the slim booklet before them. Smith and Boroweski shook their heads and looked at Price, as if mystified by his question. Love put what they were both probably thinking into his own words.

"Of course not, Jonathon; we're not all here to watch the bloody motorbike races."

"You aren't and Mr Smith here isn't," Price said, "but I am and I think there are another forty thousand like me and what about comrade Boroweski here; I thought that you came to watch your nephew race, Mikael. Isn't that true?"

The Russian's eyes narrowed just a little, but he replied without even the slightest of pauses, "This is true, Doktor Price, but I do not read English too well and of course there is no Russian translation."

"Shame really, for all of you; you don't know what you've been missing. Some excellent little articles, potted biographies on the racers, photos from last year's races, statistics and the odd little bit of paddock gossip; all most interesting and it makes a great souvenir to take home. All for the very reasonable price of six quid."

"What the hell are you going on about, Jonathon," Love said. "If you're trying to be funny, then it's not working."

"Read that!" Price exclaimed, handing his friend the programme. Love took it and rapidly fingered through the pages.

"Very interesting to spectators, no doubt," he agreed, "but it doesn't move us any further forward, does it?" Price shook his head.

"You're wrong. Read the Programme: the answer is in the Programme."

"Where?" Love asked. Price pointed to the relevant paragraph; it lurked in a page towards the end entitled *Paddock Gossip*.

Petromax, it said, *have kindly agreed to auction one of their new World Superbike replicas. The auction will take place at the rear of the Grandstand at the conclusion of the Senior Race and Mr Vladivir Illosovich, the President of Petromax, will be in attendance. Mr Illosovich will donate the money raised to a number of local Charities.*

"So?" Love asked, mystified. "He's going to raffle a bike and give the money to charity. Where's the mileage in that?"

Price smiled and shook his head. "Little bit deeper than that, Roy. Way of disposing of a bike, wouldn't you say; particularly a bike that might be a little special."

"No," Love said, "far too public. Illosovich is hardly likely to put it in the Programme if he's planning on a stunt like that. What do you think Mr Smith?"

"I've got to say I agree with you, Roy," the American said. "Jonathon's theory does sound rather difficult to swallow; it just can't be right."

"I disagree," Price said. "This is a perfect solution. Completely respectable and above board, as far as anyone watching will be able to see; nothing dubious going on there at all. Russian billionaire auctions highly sought after limited-edition superbike and then shows his philanthropic nature by giving the proceeds to charity. Very touching. It'll all be properly documented and photographs will no doubt appear in the newspapers."

"You can't be serious," Love said. "He wouldn't be that obvious."

"Why not?" Price said, "who would possibly suspect it?"

Love shrugged his shoulders and looked at the other men present within the room. The expressions on their faces suggested that they certainly would not have done.

"Okay," Love said after a moment or two's reflection, "say, for the moment we take your suggestion as a working hypothesis. What do you suggest we do?"

Price said nothing for a moment or two and then replied. "Nothing now, but prepare for plenty tomorrow. We don't know where Illosovich is, although I've a pretty shrewd idea that he's holed up in that hotel I told you about on the promenade. We certainly don't know where the plutonium is. In any event, at this stage, we don't really know why the man's here at all. Tomorrow may give us answers to all of those questions."

"And you say that now we do...nothing?"

"Unless you can suggest otherwise."

At six o' clock Louise Templeton and the undertaker arrived. They had left Professor Clarke at the airport, but they had precious little else to report. The advocate was more than a little unhappy.

"The police didn't even want to hear what we had to say," she reported bitterly, "said they'd read the Coroner's file in due course and then look into it. I tried to tell them how important this was, but they just smiled, shook their heads and looked at me as though I was a fool."

Love shook his head. "Look at it from their perspective," he said, "it *is* a little hard to believe; anyway, we're going to have to deal with this ourselves. I don't agree with his theories, but Jonathon, here, has a plan and as far as I can see it's our only way forward, so unless any of you have a better idea, let's listen to him."

Chapter Twenty-Two

Friday - Senior TT Race Day

Friday, the Senior Race Day dawned at last. It was the final day of the meeting and daybreak yet again bore a promise of blue skies and hot sunshine; only on the distant horizon did a thin rim of cloud threaten the prolonged spell of settled weather.

Price had slept little, if at all, during the night and was up and dressed long before it was light. He had finalised his plan sometime in the early hours and was now determined to put it into action. Fortunately, his allies were with him. Illosovich would probably now be aware of the identities of some of them, and it would be an easy enough task to find out where they were living or staying, but Illosovich knew nothing of the undertaker and on Price's suggestion, Love, Smith, Boroweski and Miss Templeton had spent the night in the undertaker's house. Price roused them quickly and by six am all were awake and ready. At quarter-past six they assembled around Richard's breakfast table; it would be a long day, Price warned, but he had drawn up instructions for each of them.

At seven, Mikael Boroweski left the house, followed, a short time later by the advocate. They had further to travel or more to do than the others, but at eight o' clock sharp Love set off with the American in his hired Ford Mondeo and half-an-hour later Price climbed into the undertaker's car; the black Mercedes saloon started and then purposefully pulled out of the drive.

Price had come out of hiding. He had given evidence in open court and had been seen by the Petromax lawyer and by one of the Petromax men; as he could no longer deny his own continuing existence, he felt that it would be wrong not to return to his racing duties. He had called the Chief Medical Officer the previous evening and made excuses for his absence from the Wednesday races; even to his own mind the excuses seemed rather feeble, but Dr Duffy thanked him heartily for his continued support and assistance.

"Thanks for getting in touch, Jonathon, he said; I was worried that something had happened to you. Can't tell you how glad I am you can help us tomorrow. Never known a TT like it before! After all those problems in Practice, I thought things couldn't get any worse, then I heard about the inquest on Taylor and all this stuff about radiation and opiate poisoning. Anything in it, d'you think? Would really have liked to have made the inquest myself, but couldn't get away from the hospital."

Dr Duffy was a senior consultant at Nobles; it was much to Price's relief that he had not attended the inquest and had not apparently yet learned of Price's uninvited late night visit to his hospital's mortuary.

"Don't know, Dr Duffy," Price said non-committally, "I understand that the police are looking into it; we'll just have to see what they come up with."

Dr Duffy agreed that they would just have to do that and then asked Price if he could cover Hillberry corner the following day and Price readily accepted. Hillberry was little more than a mile and a half from the finish line and could be accessed by a twisty little back lane even when the roads were closed for racing. For his purposes it was an ideal location.

Meanwhile that morning, just after seven am, Boroweski met up with the rest of his men where they had been expecting him at their campsite a few miles outside Douglas. Their task was a simple one, but it required manpower and even more importantly, manpower which would easily blend in with the rather unique current background of the Isle of Man TT Races. Mikael gave his men their orders and individually or in groups of two or three they set off in different directions. After they had all departed, the Russian, together with his lieutenant Pieter, returned to Douglas. They had a hotel to visit, a rather seedy, decaying place situated roughly halfway along the Promenade and the task they had before them was difficult and could be potentially rather dangerous.

Miss Templeton had left Richard's house at the same time as the Russian, but she went straight to her office. Her task was rather different. Unlike the others, it involved no travel, but a great deal of time on the telephone and its success was heavily dependant on her finely honed powers of persuasion.

As far as Price could guess, the two private detectives, Love and Smith, probably stood the best chance of going unrecognised by Illosovich or any of his Petromax heavies; for that reason and that reason alone, he had decided to send them to the Grandstand and at ten-past eight the blue Ford Mondeo pulled onto Noble's Park, (used as a temporary car-park for the duration of the races) and came to a halt. Love and Smith got out and began to walk slowly towards the racing paddock.

Jonathon Price had picked up his 600cc Yamaha from the hotel car park. He had inspected it carefully; maybe he was becoming a little paranoid, but after what had happened over the last eleven days he was determined to be safe rather than sorry. Thankfully, there were rather fewer places where it was possible to conceal a bomb on a motorbike than a car and after fifteen minutes he was satisfied. The bike fired up on the first prod of the starter button and he was off, via the back lane to Hillberry. By nine o' clock he was in place. Provided nobody crashed, he thought, his was by far the easiest task of the five of them.

☆ ☆ ☆ ☆ ☆ ☆

The Senior Tourist Trophy Race, the Blue Riband of the TT Meeting was about to begin.

It was one of the greatest events in the long history of motorsport; certainly the oldest, probably one of the fastest, once the richest and without doubt still the longest and most dangerous motorcycle road race on the planet. Six laps of thirty seven and three-quarter miles per lap: two hundred and twenty-six miles in total. Along tree-lined country lanes, through picturesque little villages, across heath and mountain: no run-off, no gravel traps (well only one), no slip roads and no escape. There was only one certainty: one man would win, but it was more than possible that one or more might die.

It was ten o' clock in the morning and at the Grandstand, the riders started their engines. The race began at ten-thirty: fifteen minutes to warm up and then the bikes would be called out onto the grid. All of the riders had raced there before, but that small familiarity did little to settle the nerves and butterflies which fluttered within all of their stomachs. One by one, they brought their machines out of the paddock and slowly assembled on the Glencrutchery Road. To their left, the Grandstand towered majestically above them, but to their right the gleaming white Italianate crematorium grinned silently from the centre of the cemetery. It was indeed a strange place from which to start a motorcycle race.

The riders started one by one at ten second intervals. They would accelerate down Glencrutchery Road, through St Ninian's crossroads and then plummet down the steep incline of Bray Hill. None of them took it lightly, but by ten-twenty-five in the morning on Senior Race Day, none of them would swap where they were for any grid position on any other racetrack in the world. Such was the irresistible attraction of the Mountain Circuit.

Price sat down on a low wall by the side of the road and waited. Hillberry was one of the last corners on the Course, a fearsomely quick right-hander lying at the end of a blinding fast descent from Brandish Corner. Brandish itself lay at the bottom of an even faster drop from Creg Ny Baa. The small and rather ramshackle grandstand which stood just behind the left hand kerb at the entrance to the bend was already full of spectators; they would not have long to wait: the first bikes were already well on their way towards Ballacraine and very soon, the commentary which blared out from the vintage loudspeakers mounted above them would switch to Glen Helen and they would learn who were the leaders on the road. Following the usual custom, a marshal walked over to the doctor and offered him a cup of tea. Price accepted gratefully, but his thoughts were elsewhere; not for the first time that morning, he wondered how his colleagues were getting on.

Whilst Price was sipping his tea, Love and Smith were in the paddock. They had obtained passes from the undertaker (who seemed to have contacts everywhere). The passes seemed to give them an almost unfettered freedom to wander wherever they chose. It had not taken them long to find the Petromax transporter: a tent like awning stretched out behind it, but the awning was fully enclosed and when the two men moved closer to investigate, a couple of burly Russians appeared and made it quite clear that they were not welcome. The two private detectives moved away. When Smith was quite certain that they were not being watched he pulled something from his shoulder bag and looked at it carefully.

"What's that?" Love asked.

"Geiger counter, computerised, state of the art," Smith replied, "I'm just looking at the record of activity since we entered the paddock. It's low, no more than background, even by that transporter. Wherever they're keeping the plutonium, it can't be around here, not unless they've got it pretty well shielded, that is."

"Do you believe Jonathon's theory?" Love asked suddenly.

"Dunno," the American answered, "sounds pretty far-fetched, but there again, I suppose that's its beauty; no-one would suspect it and no-one would believe it."

"Surely," Love asked, "if Illosovich wanted to supply someone with this stuff, he would just send it to them; he's got enough men and enough money to do that, hasn't he?"

"Yes," Smith replied, "but anything he sends out of Russia will be inspected by the Russian authorities and various other groups will be watching too. More than a few people have their eyes on Illosovich, so you can bet that they will take a keen interest in anything he tries to export to anyone directly. Sending a few motorcycles to the Isle of Man, though, where's the harm in that."

"This plutonium, though," Love persisted, "its radioactive so surely it would be picked up at the airports; I mean they have detectors, don't they?"

"There are detectors, certainly, but they are mainly there to pick up individuals carrying radioactive materials on their person or in their luggage. Stuff that gets sent by freight doesn't get scanned routinely. No-one would put a Geiger counter anywhere near it unless they had a tip off or were suspicious. Like I said, who's going to be suspicious of a few motorbikes. The customs authorities would probably let the sniffer dogs climb over them just to make sure there weren't any narcotics hidden in the cylinder head or something like that, but sniffer dogs aren't trained to pick out plutonium."

"So what now?" Love asked.

"We wait," Smith said, "wait and see what happens."

Some time earlier, Mikael Boroweski and his lieutenant, Pieter, had parked their motorcycles in front of a large hotel on Douglas Promenade. The hotel had obviously seen better days, but Mikael and his companion, dressed as they were, neither looked nor felt out of place when they entered the foyer. They had walked up to the reception desk; it was unmanned so Boroweski had pressed the bell. When nothing happened he pressed the button again and waited and waited. Eventually, after a long wait the drawn and anxious face of a young woman appeared behind the desk.

"Yes," she said, "can… I help you?" Her accent was faltering, foreign and scared. Boroweski detected a countryman, or countrywoman, to be more precise. He lapsed into Russian. An observer who knew little about such things may have found it impressive that he was able to match the exact dialect and accent of the person he was speaking to, but his words had the desired effect and the girl relaxed. He continued to speak to her and she began to reply. At first her words were measured and cautious; wrapped up and sealed in a dark binder of apprehension and fear, but the more Boroweski said, the more she opened up. After fifteen minutes he had learned all he needed to know, but he stood there for a few more minutes listening to the girl's worries. When she had finished, he said a few more words to her. What he said is unknown, but when she heard them her tear-flecked face bore a trace of a smile.

"Come Pieter," he said, leading his mighty confederate out of the hotel, "we have things to do and people to see."

Miss Templeton was still in her office. The telephone had scarcely moved from her ear for the last two, three, four hours, but who was counting? She had a job to do and had spoken to just about anyone she thought might listen, but unfortunately no-one had. At last, almost as an act of desperation, she dialled the number of the local trade union branch secretary. Within a surprisingly few seconds her call was answered.

"Is that you Robbie?" she asked; the voice on the other end of the line answered in the affirmative. "I've got a big favour to ask," she said, "if you say no, then I'll understand, but can you listen, first, to what I have to say?"

"I'll listen, Louise," the deep Scottish voice boomed, "but I'll promise nothing until I've heard what you have to say."

The loudspeakers announced that the leaders in the race had just passed Ramsey Hairpin on the third lap; it would only be another five minutes or so before they charged through Hillberry. Price looked up the road: the tail-enders continued to stream past, but he didn't want to miss Andre Rorletski. From what he had heard, the Russian on the black and gold Petromax was now leading on the road and leading in the race. A gaggle of rather fancied Irishmen were hot on his tail, but if Rorletski could hold onto this lead, it would be a famous, if not a phenomenal victory. The Petromax shot past and Price let out a cheer. A few seconds later the chasing pack stormed by in pursuit. After they had disappeared, one of the marshals came up to Price and started to make conversation. He was a young fellow and a local, but after a rather hesitant start, he began to make sense:

"Good rider that Rorletski," he said.

"Uh, yeah," Price replied, not really wanting to take his eyes off the road.

"And that Mr Illosovich, nice fella."

"Right," Price said, again not really listening.

"Put loads into the local community," the man continued undeterred, "Done loads for us in Laxey," he said, "especially for the Wheel."

This time Price took notice. He turned to face the young man and asked a question. "Sorry, I'm being rude. I didn't really catch that, what's your name?"

"Juan (in the Isle of Man that is pronounced Jew-ann) Quayle," came the answer.

"Okay, Juan, what exactly has Illosovich done in Laxey and what precisely for the Wheel?"

Love and Smith were there to see the end of the race. The black and gold Petromax superbike shot through the chequered flag well over a minute in the lead. Andre Rorletski had done the impossible double and the crowd seated on the grandstand leapt up to give him a deafening ovation. Rorletski trickled back along the slip road and was received and congratulated by his mechanics and pit crew. Suddenly and from nowhere, the tall black-suited figure of Vladimir Illosovich appeared from the crowd and walked over to hug and anoint his rider. Illosovich seemed happy and incredibly relaxed; Love and Smith knew that something had to be terribly wrong with Price's theory.

The rest of the leading riders were finishing now at two or three second intervals. After a few minutes the garlanding ceremony took place. Rorletski took his second victory with pride and honour; no-one sprayed the champagne further or with more vigour than he did that day and at the back of the grandstand preparations were underway for the final presentation of the fortnight: the Winged Mercury, the Senior Race Trophy, first presented by the Marquis de Mouzilly St Mars to the winner of the first TT race in 1907 and possibly the largest and most beautiful trophy in the history of sport. Whilst Rorletski's name was being cut into the solid silver to join the names of, amongst others, Duke, Hailwood and Dunlop, a small stage had been erected at the rear of the grandstand for the auction of the Petromax TT Superbike.

Love had moved to the back of the grandstand and beckoned the American over to join him. The worried expression on his face told the world that all was not well. He pointed to the prominent pressed steel stage which bore an impressive-looking black and gold motorcycle. He could already see that it was a Petromax World Superbike replica, but he could also see that no Russian heavies were in attendance. He voiced that that was where his concerns lay. "According to Jonathon's theories," he said, "that motorbike contains enough plutonium to construct a twenty kilotonne nuclear device."

"Well, we think there might be just about sixteen kilograms which is just about enough, particularly if they can construct a bomb with a neutron reflector..." Smith began.

Love cut him dead. "But there's no-one here...don't you just think that possibly someone might think of guarding it?"

"Well..."

"Look, can't you just go and check it out with your Geiger counter."

"Can do," Smith said, "just watch my back, will you?"

Love nodded and the American walked slowly over the tarmac and then up onto the stage. Smith made quite sure that the shoulder bag he was carrying came as close as it was possible to come to the black and gold motorcycle before returning to his companion's side. No-one challenged him. He disappeared behind a motorhome for a few moments before returning shaking his head.

"Nothing," he said, "the reading didn't even creep above background."

"Jonathon's got it wrong then," Love said, "that bike is a red herring. If I hadn't seen those engine parts for myself and hadn't been incarcerated at the bottom of that mine, I would be starting to have serious doubts about whether this alleged plutonium actually exists, but going on the premise that it does exist, where the hell is it?"

Smith shook his head: "I dunno," he said, "but that's why Boroweski and his men are still out looking; we'll have to wait until we hear back from them."

The area to the rear of the Grandstand was fast filling up with spectators waiting to see the Senior TT prize presentation so Love and Smith faded into the background and waited. It wasn't long before Love's 'phone rang: it was Price.

"Where are you?" he demanded.

"Back of the Grandstand," Love replied, "and Jonathon,"

"Yes?"

"Your theory about the auction is wrong; we checked the bike with the Geiger counter: it's clean."

"I know," Price said; "we've been looking in completely the wrong place, but I think I'm on the right track now. We need to meet, and soon, but not at the Grandstand: my face is too well known. Be at Richard's house in fifteen minutes and see if you can contact Mikael; I've tried his number a couple of times, but he's not answering."

The Parade Lap, run at the conclusion of the Senior Race was drawing to a close and with it that year's TT meeting. From the organisers' point of view, the parade lap could not end soon enough; they had been warned by the Met office at Ronaldsway of an approaching belt of thick low-lying cloud, but thankfully it had stayed away until the last few bikes in the Senior had made the mountain descent and the race had ended. The organisers had been forced to make a quick decision on the Parade, but word from the travelling marshals was that visibility wasn't yet a problem up on the top so the Lap went ahead on time. As the machines thundered over the mountain, however, the mist came down and by the time the prize presentation had got underway, the soft hoot of the foghorn was sounding eerily across Douglas bay.

Love and Smith made their way to Richard's place. By the time they got there, soft clammy white fingers were already caressing the cliffs on which the house stood. Although it was only a little after three in the afternoon, the sun had disappeared and the temperature had dropped. Douglas Head, on the opposite side of the bay, along with all higher ground had disappeared and the bay itself grew hazier and fainter with every passing minute. Love shuddered and recalled the thick fog which had fallen only four days earlier. If the speed at which it was falling was anything to go by, then Manannan's cloak would be even worse today.

Price's motorcycle was already parked in the drive when they arrived, but Price was alone. He had been waiting impatiently and was at the door almost before the blue Ford had stopped moving.

"Come on," he called in a hoarse whisper, "over here." The two men crossed the drive and walked into the house. They sat down in the undertaker's blue room.

"Have you been able to get hold of Boroweski?" Price asked. Love shook his head.

"No answer," he said; "he must be riding his bike. What have you found out?"

Price told them about his conversation with Juan Quayle and what he had learned about the great philanthropist, Vladimir Illosovich.

"Generous man, by all accounts; only had a house on the Island for two or three years, but according to young Juan, he's been a great benefactor to nearly all the local charities. He's passionate, though, about the Island's industrial past. Very interested in anything to do with the mines. Endeared himself to the local Mines Preservation Society and the Friends of Laxey Wheel and given them some very healthy donations to assist with the various restoration projects. In fact..." Price lowered his voice into a conspiratorial whisper, "...he's had a team of his own engineers over for several months renovating the wheel and the shafts and tunnels beneath it. Juan's not quite sure what they've been doing: well, actually, he told me, confidentially, of course, that no-one's quite sure what they've been doing and the locals have been kept away from it, for Health and Safety reasons, obviously."

"Obviously," Love agreed, acerbically.

"Anyway, that's all there is to tell, apart from one thing."

"Which is?" Love asked.

"Illosovich's eighty foot motor vessel has upped anchors and left Douglas. I don't know where it's gone, but I'd guess that the smart money would say that its lying somewhere in Laxey Bay."

"Laxey?" Love repeated mournfully; Price nodded. "And in the fog again?"

"Looks like it," Price replied.

"Well we'd better get on with it then," Love said suddenly, "but this time, Jonathon, we are most definitely not going down any mine."

The auction behind the Grandstand had not been particularly well attended. Its timing was perhaps unfortunate. The Prize Presentation had ended and with it the race meeting. That was usually the signal for the crowds to return to their hotels and campsites, pack up and make ready for the long journey home. The banks of damp swirling fog which had enveloped Douglas served to encourage such movement rather than hinder it. It was all a great pity, for it meant that that a pretty meagre crowd of thirty or so spectators were treated to what in the end developed into an enthralling spectacle.

A couple of bikers had made half-hearted bids when the auction started, but when the money became serious they dropped out, leaving two men to fight on. One of the men was a popular local collector, a balding man with a rather red face... the other man was unknown, but of middle-eastern appearance. Judging by the bids, both men had money to burn.

Price, Love and Smith were in the blue Ford driving slowly through the fog towards Laxey. For Smith it was a new experience, but for the others it was a case of déjà vu. The fog was even thicker than it had been on the Monday, but they were much earlier and so the traffic was considerably thicker. They crawled along the Groudle Road following the blood-red fog-lights of the car in front; the faint red pinpricks which were the tail lights of the cars in front of that struggled to penetrate the swirling white clouds which enveloped the road. Suddenly the pinpricks grew brighter as the cars in front braked sharply. Love, who was driving, in turn braked and brought the blue Ford to a halt. After a couple of minutes, it was obvious that something had happened on the road ahead. Love got out of the car to investigate. He was gone for some time; when he returned, the expression on his face told them that the news was not good.

"Accident," he said, "bad one, on the main road just after the junction a hundred yards or so further on, cars are bumper to bumper. We're going to be stuck here for hours. The only alternative is to turn around and drive back to Douglas and then try and get to Laxey via the Creg, but I must say I don't fancy it in this fog."

"Won't that take hours?" the American asked.

"Probably," Love said, " but I can't think of any other way".

"Unless..." Price began. Suddenly a bell clanged behind them; it was dulled and muffled by the fog, but Price knew exactly what it was.

"The Electric Tram," he exclaimed. "The fog won't stop that," he continued, "come on, out of the car; let's flag it down and hitch a ride - it can't be more than three or four miles."

They jumped out of the car. The tramlines ran by the side of the road and a dark shape loomed out of the fog from the direction of Douglas. Fortunately, the driver had seen the queue of stationary cars and the tram had slowed almost to walking pace. The men jumped on board and the carriage rattled and banged over the level crossings which took the tracks firstly over the Groudle road and then, a few minutes later, over the main Onchan to Laxey Road. Mercifully the crossings were free of traffic and with a bump and a clang the Victorian tramcar picked up speed. It would probably be hard pushed to travel at more than twenty five miles an hour, but it would get them where they wanted to go and, given the prevailing weather conditions, that was all they could possibly ask.

The journey took twenty minutes, far longer than Price had predicted, but at last the tramcar pulled into the Station in the centre of Laxey village and the three men disembarked. The fog had shown no signs of lifting and now, in all probability, had set in for the night.

"Where now?" the American asked, looking at the other two.

"The Wheel, I think," Price decided, "yes, let's make for the Wheel."

Normally, the Lady Isabella would have been easy to find. A quick glance at the slopes of Snaefell Mountain would have shown the way, but with visibility down to little more than a few yards, Price struggled for a moment to get his bearings.

"Come on," he said, seizing the initiative, "follow the tram lines to the other side of the road and then along the line of cottages. We'll get there, even if we have to crawl on our hands and knees."

The giant waterwheel, known affectionately as the Lady Isabella and named after a former Lieutenant Governor's wife, sits in the hills above Laxey and is the largest working waterwheel in the world. It has a diameter of seventy-two feet and was built in 1854 to pump water out of the vast labyrinth of mineshafts, levels and tunnels which riddle the ground beneath it. It was normally open to the public on payment of an entrance charge, but had been closed a couple of days earlier to allow certain essential maintenance work to take place. What exactly that work entailed had never really been made clear, but a couple of unmarked white vans had been standing in the car park beside the wheel all day.

Sometime in the late afternoon, as the impenetrable bank of fog crept down the lower slopes of Snaefell, a four-wheeled drive vehicle pulled into the car park and came to a halt. A man in a dark suit got out, looked at the Wheel and smiled. It was Illosovich and today, for once, he was happy. His machine and rider had won the Senior Race: only a little thing in the great scheme of things, but it gave him a certain sense of satisfaction. Of more importance, his other, larger project was drawing to a successful close. Just a few hours more and he would be gone. He had planned to use the helicopter, but the fog had put a stop to that. Not to worry, he would make his departure by sea and the fog would help cover his tracks, but first certain materials would need to be removed from the mine.

He nodded at the men who accompanied him, pointed towards the entrance to the mine and barked a terse string of words of command; the men moved into action. The words were in Russian, but their urgency would have been clear to anyone.

At about the same time Price, Love and Smith were making their faltering way up the short, but steep and narrow lane that led to the Wheel. Although they were only a few hundred yards from the nearest dwelling, the silence and the sense of isolation was intense. They could just make out the vague shapes of trees by the side of the lane and every now and then the ghostly arms and fingers of branches, twigs and leaves touched their heads or rubbed against their shoulders. Fortunately it was still light, but the light was faded and subdued, dimmed and lessened by the thick white shroud which lay across their path. They kept their thoughts to themselves and carried on until they suddenly came across a wide open space: it was the visitors' car park.

The visibility was a little better there, out from under the trees and the fog just a little less intense. Smith, the American, seemed to have better eyesight than the others and saw the two vans and the four wheel drive vehicle. He nudged his companions and whispered, "Petromax; take care!"

The two men beside him glanced at him and then at each other. Whatever they were looking for must now be close to hand.

Love ventured a hoarse whispered question, "Where now?"

Price shrugged his shoulders and then nodded forward.

"The Wheel, I still think we should try the Wheel."

The men crept slowly past the deserted kiosk, where visitors were normally expected to pay the entrance fee and buy an official guide book or a souvenir or two, and passed through an open gateway onto a shadowy path. Price had never been there before, but knew that the gateway should have been closed and locked. Not far ahead something massive towered above them; they could not see it, but they sensed that it was there.

"Shsss," Love whispered, "someone's coming."

They froze and listened. They could hear the sound of heavy footsteps approaching from somewhere up ahead and the footsteps were not far away. At that moment one of them shifted his footing; a twig snapped; it was the slightest of noises, but it broke the gloomy silence like a rifle shot. The footsteps ahead of them stopped.

"Who is there?" a voice called out. It was a voice with an unmistakeable accent. There was a breath of wind and the shadowy veils were briefly drawn away to reveal a clear window in the white wall of fog. Price, Love and Smith were standing no more than thirty yards away from Illosovich and half a dozen of his men.

The window was only there for a moment, but that moment was long enough. Illosovich's men seemed to be carrying a number of long wooden boxes. What they contained was anyone's guess, but they seemed heavy for it took two men to carry each box. The contents could not have been too delicate or sensitive, though, for on seeing Price and his companions, one of the men gave a shout and two of them dropped the box they were carrying giving pretty clear signals as to what they were about to do next.

"Let's get out of here," Smith urged, "they're armed."

Mercifully the shroud of fog swept over them again, but as it did, the soft flat report of a silenced firearm cut through the air.

"Get down." Smith whispered, "and disperse, hide; find somewhere away from this track. With any luck this fog will hold; they won't be able to shoot what they can't see!"

The three men separated and Price broke into a run. From the shouts behind him, the Russians had realised what was happening and had also split up to give chase. Price ran on and up a slope, then suddenly his foot hit something causing him to trip and fall. He swore, but was immediately on his feet again. Looking down he noticed a step, the first of a flight of many. Above him he could see the ghostly outline of the gigantic wheel of the Lady Isabella, it seemed as good a place to hide as he could think of in the circumstances and he began to climb.

Love and Smith ran downhill, back to the car park and then on to silently merge into the camoflage of the woodland beside the stream which ran from the outflow of the Wheel. They heard the sound of running feet, but the footsteps slowed and then stopped. Someone spoke. It was a Russian voice and had a definite air of authority. Then there were a number of dull thuds, doors were slammed and engines started. Suddenly three pairs of headlights appeared and three vehicles pulled out of the car park and moved off down the hill towards the village.

"What did he say?" Love asked the American. He had never actually been told, but had assumed that the man, if not actually a fluent Russian speaker, had at least some rudimentary knowledge of the language.

"Haven't a clue," Smith replied tersely, "but they seem to have pulled out. Let's find Price; did you see where he went?"

"I think he ran up the hill," Love said, "towards the Wheel."

Price had climbed the first flight of steps, a straight and relatively short flight, but even before he reached the top, he heard the sound of footsteps behind him. He was being pursued. At the top of the flight, a platform ran horizontally to the left along the

206

base of the mighty waterwheel. An iron railing to his left and a wall of solid masonry to his right ensured that he could take no other turn, until the masonry came to an end and he saw a spiral staircase. The footsteps behind him were getting closer and sounded more than half way up the straight stair. There was no time to think or reconsider his position, he could only go onwards and upwards, there was no alternative. He turned right and began to climb the spiral stair. At first he ran, but after he had completed the first three hundred and sixty degrees his pace fell to a brisk walk. Suddenly, a thought hit him like a bullet; these were the steps to the top. He had seen it from a distance: the narrow platform jutting out over the majestic waterwheel. A cul-de-sac, a dead end; there was no other way down. Price continued to climb thinking desperately of a means to escape; he flirted with the idea of jumping onto the wheel itself and somehow riding it down, but a mental picture of a crushed and mangled body seemed somehow to intrude into his thoughts. Behind him footsteps were now climbing the spiral staircase. There was only one answer; at the top of the steps he would have to stand and fight. He reached the top, turned and steeled himself; with any luck he would enjoy the element of surprise. The footsteps were getting closer, but when they were almost upon him they slowed and a voice called out in a hoarse whisper:

"Doktor Price?" Price breathed a deep sigh of relief. It was the voice of Mikael Boroweski.

At the base of the Wheel they found Love and Smith.

Boroweski spoke forcibly and rapidly. "Come, now there is no time to talk; Illosovich and his men must not make their escape."

"Where are we going?" Love asked, putting all of their questions into words.

"The harbour," Boroweski replied breathlessly from some way in front of them. He was already running down the slope. "Quick, I have motorcycles, but we must hurry."

Price, Love and Smith started after him. At the bottom of the slope, Pieter was waiting and beside him stood Boroweski's Cossack and the ancient Ural combination.

"Quick, quick," Boroweski commanded, "two of you with Pieter, one with me. There is no time to lose; they already have big start on us."

They did as he said, the Russians jumped on their kickstarts and the elderly machines burst into life. Down the hill, they thundered and then on down the road to the village. It was a blind, reckless, but exhilarating charge through the swathes of swirling grey blanket of fog which still filled the valley. Price clung onto Boroweski for dear life as the Cossack swept across the main Ramsey road and then plunged down the lane towards the harbour. It was a journey of no more than a mile or two, but the lack of visibility made it impossible for Price to get any sort of bearing. He marvelled at how the Russians managed to find their way, but more so at how they managed to avoid what he felt was an inevitable accident. At last Boroweski pulled the motorcycle to a halt, jumped off and ran to the edge of the quayside.

The fog was still thick, but a little less so than it had been earlier. A small motor launch had cast off from its mooring and was making its way out of the harbour. The dim figures on board were too far away to make out clearly in the murkiness, but neither Boroweski nor Price had any doubt who they were. Suddenly a shout went up from the boat; one of its crew had noticed the figures stood on the quayside.

A distant voice floated across the water. "Goodbye, Doctor Price. You try hard, but I am afraid you must lose." The voice laughed and then disappeared into the mist.

Boroweski swore.

The ancient motorcycle and sidecar combination thundered onto the quayside and stopped. Its rider and passengers got out and Price explained the situation.

"It's Illosovich," he said, "he's got away in his boat – god knows where he's heading for now. It'll have to be a job for the Coastguard or the Navy to find them."

Love laughed. "What are you going to tell them," he asked, a touch bitterly. "We still have no evidence, nothing, only vague unsubstantiated theories. Can you really see the Coastguard or the Navy acting on those, particularly given the identity of our suspect?"

"I still don't see," Price began, "why Illosovich would bring the stuff onto the Island only to take it away with him again; seems pointless. My idea of him using the TT as a way of passing it on to another party made a whole lot more sense."

"Well, he didn't," Love said; "maybe you should call him back and tell him what he's done wrong."

Price ignored the sarcasm and continued. "That auction, now, I wonder what happened in the end. Did you see who bought the bike?"

"We didn't hang around to watch, Jonathon," the American replied. "I checked it out with the Geiger counter; it was clean, so we came over to join you."

"When you say *checked it out*, what exactly do you mean?" Price asked. He could feel the hairs on the back of neck begin to stand on end. Smith explained what he had done.

"You told me before that you can shield this stuff; how would you go about doing that?" Price demanded.

Smith shrugged his shoulders. "I suppose if you encased it in a lead box, about an inch thick, that'd do the trick," he said.

"How about a lead engine block?" Price asked excitedly, "an engine block made to look exactly like the engine block of a Petromax World Superbike replica machine."

Smith thought for a moment and then answered.

"I suppose that would do," he said, "but technically it would surely be difficult?"

Price shook his head and called for Roy Love's mobile. His fingers were trembling as he punched in the number. The 'phone rang for no more than a couple of seconds before it was answered.

"Hello, Louise," he said, "did you get anywhere with what I asked you to do?"

"I've been on the 'phone all day," she said; her voice sounded tired and almost breaking with emotion, "but I got nowhere with the police, the government or any of the authorities. In the end things were looking desperate so I called red Robbie."

"Who the hell is he?" he asked.

"The local union supremo," she replied.

"Can he help? Can he do anything?" Price demanded.

"As much as anyone," she said; "I've told him all we know and he's passed it on to his members. Every boat that leaves the Sea Terminal and every 'plane that leaves the airport will be thoroughly inspected. Don't worry, Robbie doesn't give his word lightly, but when he says it will be done, trust me, it will be done."

"Even at this time of year?"

"Even at this time of year."

Price turned to the others. "We can do no more here," he said, "Mikael, can you and Peter take us back to Douglas?"

Boroweski nodded. "Where do you want to go?" he asked.

"The Grandstand," Price answered, "then at least we can find out what happened to the Petromax bike."

"We can take you there," the Russian said, "but then we must go; we, my comrades and I, are booked on ferry that leaves for Liverpool tonight."

The fog was still swirling thickly around the Grandstand by the time the two Russians stopped to let off their passengers. They said heartfelt goodbyes, but by now the sun had set and it was growing dark. The paddock area to the rear of the building was full of vehicles and people, but they were all packing up and making ready to leave. The TT Races had ended and everyone who had been involved in the festival now had somewhere else to go. Price, Love and Smith wandered around in the misty gloom, without being really sure of what they were looking for. After twenty minutes or so, they came across the main Petromax transporter. The awning had been dismantled, but the race winning bike still stood proudly on a stand behind it wearing the garland that pronounced its pedigree. Price looked around and spotted a figure sitting quietly in the background; it was a tall and powerfully-built man wearing black and gold motorcycle racing leathers. He was alone, but Price recognised who he was.

"Andre," he said, "Andre Rorletski. Well done! Congratulations on your double victory!" The man jumped up and walked over. When he came into the light, he looked tired and a little depressed. He recognised Price and shook his hand.

"So, Andre," Price said, "why aren't you out celebrating? Two TT victories on your first ever appearance! I would have thought that was worth a vodka or two?"

Andre Rorletski looked at Price and shook his head mournfully.

"TT victory one thing, Doctor Price," he said, "but I would rather have my job. I am told at end of the race that I am fired and I must now make my own way back to Russia."

"What," Price said, "that's impossible; no rider could have done any better. Who told you you're fired?"

"Boss man," Rorletski replied, "Mr Illosovich. He say, thank you Andre, you have won famous victory, but there is no place for you in my team anymore. Please find your own way home….."

Price tried to think of something positive to say. "Never mind, think of the prize money: two major wins, that's got to be…(Price calculated rapidly)…at least fifty or sixty thousand quid in your hand."

"Doctor Price," Rorletski replied, "when I signed contract to race for this team, I sign over all of my prize money to them."

Price tried again, but could only think of one more thing to say. "I've spent a lot of time with your uncle Mikael over the last few days, Andre, don't worry, I'll give him a ring and I'm sure he'll help sort everything out."

"Uncle?" the young Russian said, genuinely mystified. "I have no uncle. I never knew my parents, I am an orphan and have no family."

While Price was talking to the young Rorletski, his companions scoured the paddock, searching for news of the Petromax Replica and the auction. It was hard to find any answers for the place was emptying rapidly. Everyone seemed to have hurried work to do and/or a boat to catch. A few scraps of information found their ears, the main one being that the bike had been sold and for a fantastic sum. The buyer was some sort of rich collector and had paid the full price in cash. As soon as the money had been paid a few heavy-looking dudes (the witness's own words) had turned up, put the bike in a van and driven it away. No-one knew who they, or the purchaser was.

Love tried to get a description, but it was no use. This year's TT meeting was over, life was moving on and no-one really had time for what seemed like idle chat. He passed on what he had learnt to Miss Templeton and she in turn passed it on to Red Robbie. There was precious little else they could do.

At last, reluctantly, Price, Love and Smith gave up. They summoned a taxi and asked to be taken to a large house on a cliff top in Onchan. As young Rorletski had nowhere else to go, they took him with them. As the taxi pulled into the drive, they could see through the drifting clouds of mist, the silhouette of a man sitting on the veranda with a glass in his hand. They got out and the man shouted a greeting.

"What took you so long? I've been waiting here for hours. Just poured myself a little Canadian Club Whisky to pass the time."

Richard was obviously more than pleased with himself. He welcomed his guests into the house and then without further ado ushered them through the hallway into his blue room. There, resplendent between the Rem Fowler Norton and the Mike Hailwood Ducati, on its own special stand, stood the Petromax World Superbike replica.

"How the…?" Price asked. The other men were speechless.

"Cost a few quid," the undertaker said, "but I bid more than the other fella. When it got to silly money, I had to point out that in the Isle of Man auctions have to be paid in cash. Other fella wanted to use cheques, promissory notes, electronic transfer, all that rubbish, but fortunately, the auctioneer was a decent chap from Ramsey - second cousin of mine, actually - and I had enough cash to support my bid so I bought the bike. What do you reckon… looks rather nice, doesn't it?"

"You do, er, remember why we were interested in it, don't you Richard?" Price enquired.

"Can't say I do," the undertaker replied, "I know you were talking about it, but I was a little tired and I think I may have fallen asleep."

Price looked at the others. "What do you think?" he asked.

The American nodded and walked over to the machine. He produced a small penknife, opened the blade and drew it slowly across the top of the engine block. The knife cut into the metal like butter.

They told Richard what they wanted to do and he produced a selection of tools. Smith volunteered to take the engine apart, but after a few minutes it was clear that he didn't really know enough about what he was trying to do. A young man who had been quietly sitting in the background stood up, walked across the room and politely took over. After fifteen or twenty minutes the engine had been partially disassembled and Rorletski stood aside. Price, Smith and Love went over to look, but what they found was not what they had hoped: a camshaft was missing together with a number of other parts. Either Illosovich had never put them in the engine or…

"Richard?" Price asked.

"Yes?" the undertaker replied, looking around. He had just offered Rorletski a ride on one of his bikes for the following year's TT. At long last the young Russian was smiling.

"How, er, did you actually get this bike here. I mean, you obviously didn't ride it and it's a hell of a long way to push it from the Grandstand?"

"Easy," the undertaker replied, "those friends of yours were there, the Russian guys, er, Mikael's friends. They were up at the auction and when I got the bike, they offered to bring it down. They had a van."

"Did they take long?" Price asked.

"Dunno," Richard replied. "I was pretty pleased with what I'd done so I gave them the keys to my house and left it all to them. I met a few fellas I knew; we decided to have a small celebration so we wandered over to the hospitality tent...."

As the undertaker was speaking, a Russian trawler which had been berthed by the outer breakwater in Peel cast off its moorings and slipped quietly out into the Irish Sea, then turned and headed northwards. The mist was lighter now, but the sun had long-since set on the far western horizon. The darkness was relieved by only a few last fleeting rays of pink and orange sunset light reflected from the lifting clouds. The captain of the vessel glanced at his charts, then at the sea and finally at the rapidly darkening sky. He was glad to be on his way.

In a cabin below him his two passengers opened a bottle of Vodka and raised their glasses in a silent victory salute. As two of Russia's greatest special agents, they had particular reason to be pleased that night: their mission had been successful, the rather special engine parts had been retrieved and were now secure in the hold of the vessel, a despised enemy had been thwarted and a son of mother Russia had won the fabled and legendary Senior TT.